LEGENDA MARIS

"'The Birthgrave', Tanith Lee's first novel changed British fantasy. Here was an author who charged fantasy with dark fire, but also convincing realism. Her characters were not stereotypes, but living, breathing people. The writing itself was beautiful, flowing like poetry. I was not the only young writer greatly influenced and inspired by Tanith Lee. Her love of language taught us how to shape our own words into living textures. Her ability to see beyond the ordinary guided us to peer beyond the veils of the mundane world and to report what we found there. As both a writer and a mentor, Tanith Lee is irreplaceable."

—Storm Constantine, author of *'The Moonshawl'*,
publisher of Immanion Press books.

"We always live in the Age of Legends without knowing it. In such times living gods and goddesses walk among us, and share this Flat Earth and mold its shadow fabric. It is only when the gods depart do we realize in retrospect what fragile miracle we've been privileged to observe, and what is now gone from the world... The divine Tanith Lee has slipped away. And yet, both legends and deities leave a permanent brand in the hearts of mortals. The brand is seared with the wild flame of Story, and it holds a fragment of elusive divine Wonder. Here is one remarkable collection. And now it breathes in her stead, as it will always – in tandem with every last one of her stories and books and poems and images, a great holy bellows of fire. Forgive me if I speak in such exalted language, but none other will do when it comes to Tanith Lee."

—Vera Nazarian, author of *Cobweb Bride*,
publisher of Norilana Books

Title   LEGENDA MARIS
Condition   Acceptable
Location   Books   Row G 4 Bay 5 Item 4735
Description   The cover and pages are in good condition shows signs
               of normal wear. The cover is clean but does show some
               wear. Fast Shipping from California. Supports Goodwill
               job training programs.
Source   EBOOKS
SKU   3ZHD73006JGT
ASIN   1907737677
Code   9781907737671
Employee   kevinth
Date Added   10/7/2019 10:10:59 AM

3ZHD73006JGT

Books   Row G 4 Bay 5
LEGENDA MARIS

4735

4735

LEGENDA MARIS

Tanith Lee

IMMANION
PRESS
Stafford England

Legenda Maris
By Tanith Lee
© 2015

This is a work of fiction. All the characters and events portrayed in this book are fictitious, and any resemblance to real people, or events, is purely coincidental.

The right of Tanith Lee to be identified as the author of this work has been asserted by her in accordance with the Copyright, Design and Patents Act, 1988.

Cover Art by Tanith Lee and John Kaiine
Cover Design by Danielle Lainton
Frontispiece illustration by Tanith Lee
Interior layout by Storm Constantine

Set in Palatino Linotype

ISBN 978-1-907737-67-1

IP0121

New (future) Author Web Site, as the original has been stolen:
http://www.tanith-lee.com

An Immanion Press Edition
http://www.immanion–press.com
info@immanion–press.com

Books by Tanith Lee

A Selection from her 93 titles

The Birthgrave Trilogy (The Birthgrave; Vazkor, son of
Vazkor, Quest for the White Witch)
The Vis Trilogy (The Storm Lord; Anackire; The White
Serpent)
The Flat Earth Opus (Night's Master; Death's Master;
Delusion's Master; Delirium's Mistress; Night's Sorceries)
Don't Bite the Sun
Drinking Sapphire Wine
The Paradys Quartet (The Book of the Damned; The Book of
the Beast; The Book of the Dead; The Book of the Mad)
The Venus Quartet (Faces Under Water; Saint Fire; A Bed of
Earth; Venus Preserved)
Sung in Shadow
A Heroine of the World
The Scarabae Blood Opera (Dark Dance; Personal Darkness;
Darkness, I)
The Blood of Roses
When the Lights Go Out
Heart-Beast
Elephantasm
Reigning Cats and Dogs
The Unicorn Trilogy (Black Unicorn; Gold Unicorn; Red
Unicorn)
The Claidi Journals (Law of the Wolf Tower; Wolf Star Rise,
Queen of the Wolves, Wolf Wing)
The Piratica Novels (Piratica 1; Piratica 2; Piratica 3)
The Silver Metal Lover
Metallic Love
The Gods Are Thirsty

COLLECTIONS

Nightshades
Dreams of Dark and Light
Red As Blood – Tales From the Sisters Grimmer
Tamastara, or the Indian Nights
The Gorgon
Tempting the Gods
Hunting the Shadows
Sounds and Furies

Also Published by Immanion Press

The Colouring Book Series
Greyglass
To Indigo
L'Amber
Killing Violets
Ivoria
Cruel Pink
Turquoiselle

Ghosteria Volume 1: The Stories
Ghosteria Volume 2: The Novel: Zircons May Be
Mistaken
A Different City

CONTENTS

INTRODUCTION TO 'LEGENDA MARIS'

'Legenda Maris' is the first of a series of themed short story collections that Tanith Lee planned to publish through Immanion Press. Tanith died on 24th May 2015 at the age of 67. We see the publication of this book as our tribute to a remarkable author with whom we were privileged to work for several years and whose writing I personally have adored and found inspiring since I began reading it back in the 70s. While some of these stories have been in print before, Tanith always ensured that any new collection of her work included unpublished pieces. The new tales in this book were written only a few months ago, and are among the last ones she wrote. By collecting her stories within a theme, Tanith produced a new work entirely – almost like a series of chapters in a novel where the characters of each chapter never meet. In this work particularly, the only recurring protagonist is the sea. And the sound of it, the smell of it, permeates every story.

As most people who are familiar with Tanith's work will know, to say she was a prolific writer is an understatement. She lived and breathed writing, and even when incapacitated by illness endeavoured to keep working. She was reading the proofs of this book and marking corrections on them only a week or so before she died. Producing words almost continually never meant a lessening of standards. Tanith's stories were – and are – always fresh and innovative. She had an ability to conjure atmosphere in a way that only the best writers can. To read her work is to immerse yourself in her dreams and visions. She accomplished what many aspire to: virtual realities, magical worlds, in which you simply forget you are reading. You are there.

Tanith described her writing as 'channelling'. Stories poured out of her, characters spoke through her. While for some authors, writing can be like a war with their ability to describe accurately what they see so vividly in their minds, for Tanith writing was never a struggle. This was a wonderful gift, almost an extra sense. It speaks to me of a serene confidence; she never doubted for a moment that she was a story-teller to her very core – it was her *purpose* – and the buffets and blows of the publishing industry, which quite frankly was not always good to her, never undermined that confidence nor damaged her creativity.

The new stories in this book, 'Leviathan' and 'Land's Edge, The Edge Of The Sea', were written when Tanith was aware she didn't have much time left in this life, and this makes them particularly poignant. They explore passing and change, but also eternity and cycles, the *sureness* of life, as well as its ebb and flow. They are written with dignity and strength. With Tanith's passing, the world has lost a great writer, but many of us have also lost a beloved friend. The words of some of these friends can be found at the beginning of this book.

The less recent stories in *'Legenda Maris'* include a couple of my favourite Tanith tales 'Magritte's Secret Agent' and 'Because Our Skins Are Finer'; like strange dreams washed up on the shore of sleep, they stay with you long after you've finished reading. Several of the other pieces are uncollected, and I'd not even read them myself before Tanith sent me the manuscript for the book. These had been published previously in magazines or anthologies, so I suspect they will be new to many other readers of this collection too. The cover was created from an original collage by Tanith, which I scanned into the computer in two parts, (it was a long picture!), and which Immanion artist Danielle Lainton then 'stitched' together deftly so you cannot see the joins. Tanith's husband, John Kaiine, then worked on the picture some more to create the beautiful finished image that now adorns this book.

John wishes Tanith's work to continue, and part of this will be to go forward with the collections she planned to publish through Immanion Press. For now, though, please enjoy this jewel-spilling treasure chest of tales. And listen to the sea.

Storm Constantine
16th June 2015

"Though we come and go, and pass into the shadows, here we leave behind us stories told – on paper, on the wings of butterflies, on the wind, on the hearts of others – there we are remembered, there we work magic and great change – passing on the fire like a torch – forever and forever. Till the sky falls, and all things are flawless and need no words at all."

Tanith Lee

GIRLS IN GREEN DRESSES

This is for John Kaiine, who, on my mentioning the story-less title, told me who they were, and promptly recounted most of the tale of Elrahn.

In the dim diluted light an hour before the dawn, the girl's father took her hand. And soon after they set out on the long walk to the lake among the reeds.

The river flows into the lake from the hills, then flows away again, down to the sea. It is a green river, and the lake, tidal but also capable of deep stillness, is green too. The tallest reeds grow there, taller far than a child-girl of thirteen years, as was Elaidh that morning. Men and women, and children too, go there now and then to cut the reeds for the thatch, and for their healing value. But not so often any more. Since the lake is thought an unsafe and mysterious place, not gentle with humankind.

Yet it looked well, that morning, the water a milky green among the circle of the round hills, and the mist just stealing away as the sun came up unseen, only the sky lighting to show its path. A heron rose from the reeds, steel-pale in the twilight, but every stem shivered, and the ripples fled over the lake as a woman gathers her stitches when she sews a cloth. But then the reeds were once more still as if made of iron, and the lake was like a plate of misty glass. And silence spoke with its own voice.

"Are you cold?" asked the father, Elrahn.

"No, dadda."

"Are you afraid?"

"No, dadda."

"We'll sit, then. We must wait. We'll eat our breakfast on the shore."

So in the lea of a willow they ate their bread, dipped in sweet black tea. They waited. He did not tell her the story then, for he had already told her, over and over, all the years of her life that she could listen. Only the silence spoke, then sang

He had been a baby, Elrahn, when he took the snow-sickness Not many take it, nor live that take it. Those that do are ever after marked.

And that was how he grew up then a fine young man, but with hair and skin so white, and his face and body, all his fleshly surface, pitted by the silvery pocks the fever had made on him, that are like a mountain leopard's paw-marks in the snow.

"He will have second sight," said the old women. But he did not.

"He'll go off for a soldier," said the men. He never did.

"Religion is always a refuge and consolement," said the priest, standing lonely under the church's dome. But Elrahn did not come to be taught about God.

"He will never wed," said the girls, "though we should like him, if it were not for his snow-leopard skin."

And Elrahn did not court or marry. He did not even glance at the girls, and if he thought of them when he was not with them, it was impossible for them to say.

His mother was a widow—his father was long dead of the spirit that he had brewed at his own still. But when Elrahn was seventeen or so, the mother too died. And besides she had never liked Elrahn much nor been very kind to him, preferring her other sons. These presently kicked him out, and it was winter too. "Go cuddle the snow or find a leopard to live with, or a wolf, Elrahn. It's sick of the sight of your white scales we are."

Elrahn did not answer. He seldom said a lot. He picked himself up and walked off along the village street through the snow, not looking back once. Only the priest followed him a little way, shouting, "Return, dear Elrahn. God loves you." But Elrahn did not return.

Elrahn walked all through the dark, white day, and when he was hungry and thirsty, he took up some of the snow, or plucked an icicle and sucked it. Later he found a barn to sleep in and there was a cow there with a calf, and he had a little of the warm milk

The next day Elrahn met a kind of travelling show. There were three painted wagons strung with bells, and drawn by shaggy ponies, and in the wagons were those who danced or jumped through fire, or performed magic tricks for money. And also there was a woman pretty enough to make you blink, but she was only the height of the back of a young dog. And also there was a dog, that had wings. Though it could not fly until hoisted up in a harness from invisible wires by night, to deceive the ignorant in various villages.

The show-master was a man in a fine coat with brass buttons. He gave Elrahn a piece of cheese with bread and a cup of liquor. "Well, my handsome fellow, are you marked like that all over? What do you say to going with us? You can be our serpent prince, the child of a man and a female snake. Your food, and one hundredth of whatever we'll take in coins."

Elrahn was staring at a blue ape that could walk across the tops of narrow sticks and was doing so. The cheese was tasty, and besides the pretty dwarf had given him a sort of look he had never been given—or noticed he was given—before.

"I will," said Elrahn.

Some while Elrahn was with the show-wagons. In the villages and little rambling stone towns, he stood naked but for a kilt and some ornament painted to look like gold. The people gaped, for in those parts they had never even heard of the snow-sickness. And when he stuck out his tongue, stained black for purpose, they gasped.

Life among the wagons was not bad. It was better than it had been in the village and with the mother and her other sons.

The blue ape was full of jokes and the winged dog liked running, and would warm your feet by the fire. The troupe were daring. And besides, there was the lovely dwarf.

But then one day, in a town above a high forest, a rich man saw the dwarf and he made her an offer of love and marriage.

"Elrahn," said she, "we have been good friends, but I would be a fool to refuse this chance. He is a kind man, if not good-looking or young. And I am coming to the end of my bloom. You'll tire of me, in any case."

Another man in Elrahn's place might have said, Never! But Elrahn said nothing like that. Nor did he say, You are breaking my heart, or, You are a bitch. Only his eyes filled with tears, but he looked away, and she did not see, or if she did she did not say. Instead he answered, "I wish you well and happy."

After the dwarf woman was gone, Elrahn had less interest in the wagons. He told the master so.

"Ah, then, just come down to the reedlands with me," said the man, "for they say there you can find a mermaid, and I should like, I would, to have a mermaid among my show."

Elrahn agreed to this. He thought he might as well go on with them until he found some other thing to do.

The spring was begun, and the reedlands were green. The greenest place on earth they seemed, as they always do then, and in the summer. Even the sky looks green, in its way, between the stems, and from willow islands in the rivers, the emerald ducks fly out in swarms like bees.

There was a big old inn, and here the three wagons stopped for several days.

As he drank beer under the low beams, the show-master asked to hear the local tales.

So then they were telling him everything, of giants in the hills who had left the ruins of their castles there, of ghosts that dance on the thirteenth night of every month and of the demon-fox that steals babies left in the fields and changes them to foxes.

The show-master and his troupe listened to all this, but Elrahn could see the master was impatient. Elrahn wondered why the master did not ask straight out for the tale he wanted, the story of the mermaids. But as Elrahn never said a lot, he never said a single word now.

And then an old man came over and held out his mug for some beer.

"Welcome, grandda," said the master. "What tale do you have, then?"

"No tale at all," said the old man. "Only this warning. Do not go down to the lake in these days of the spring."

"And why is that, grandda?"

"If you do, you may see there the girls in green dresses. And then no man alive, nor God in His sky, can save you."

A great thick hush had fallen. Even the fire dropped down on the hearth, and the winged dog folded his wings close, and went under the table.

"Why is that, then, grandda? Are they so terrible, these girls in green dresses?"

"So they are."

"And *why* are they?"

The old man said, "Ask the dead, for they know."

Then the show-master nodded, and refilled the old man's beer-mug, and said the ape would dance on the rafters upside down, which it did. And the other matter was let go.

Except that, near midnight, as they were all in bed, the master woke Elrahn up. "Tomorrow, at first light, we walk to the lake, you and I."

"Do you want?"

"Are you a dunce, or what? Do you not know what the old man said?"

Elrahn said he did not.

"Listen then. They call them that here, girls in green dresses. There are *mermaids* in spring in this lake. And we shall catch one or I'll be hanged by my tassel."

They say the mermaids would come in from the sea, up the river to the lake, in spring. As salmon come in, to spawn. But a mermaid is a fish only up to her middle, and from there she is a naked woman. So, if she should stand upright on her tail out of the water among the green reeds, she may look like a girl clad in green...

All this the master explained to Elrahn as down to the lake they went, brushing through the spangle-dew before sunrise.

The sun was just opening its eye when they reached

the shore. A sight of beauty it was, the coin of water lying there so still among the misty hills, and the rim of the flame-green reeds, and the sun just touching the world with one crystal finger. And then the dawn wind stirred and blew on the reeds, and they rattled like harp-strings struck by an unseen hand.

But when the wind was gone, all was still again. And Elrahn was taken with the idea that human things and animals breathe, and so are always in a sort of motion, while they live. But the land and the heaven and the water, which do not breathe at all, may lie as still as if turned to glass.

Then the master spoke in a fierce quick whisper. "See! Do you see, *there*?"

Elrahn looked. A duck was swimming along the lake. No, it was a great fish. And he thought they might have brought a rod or net, to catch some fish for breakfast. And then he thought, curiously, of the Bible, which the priest had kept telling him of, and of the thing spoken to a fisher-man, saying he should be a fisher of men.

Just then the fish broke the surface of the lake, and oh, it was not any fish at all, but a young girl with skin as white as winter snow and hair as green as water. And then down she dived again and there was the flip of her tail, and the unbreathing lake was turned once more to glass.

Elrahn was amazed, but the show-master was already going out between the reeds, standing himself on the shore. And in his hands he held a shining string that looked like gold, but Elrahn knew it would only be painted.

He thinks that will catch her, thought Elrahn. But he himself knew nothing about mermaids, and perhaps it would.

Presently there came again a rippling and whirling in the water, and suddenly the water broke in a hundred pieces, and up out of it burst two creatures, and they were, without any doubt, mermaids, the pair of them.

"See my sweet girls—" boldly cried the master, "look—a golden chain! I have heard how you like to gather treasures. Should you like this golden chain?"

And then they looked and they laughed, the two mermaids.

Elrahn thought he had never heard a sound so charming or so cruel.

It was true they were naked to the waist, and a little below. They had long slim arms and throats, and round white breasts with centres pink as coral. Their lips were pink like that, and the long nails on their hands, and as they laughed he saw their teeth, which were white and very sharp. And Elrahn remembered he had heard once a sailor speak of big fish in the sea with teeth, called sharks.

Their hair was long and green and wrapped them over as they moved and then uncovered them. Their tails were a silvery green, and utterly the tails of fish, with silver fins like fans. Their eyes were pale so he could not be sure of their colour, but it was somewhere between the other colours of them, green and white and silver—and also pink.

"Come, sweetlets, come to me and take the chain—" cried the show-master, gambolling along the shore and jinking the painted string, and the mermaids laughed, and dived and whirled and came up again, always nearer the shore, and then they clove through a reed-bank and stood up among the reeds, tall on their tails, and they were two girls in green dresses.

"Come away," called Elrahn to the show-master.

But the master did not hear. He thought he fished for mermaids and held out the bait, and would soon catch both—and once on land they would be helpless as any fish thrashing and rolling and at the mercy of anything on legs. Yet Elrahn saw their playful strength and suppleness and their sharp teeth and the pink under the green of their eyes. Elrahn heard the old grandda at the inn saying, "Then no man alive, nor God in His sky, can save you."

"Master—come away!" called Elrahn, now loudly.

And when he did this the mermaids both turned their heads as one, and stared right at him.

And under the silver-green and pink of their eyes, was black, a black as deep as the unsounded depths of the outermost seas, from which they had come.

What a journey it must be for them, with all the trial and danger the in-running salmon finds. The terrible currents and waiting enemies, the rocks and tides, the change from salt to soft water. Yes, they were strong, these girls, and cunning too, for they had survived. Yet why, he wondered, why did they come in at all? For the salmon came to mate, but surely these ones—*their* kind lived in the sea?

Right then, one of the mermaids dived down under the reeds. She vanished, but the other lingered there flirting still and smiling at the master, and at Elrahn too, and waving her hands now, in a sort of amorous half-embracing way.

Elrahn strode out towards the master. This man had, after all, taken him in even if for profit, fed him, and been polite, and even bought him drink the night the dwarf lady was wed.

When she saw Elrahn also was striding towards the lake, the mermaid in the reeds shook her shimmering hair for pleasure. Then Elrahn broke into a run.

But he had not yet reached the master when out of the purling water at the master's very feet, the first mermaid broke like a shining spear up from the lake.

The master shouted and held the golden string high to entice her on. But in the next moment, she seemed to sink down over on him like a wave. Elrahn saw her arms about the master's neck, and her hair falling all across him, and then the gleaming fish's tail swung up and round, and the master, held in the coil of it as if in the coils of a snake, was falling over. Over into the lake he fell, all twined in tail and hair and arms. There was a sparkling slither and a splash. Elrahn beheld the fan-like tail-fins flash from the water once, then go under.

Both had gone under, the mermaid-girl and the show-master—gone without a trace. And the water closed shut upon them.

Elrahn stood there with his heart drumming, and he thought he must run back now to the inn and get what help he could. And as he thought this, he knew there was no use at all in it. But he had forgotten the other one, the other mermaid, and in that very instant in her turn she was there.

What he had only seen with his eyes a moment ago, now happened to him.

Her arms were cool and silken and her clasp unbreakable, and her hair like the green reeds and smelling of spring flowers and mud. Her mouth, which was a woman's, laughed in his face and her breath smelled of the open sea. Then the horror of her tail, muscular as the body of a leopard, seized him. And he was pulled over at once before he could do anything, into the white slap of the water and down into the dark of the dark below.

If he had thought a single last thing, which he had not, Elrahn would have said a prayer, knowing it must be death he went to. And, it is no lie, in any other case it would have been death.

The mermaids came up the river to the lake in spring to fish for men. And when they caught them, they ate them—but this Elrahn only learned later, when he had learned too something of the mer-language. They told him then, or *she* told him, the one who caught him, that just as men relished fish, so certain fish relished the flesh of men. Indeed, she said, a mermaid would not eat a fish, for mermaids were themselves partly of fish-kind. "But you are also of mankind!" exclaimed Elrahn. She said this was not so. Mermaids in their other half were of *woman*kind. And so they would not eat a woman either. Not a fish or a woman or a human child. Only a man. And they preferred, as some humans prefer fresh-water fish—fresh-water men.

The name of this mermaid, who had caught and thereafter owned him, was Trisaphee. Hers was the only name among them he ever learned, for the sounds of their tongue still bewildered him even after he came to understand it somewhat. Their voices too, under the lake, were also like water. He never heard them speak or sing or call in the sea, for when the time came for them to return there, his days with them were over and done.

That *first* day, Elrahn woke up lying not, in darkness, but in dimness. What he could see was water, and there could be no doubt of what it was. The movement of it was like that of thin cloths drawn over and against each other, but bubbles littered through, all bright. And even the sun shone in with one smoky shaft, though far off.

And he saw too that *they* were going to and fro, swimming over and about each other in an endless dance.

There were many hundreds of them. A clan of them. A host. All were female, with breasts and long, long hair, and all were fish from a little below the waist.

They were very lovely, to be sure. The loveliest thing he ever looked on, apart from the full moon. But at this hour he thought of their beauty less than his own terror and the place he was in.

After a while, he next realised that he, a breathing thing of the world, still breathed.

Then he got up, and he went about to see how it was that he could. And *then* he found he had been shut up in a cage, but it was a cage of air, a great round bubble that somehow had been formed, and when he put his fists against it, its walls did not rupture, only trembled.

All this while the mermaids swam about him, some paying him no attention, but some staring in. And their eyes, like this, under the lake, were sombre green and beautiful and quite human in their shape and form—yet too, they were luminous as the eyes of cats or *demons*.

Soon, *she* was there. That is, Trisaphee, only then he did not know her name. She came and she shook her hair at him, which underwater was like a sequinned veil.

"Let me go, you witch," said Elrahn.

But the instant he said it he thought he had been a fool. For though she seemed to grasp what he said—and many of them, he after found, knew the language of men—she was the more powerful, and his foe.

However, even through the vast bubble of air, she said something to him. He knew not a word of it, even if he could make out the liquid sounds. But then she spoke in his own tongue, and she said, "Stay still, you Man. You belong to me, and we will not harm you."

This done, she swam away.

Then all of them swam off, and not long after the shaft of sun faded, and everything was darkness.

Perhaps he slept, or simply lost his wits again from fear. Waking once more, he saw the moonlight pierced the water as the sun had done. And in the rays of the moon, more dreadful than any sight he ever saw before or after, Elrahn made out the skull and bones, and something of the body, what had been left of it, of the show-master, lying there on his own fine coat with the brass buttons, with the gold-painted string of bait tangled between.

How long exactly Elrahn lived in the bubble he was afterwards unsure. But he said that he kept some count, by the gilded shaft of sun and the bluish one of the moon, and maybe it was a fortnight.

The very second day, the master's bones were cleared. But he knew that was not for any Godly burial, for he saw one of the mermaids gnawing at a thigh bone—and some while after this one returned, and lo and behold, she had refashioned the bone as a pipe and she played on it a low, mournful, underwater song, which Elrahn took a mortal hatred for.

But then too, Elrahn thought, the master would have caught a mermaid if he could and put her in his show. Perhaps she would have had less kindness than he gave the dog or the ape—she would have been a slave, and crippled on the land by her tail.

It was Trisaphee who took care of Elrahn.

She brought him fresh fish, newly killed and cleaned, and though he must eat them raw in the bubble, they were not so bad. Also she brought him ducks' eggs, and once or twice human bread, and once a bottle of tea with some berry jam stirred in—but these last things he would not bring himself to swallow, for they had certainly come from others who had been killed and devoured.

Why had she not slain and eaten Elrahn? He never had to ask her, for in the end, he fathomed it for himself. It was his skin. His skin which, though that of a man, stayed—save at the head and groin—hairless and clear white as any mermaid's. Also was he not, from the snow-sickness, pocked and scaled like a snake or a fish?

He came to see, between the clocks of the sun and the moon, that he was kept by Trisaphee as her pet. She fed him, and even she pushed in—like the food through the sides of the bubble, by some uncanny aperture of which he was never certain—lake water in a crock that, he might drink and wash himself.

As a prisoner will, where they are able, he tried to keep himself in health, and keep his brain in sanity and his soul in hope.

But one morning, by the sun-shaft clock, Trisaphee came and she lashed the side of the bubble with her tail, and the lake gushed through. The water covered all and in a minute or less, Elrahn was drowned.

And then he thought, *But I am not*. Nor was he. And so he found that, by a magical means in the bubble, which was itself, maybe, part air and part water, he had mastered the art of breathing liquid. Then out he swam, and in the marvel of this wonder, he turned and saw

Trisaphee was smiling at him in a loving, tender way. And she stroked his hair and kissed him with her icy mouth, between the eyes, before she put on to him the harness and the lead.

He was her dog, then. Where she went, he might go with her, if so she wished. But when she did not wish it, she tied him to some post or rock or curious aqueous stalagmite under the lake.

To the surface they never ascended. But now and then into the depths they did go, where it was so black he could not see, and then she shortened the leash, and guided him, with her other hand resting on his neck.

What did he think of this? He was angry, but also he liked her touch. Yes, even though she was what she was and had done what she had done. And not long after, as he learned from her pieces of her language and she spoke somewhat in his own, she announced to him she herself had not eaten any of the body of his friend, the show-master. And when Elrahn, hearing that, swore an oath, she too swore she was blameless of it, and this in his own tongue. And she swore on the name of God.

This gave Elrahn pause. For the priest in his birthplace had once assured him no soulless or evil thing could speak God's name.

Then again, Trisaphee gave Elrahn presents. He did not, of course, want the leash, though it was plainly of real gold, a very proper metal, and set with pearls. But also she gave him a silver ring fixed with a jewel like a fox's eye, and then she regaled him with stories of treasure hoards in the seas to which her kind had access. And when his clothes wore out in the water, she brought him leggings of some strange stuff. She said they had been made from the skin of a shark her kind had killed in war.

"Do you fight, then, Trisaphee?"

She assured him they must, to live.

"How were you born?" he asked her once, one time when they rested under a cliff far down in the lake to watch the clouds of fish, which blew about there.

"In the usual way," said she.

"But," he said, "seeing you are a woman but also—a fish, like these, and also because you say your kind are *only* female—"

But she would not answer him directly, and only said she had lived many hundreds of years and would live many hundreds more, and could not recall her start.

At this time, it must be admitted, he felt he understood the tongue of her kind better than perhaps he did, and so may have mistaken her words. But also she had spoken partly in his own tongue, and he could have had the right of it.

Always he had been an outcast. And even when he had journeyed with the wagons, Elrahn had not existed as most men do, nor lived by the normal laws. In this way, for him, this being under the lake among the green fish-girls was only another eccentric phase of his odd life. While he himself had been well taught he was a monster of some type.

He flowed along with his fate therefore, resisting only a little, and that only in the matter of the harness and lead, and those moral issues to do with eating human flesh. He flowed with the currents, and in the company of Trisaphee. And now and then he saw not only that she was beautiful but that she was a living thing, and even under the lake she breathed, as he did, and was not made of glass or water.

One morning—the sun shaft was there—Trisaphee took him away up the lake to a spot they had never before swum to. Wide watery caves ran into the under-side of the hills above. They were black as night, yet things clung in them, lichens and weeds and stones that glowed.

Trisaphee sat herself on a rock, and only her hair kept up its furling spun-silk motion. A mermaid's hair is never so beautiful above the water as it is below.

Presently she spoke in Elrahn's language, which—as only years later he came to see—she had grown more accomplished at as her time with him progressed.

"You have been with me now a while, my Man. If I were to ask what you would like most in the world that I could give you, what should it be?"

Elrahn looked at her. He said not a word.

"Well," said she, "it's tired out by the lake you must be. And so it is with us. Soon we shall be turning down the rivers to the sea. And there I will not take you, for there I could never keep you safe. What shall I be doing with you, then?"

When it seemed she would wait on and on for his answer, he looked her in the eye and he said, "So *now* you will murder me."

"No," said Trisaphee. "You shall live. But what would you like?"

"To live, then," he said, "and to go free."

"It's tired of me too, so you are," she said.

"How not, seeing you keep me on a chain like your dog?"

"Have I not fed and cared for you, am I not kind and loving to you?"

"As to your dog."

Then she stretched out her hand and tapped the harness where it circled him, and it flew off and went bounding away through the water.

"Be free," said Trisaphee, "and not my dog."

He thanked her.

"But what will you have?" she inquired.

"You have given it. And if you'll let me go up now to the light and air—that is all I ask."

"Ask for something more," said she.

Elrahn showed her the ring on his finger. "I have this of you, which is worth money in the world. That is enough, if I can keep it."

"Oh, keep it, keep it, sell it and forget me," said Trisaphee.

"How can I *forget* you?" he angrily asked. "Do you think I am *mad*? You are a mermaid of the deeps."

Then she smiled. "Then what would you have?" she asked again.

Elrahn had not been much with women, but he had been with one, the dwarf lady, and so at last, a tinkling bell rang somewhere in his brain. He widened his eyes at Trisaphee, wondering if he could be mistaken. And if he were not, whether he wished he were.

"I do not presume," said Elrahn prudently.

Then Trisaphee left the rock and she came and wrapped him round with her arms and body and hair and tail. It was as it had been that first time when she caught him and pulled him over into the lake. Yet, much more gentle, and to say he did not care for it would be to speak falsely. Then she kissed his mouth, and it was the kiss a woman gives her lover, though her lips tasted of brine and her tongue of silver water.

32

And could there be any man in such an embrace who would not wonder what he must do next, seeing she was formed as she was. But before he could attempt a single thing with her, she suddenly let him go, and floated from him with a look so sad and ancient now, he believed at last she was old as the oceans and full of sorrow, and the salt in her was not only sea but unshed tears.

"I will tell you now, my Man. You may swim up to the land. And not one of us will harm you. But when you come ashore you will feel a hurt in your chest. Have no fear of it. It is only the air coming back into your body. Spit the moisture from your mouth and void it from your nose and all will be well with you. But never again will you be able to breathe in the water."

"Very well." said Elrahn "but—"

"I am not done," said she. "Listen well to me. Tonight you will dream of me, and everything you might like to have of me you will have, but only in sleep. When you wake you will discover there is yet something left with you that is ours, yours and mine. And heed me now, care for it, that thing, or I will curse you. Thirteen years from this day's night, you must come back to this water's-edge, and prove to me you have done as I say. And on that night before that morning, distant by thirteen years, which to me are like thirteen quarters of an hour, you will see me again in a dream. But in the daybreak you will see and meet me among the reeds. And you will have with you that thing I have left with you now. Or else woe betide you."

All the while she spoke to him in this way, Elrahn felt his skin crawl with a strange thin fear. And even as he felt the fear he felt a sort of love for her and a sadness for her, and besides, he lusted for her.

"Say yes, now," she said. "Let me hear you say yes, so that I know I have made you understand."

"I understand nothing, but I will say yes, to make you happy."

"Ah," said Trisaphee, "what is happiness? I am familiar with a joy your kind can never know, except in heaven."

And then she turned in the water, brilliant as a star, and swift as a dart she shot away.

Elrahn hesitated only a moment or so. Then he too raced from the cave, and raising his arms, he rushed for the surface.

All the while he was diving up, with the little fishes storming off before him, he was certain others of her tribe might come and attack him. But he saw none of them, and in a space of minutes, the water turned from sable to fair and then to jade and so to gold. And then he broke the skin of the lake and swam wildly for the nearest shore. And a pain began in his chest and lungs as if he breathed in molten bronze.

When at last he fell out among the reeds, he coughed and choked and hawked and spat away the spell and the water. And then he lay a time under the sun, until he was able to get up and go on his way.

Elrahn did not walk towards the inn, nor did he really recognize the place where he had beached, to find that inn. He walked away from the reedlands, and up into the hills, and everything he saw was a great marvel to him, from the tall trees to the little sparrows, and the grey hares that sprang along in the fields. As for the sky, he could hardly bear to look at it, it was so mighty and so lighted up, so *blue*. When night came on, the stars made him weep. It seemed, even by starshine, he had never seen such colours.

How long had he been in the lake? A week or two, a month or two. But he might have been gone a lifetime.

And he resolved he would tell no one the story of what had befallen him, for who would believe it but for the people of the inn, or the people from the wagons who would blame him for the death of their master?

Last of all he thought he might not sleep, but keep himself awake, and he was hungry enough he fancied that would not be so difficult. Truth to tell, he was frightened now by what she had said to him, the mermaid, about the dream and that something would be left between them, and he must care for it and show her, in thirteen years, he had, or be cursed. He was afraid at last, if *all* the truth be told, of everything that had happened.

But in the end, sitting up staring under the burning stars, he slept.

And he dreamed what many a man would, things being as they were. He dreamed of Trisaphee, and that he lay in the reeds above the lake with her, and she had wrapped him in her reedy hair and her fish's tail, caressing him while he caressed her, and without possessing her, yet he *possessed* her. And so vast was the pleasure that he cried out loud. And in a while he looked her in her fiery eyes, and he said, "Yes, there is one other joy, under heaven, that I know."

But waking a second later, he was aware that he had *not* possessed her in any way, but only given his seed to the grass. And with a bitter sigh, he moved his sleeping place. And after that he slumbered dreamless till the morning.

The sun was over the trees by the time he roused again. The birds were singing, and he lay in rapture to hear them, after all those shadow days of the mournful, heartless songs of the mermaid kind.

When he got up, he saw how in parts the dew still sparkled on the grass. And then he saw that one bead of dew was larger than all the rest. And when he went to see, he found a big gleaming pearl that lay in the lap of the earth. But even as he stood there watching it, the pearl swelled larger and greater and soon it was the size of a thumbnail, and then the head of a spoon and then of a cup and then of a plate, and then it cracked open, and out fell a tiny child, white and translucent as an asphodel.

This child, a girl, lay in the grass with her dreamy eyes gazing at him. Next she seemed to harden over, her flesh losing its fairy look of flowers. Soon she was opaque, and big nearly as a baby two months old. She breathed, and she hiccupped, and then she cried.

"What on God's earth shall I do with this?" said Elrahn. But anyway he picked her up, and took her where they could both find food and shelter. And here he told the people a tale not the facts. Such fact he told to her alone, to the child from the pearl, that in a while he called Elaidh, his daughter, through a kind of birth, by the mermaid Trisaphee.

Now, as they sat on the shore of the morning lake, to which they had come back in her thirteenth spring, Elaidh looked up when again her father spoke.

"These have been good years together, child."

"Yes, dadda."

"I have loved you, Elaidh. But you were never more than half mine, and this I have told you often, from as soon as you might hear."

"I am a mermaid's daughter," said Elaidh.

She was solemn as the quietness of the lake, and her long hair was the pale brown of a duck's wing, but her eyes were green.

"Now and then," said Elrahn, as if idly, but not looking at her at all, "I thought I would see you grow to be a woman, and I should dance at your wedding when the fiddler played his best tunes."

Elaidh said "I would like that, dadda. But now I love you first."

"Do not be loving me," said Elrahn, "and I must not love you, for it's your mother loves you best. She made you with me, which is how all her clan make their children, by a sort of magic, and they are always daughters. Last night I saw her again in a dream, only the second dream I ever had of her. I never saw her all these years till then. But it was as she promised or she warned me. She told me this, Elaidh. And she told me she will swim up in a while today, out of the lake. And when you see her, she is that lovely, Elaidh, and young still as when I met her last. She will never grow old, and not for an age will she die. Her kind live for centuries, perhaps they do for ever. And this too she said I must say to you: How they roam all the waters, the fresh and the salt, the endless oceans that lead one into another, and the rivers and the lakes that pierce and cross the land. How they own vast treasures, huge rubies and diamonds and hoards of golden coins that have gone down with ships, and pearls that grow in the shells of creatures in the sea. How they play on sands miles under water, lit at night by a moon so vigorous its light is as the summer at midday. And how they sing and make music. And how they are free as the tides. And their beauty, Elaidh, and I should know it, is like a secret of the heart."

"Yes, dadda?" asked the child, all attention.

"You and I," said he, "have had our life together. A chancy travelling existence. Doing this and that, mending, fetching, or pulling trick birds from a scarf to tickle crowds. I have taught you the little I know, little enough it could fit inside an acorn. That was all I could do, but it was given to me to do it. And at first it seemed too much for me, the task. And then it was only simple as to breathe. And now, it's done. For when she comes from the lake, your mother Trisaphee, she will offer another life to you. She will offer to take you among her own kind, half of which kind you are. By her spell, your hair will turn to the colour of the reeds, and you will have a tail like a fish, strong as a leopard. And water and air will be alike to your lungs. You will live for centuries never growing old. You will journey through the oceans, free as the tides, playing with rubies and pearls. You will be a mermaid, if so you wish it."

The child stared. She said, "But if not?"

Elrahn said. "Then you'll stay with me and be my daughter. You will wed a man and bear his children, not as she and I bore you, but in pain and labour. You will likely be poor, and certainly hard-worked, and you will wither with the years, a piece of time which to a mermaid is like an afternoon. Then you will die and be dust. Unless, as the priest said, you have a soul. We have been good friends—but oh, a mermaid—you would be a fool to refuse this chance."

Then all at once Elaidh had turned from him and Elrahn knew why. He heard the murmur of the water, the flutter of it as if a great fish swam just under the surface.

Then came a dash of light and water-drops.

Turning himself, he saw Trisaphee standing there, as in the second dream he had, lifted on her tail in the reeds, a girl dressed all in green.

And she held out her smiling arms, not to him, but to Elaidh, and Elaidh jumped to her feet and ran towards her mother and the lake, the centuries and the shadows, to sing and laugh, and to bite the bones of men.

Elaidh had her foot even on the water's hem. She had let her hand almost into the hand of the tall green girl, her mother, who seemed only five or seven years her older. Already Elaidh felt the coolness of the lake, the freedom of a fish, she smelled the ocean and the opening of infinity.

But then, she glanced back.

There *he* stood, her father, straight and scaled and calm, no longer young. And he raised his hand in farewell. "Elaidh, my love, I wish you well and happy."

But she saw his eyes, they were full of salty water, full of tears.

Elaidh took her foot out of the lake's edge, and put down her hands. She stood on the lakeshore and looked at her wonderful mother, the mermaid.

"Mother," said Elaidh, "thank you so kindly for your queenly offer. But I will stay here with mankind. I'll stay with my da."

And Trisaphee made a sound, that might have been the human word *Why?*

"Oh," said Elaidh, "because they kept me when you let me go, and he lets me go when I *would* go and you would take me. Because they can cry salt water. Tears—that is ocean enough for me. I will stay with my da."

And turning, Elaidh walked back along the shore, into

the land.

Behind her came a splash they say, as if every mirror in the world had been smashed in fragments. No more but that, and the reeds again were empty, green, and silent as the moon.

MAGRITTE'S SECRET AGENT

You asked me about it before, didn't you, the picture?
And I never told you. But tonight, tonight I think I will.
Why not? The wine was very nice, and there's still the
other bottle. The autumn dusk is warm, clear and
beautiful, and the stars are blazing over the bay. It's so
quiet; when the tide starts to come back, we'll hear it.
You're absolutely right. I'm obsessive about the sea. And
that picture, the Magritte.

Of course, it's a print, nothing more, though that was
quite difficult to obtain. I saw it first in a book, when I
was eighteen or so. I felt a strangeness about it even then.
Naturally, most of Magritte is bizarre. If you respond to
him, you get special sensations, special inner stirrings
over any or all of what he did, regardless even of whether
you care for it or not. But this one – this one.... He had a
sort of game whereby he'd often call a picture by a name
that had no connection—or no apparent connection—
with its subject matter. The idea, I believe, was to throw
out prior conception. I mean, generally you're told you're
looking at a picture called 'Basket of Apples', and it's
apples in a basket. But Magritte calls a painting 'The
Pleasure Principle', and it's a man with a kind of white
nova taking place where his head should be. Except that
makes a sort of sense, doesn't it? Think of orgasm, for
example, or someone who's crazy over Prokofiev,
listening to the third piano concerto. This picture, though.
It's called 'The Secret Agent'.

It's one of the strangest pictures in the world to me,

partly because it's beautiful and it shocks, but the shock doesn't depend on revulsion or fear. There's another one, a real stinger—a fish lying on a beach, but it has the loins and legs of a girl: a mermaid, but inverted. That has shock value all right, but it's different. This one.... The head, neck, breast of a white horse, which is also a chess piece, which is also a girl. A girl's eye, and hair that's a mane, and yet still hair. And she—it—is lovely. She's in a room, by a window that faces out over heathland under a crescent moon, but she doesn't look at it. There are a few of the inevitable Magritte tricks—for example, the curtain hanging *outside* the window-frame, instead of in, that type of thing. But there's also this other thing. I don't know how I can quite explain it. I think I sensed it from the first, or maybe I only read it into the picture afterwards. Or it's just the idea of white horses and the foam that comes in on a breaker: white horses, or mythological kelpies that can take the shape of a horse. Somehow, the window ought to show the sea and it doesn't. It shows the land under the horned moon, not a trace of water anywhere. And her face that's a woman's, even though it's the face of a chess-piece horse. And the title. 'The Secret Agent', which maybe isn't meant to mean anything. And yet—sometimes I wonder if Magritte—if he ever—

I was about twenty-three at the time, and it was before I'd got anything settled, my life, my ambitions, anything. I was rooming with a nominative aunt, about five miles along the coast from here, at Ship Bay. I'd come out of art school without much hope of a job, and was using up my time working behind a lingerie counter in the local chain store, which, if you're female, is where any sort of diploma frequently gets you. I sorted packets of bras, stopped little kids putting the frilly knickers on their heads, and averted my eyes from gargantuan ladies who were jamming themselves into cubicles, corsets and complementary heart-attacks in that order.

Thursday was cinema day at the Bay, when the movie palace showed its big matinee of the week. I don't know if there truly is a link between buyers of body linen and the matinee performance, but from two to four-thirty on Thursday afternoons, you could count visitors to our department on two or less fingers.

A slender girl named Jill, ostentatiously braless, was haughtily pricing B cups for those of us unlucky enough to require them. I was refolding trays of black lace slips, thinking about my own black, but quite laceless, depression, when sounds along the carpet told me one of our one or two non-film-buff customers had arrived. There was something a little odd about the sounds. Since Jill was trapped at the counter by her pricing activities, I felt safe to turn and look.

I got the guilty, nervous, flinching-away reaction one tends to on sight of a wheelchair. An oh-God-I-mustn't-let-them-think-I'm-staring feeling. Plus, of course, the unworthy survival-trait which manifests in the urge to stay uninvolved with anything that might need help, embarrass, or take time. Actually, there was someone with the wheelchair, who had guided it to a stop. An escort normally makes it worse, since it implies total dependence. I was already looking away before I saw. Let's face it, what you do see is usually fairly bad. Paralysis, imbecility, encroaching death. I do know I'm most filthily in the wrong, and I thank God there are others who can think differently than I do.

You know how, when you're glancing from one thing to another, a sudden light, or colour, or movement snags the eye somewhere in between—you look away then irresistibly back again. The visual centre has registered something ahead of the brain, and the message got through so many seconds late. This is what happened as I glanced hurriedly aside from the wheelchair. I didn't know what had registered to make me look back, but I did. Then I found out.

In the chair was a young man—a boy—he looked about twenty. He was focussing somewhere ahead, or not focussing, it was a sort of blind look, but somehow there was no doubt he could see, or that he could think. The eyes are frequently the big give-away when something has gone physically wrong. His eyes were clear, large, utterly contained, *containing* like two cool cisterns. I didn't even see the colour of them, the construction and the content struck me so forcibly. Rather than an unseeing look, it was a seeing-through—to something, somewhere else. He had fair hair, a lot of it, and shining. The skin of his face had the sort of marvellous pale texture most men shave off when they rip the first razorblade through their stubble and the second upper dermis goes with it forever. He was slim, and if he had been standing, would have been tall. He had a rug over his knees like a geriatric. But his legs were long. You see I've described him as analytically as I can, both his appearance and my reply to it. What it comes to is, he was beautiful. I fell in love with him, not in the carnal sense, but aesthetically, artistically. Dramatically. The fact that a woman was wheeling him about, helplessly, into a situation of women's underwear, made him also pathetic in the terms of pathos. He preserved a remote dignity even through this. Or not really; he was simply far away, not here at all.

The woman herself was just a woman. Stoutish, fawnish. I couldn't take her in. She was saying to Jill: "should have been ready. I don't know why you don't deliver any more like you used to."

And Jill was saying: "I'm sorry, maa-dum, we don't deliver things like this."

It was the sort of utterly futile conversation, redolent of dull sullen frustration on both sides, so common at shop counters everywhere. I wondered if Jill had noticed the young man, but she didn't seem to have done. She usually reacted swiftly to anything youngish and male and platitudinously in trousers, but presumably only when trousers included locomotive limbs inside them.

"Well, I can't stop," said the woman. She had a vague indeterminate Ship Bay accent, flat as the sands. "I really thought it would be ready by now."

"I'm sorry, maa-dum."

"I can't keep coming in. I haven't the time."

Jill stood and looked at her.

I felt blood swarm through my heart and head, which meant I was about to enter the arena, cease my purely observational role.

"Perhaps we could take the lady's name and phone number," I said, walking over to the counter. "We could call her when her purchase arrives."

Jill glowered at me. This offer was a last resort, generally employed to placate only when a customer produced a carving knife.

I found a paper bag and a pen and waited. When the woman didn't speak, I looked up. I was in first gear, unbalanced, and working hard to disguise it. So I still didn't see her, just a shape where her face was, the shadowy gleam of metal extending away from her hands, the more shattering gleam of his gilded bronze hair. (Did she wash it for him? Maybe he had simply broken his ankle or his knee. Maybe he was no longer there.)

I strove in vain towards the muddy aura of the woman. And she wouldn't meet me.

"If you'd just let me have your name," I said brightly, trying to enunciate like Olivier, which I do at my most desperate.

"There's no phone," she said. She could have been detailing a universal human condition.

"Well... " I was offhand "...your address. We could probably drop you a card or something."

Jill made a noise, but couldn't summon the energy to tell us such a thing was never done. (Yes, he was still there. Perfectly still; perfect, still, a glimpse of long fingers lying on the rug.)

"Besmouth," said the woman, grudging me.

It was a silly name. It sounded like an antacid stomach preparation. What was he called, then? Billy Besmouth? Bonny Billy Besmouth, born broken, bundled baby-like, bumped bodily by brassieres—

"I'm sorry?" She'd told me the address and I'd missed it. No I hadn't, I'd written it down.

"19, Sea View Terrace, The Rise."

"Oh yes. Just checking. Thank you."

The woman seemed to guess suddenly it was all a charade. She eased the brake off the chair and wheeled it abruptly away from us.

"What did you do that for?" said Jill. "We don't send cards. What d'you think we aar?"

I refrained from telling her, I asked instead what the

woman had ordered. Jill showed me the book, it was one of a batlike collection of nylon-fur dressing gowns, in cherry red.

At four-thirty, ten women and a male frillies-freak came in. By five-forty, when I left the store, I should have forgotten about Bonny Billy Besmouth, the wheelchair, the vellum skin, the eyes.

That evening I walked along the sands. It was autumn, getting chilly, but the afterglow lingered, and the sky above the town was made of green porcelain. The sea came in, scalloped, darkening, and streaked by the neons off the pier, till whooping untrustworthy voices along the shore drove me back to the promenade. When I was a kid, you could have strolled safely all night by the water. Or does it only seem that way? Once, when I was eight, I walked straight into the sea, and had to be dragged out, screaming at the scald of salt in my sinuses. I never managed to swim. It was as if I expected to know how without ever learning, as a fish does, and when I failed, gave up in despair.

You could see The Rise from the promenade, a humped back flung up from the south side of the bay, with its terraced streets clinging on to it. He was up there somewhere. Not somewhere: 19, Sea View. Banal. I could walk it in half an hour. I went home and ate banal sausages, and watched banal TV.

On Saturday a box of furry bat-gowns came in, and one of them was cherry red.

"Look at this," I said to Jill.

She looked, as if into an open grave.

"Yes. Orrful."

"Don't you remember?"

Jill didn't remember.

Angela, who ran the department, was hung over from the night before, and was, besides, waiting for her extramarital relationship to call her. I showed her the dressing gown and she winced.

"If she's not on the phone, she's had it."

"I could drop it in to her," I lied ably. "I'm going to meet someone up on The Rise, at the pub. It isn't any trouble to me, and she has a crippled son."

"Poor cow," said Angela. She was touched by pity. Angela always struck me as a kind of Chaucerian character—fun-loving, warm-hearted, raucously glamorous. She was, besides, making almost as much a mess of her life as I was of mine, with a head start on me of about ten years.

She organised everything, and the department did me the great favour of allowing me to became its errand-person. I suppose if the goods had been wild-silk erotica I might not have been allowed to take them from the building at all. But who was going to steal a bat-gown?

"You aar stew-pid," said Jill, "You should never volunteer to do anything like that. They'll have you at it all the time now."

At half past six, for Saturday was the store's late closing, I took the carrier and went out into the night, with my heart beating in slow hard concussions. I didn't know why, or properly what I was doing. The air smelled alcoholically of sea and frost.

I got on the yellow bus that went through The Rise.

I left the bus near the pub, whose broad lights followed me away down the slanting street. I imagined varieties of normal people in it, drinking gins and beer and low-calorie cola. Behind the windows of the houses, I imagined dinners, TV, arguments. It had started to rain. What was I doing here? What did I anticipate? (He opened the door, leaning on a crutch, last summer's tennis racket tucked predictably under the other arm. I stood beside his chair, brushing the incense smoke from him, in a long queue at Lourdes.) I thought about his unspeaking far-awayness. Maybe he wasn't crippled, but autistic. I could have been wrong about those strange containing eyes. Anyway, she'd just look at me, grab the bag, shut the door. She had paid for the garment months ago, when she ordered it. I just had to give her the goods, collect her receipt. Afterwards, I'd go home, or at least to the place where I lived. I wouldn't even see him. And then what? Nothing.

Sea View curved right around the bottom of The Rise. Behind its railing, the cliff lurched forward into the night and tumbled on the sea. Number 19 was the farthest house down, the last in the terrace. An odd curly little alley ran off to the side of it, leading along the downslope of the cliff and out of sight, probably to the beach. The sound of the tide, coupled with the rain, was savage, close and immensely wet.

I pushed through the gate and walked up the short path. A dim illumination came from the glass panels of the door. There was no bell, just a knocker. I knocked, and waited like the traveller in the poem. Like him, it didn't seem I was going to get an answer. An even more wretched end to my escapade than I had foreseen. I hadn't considered the possibility of absence. Somehow I'd got the notion Mrs. Besmouth-Antacid seldom went out. It must be difficult, with him the way he was, whichever way that happened to be. So, why did I want to get caught up in it?

A minute more, and I turned with a feeling of letdown and relief. I was halfway along the path when the front door opened.

"Hi you," she said.

At this uninviting salute, I looked back. I didn't recognise her, because I hadn't properly been able to see her on the previous occasion. A fizz of fawn hair, outlined by the inner light, stood round her head like a martyr's crown. She was clad in a fiery apron.

"Mrs. Besmouth?" I went towards her, extending the carrier bag like meat offered to a wild dog.

"Besmouth, that's right. What is it?" She didn't know me at all.

I said the name of the store, a password, but she only blinked.

"You came in about your dressing gown, but it hadn't arrived. It came today. I've got it here."

She looked at the bag.

"All right," she said. "What's the delivery charge?"

"No charge. I just thought I'd drop it in to you."

She went on looking at the bag. The rain went on falling.

"You live round here?" she demanded.

"No. The other end of the bay, actually."

"Long way for you to come," she said accusingly.

"Well... I had to come up to The Rise tonight. And it seemed a shame, the way you came in and just missed the delivery. Here, do take it, or the rain may get in the bag."

She extended her hand and took the carrier.

"It was kind of you," she said. Her voice was full of dislike because I'd forced her into a show of gratitude.

"People don't usually bother nowadays."

"No, I know. But you said you hadn't got time to keep coming back, and I could see that, with—with your son..."

"Son," she interrupted. "So you know he's my son, do you?"

I felt hot with embarrassed fear.

"Well, whoever—"

"Haven't you got an umbrella?" she said.

"Er— no—"

"You're soaked," she said. I smiled foolishly, and her dislike reached its climax. "You'd better come in a minute."

"Oh no, really that isn't—"

She stood aside in the doorway, and I slunk past her into the hall. The door banged to.

I experienced instant claustrophobia and a yearning to run, but it was too late now. The glow was murky, there was a faintly musty smell, not stale exactly, more like the odour of a long closed box.

"This way."

We went by the stairs and a shut door, into a small back room, which in turn opened on a kitchen. There was a smokeless-coal fire burning in an old brown fireplace. The curtains were drawn, even at the kitchen windows, which I could see through the doorway. A clock ticked, setting the scene as inexorably as in a radio play. It reminded me of my grandmother's house years before, except that in my grandmother's house you couldn't hear the sea. And then it came to me that I couldn't pick it up here, either. Maybe some freak meander of the cliff blocked off the sound, as it failed to in the street.

I'd been looking for the wheelchair and, not seeing it,

had relaxed into an awful scared boredom. Then I registered the high-backed dark red chair, set facing the fire. I couldn't see him, and he was totally silent, yet I knew at once the chair was full of him. A type of electric charge went off under my heart. I felt quite horrible, as if I'd screamed with laughter at a funeral.

"Take your coat off," said Mrs. Besmouth. I protested feebly, trying not to gaze at the red chair. But she was used to managing those who could not help themselves, and she pulled the garment from me. "Sit down by the fire. I'm making a pot of tea."

I wondered why she was doing it, including me, offering her hospitality. She didn't want to, at least, I didn't think she did. Maybe she was lonely. There appeared to be no Mr. Besmouth. Those unmistakable spoors of the suburban male were everywhere absent.

To sit on the settee by the fire, I had to go round the chair. As I did so, he came into view. He was just as I recalled, even his position was unaltered. His hands rested loosely and beautifully on his knees. He watched the fire, or something beyond the fire. He was dressed neatly, as he had been in the shop. I wondered if she dressed him in these universal faded jeans, the dark pullover. Nondescript. The fire streamed down his hair and beaded the ends of his lashes.

"Hallo," I said. I wanted to touch his shoulder quietly, but did not dare.

Immediately I spoke, she called from her kitchen: "It's no good talking to him. Just leave him be, he'll be all right."

Admonished and intimidated, I sat down. The heavy anger was slow in coming. Whatever was wrong with him, this couldn't be the answer. My back to the kitchen, my feet still in their plastic boots which let water, I sat and looked at him.

I hadn't made a mistake. He really was amazing. How could she have mothered anything like this? The looks must have been on the father's side. And where had the illness come from? And what was it? Could I ask her, in front of him?

He was so far away, not here in this room at all. But where was he? He didn't look—oh God what word would do? —*deficient*. Leonardo da Vinci, staring through the face of one of his own half-finished, exquisite, lunar madonnas, staring through at some truth he was still seeking.... that was the look. Not vacant. Not.... missing—

She came through with her pot of tea, the cups and sugar and milk.

"This is very kind of you," I said.

She grunted. She poured the tea in a cup and gave it to me. She had put sugar in, without asking me, and I don't take sugar. The tea became a strange, alien, sickly brew, drunk for ritual. She poured tea into a mug, sugared it, and took it to the chair. I watched, breathing through my mouth. What would happen?

She took up his hand briskly, and introduced the mug into it. I saw his long fingers grip the handle. His face did not change. With a remote gliding gesture, he brought the mug to his lips. He drank. We both, she and I, looked on, as if at the first man, drinking.

"That's right," she said.

She fetched her own cup and sat on the settee beside me. I didn't like to be so close to her, and yet, we were now placed together, like an audience, before the profile of the red chair, and the young man.

I wanted to question her, ask a hundred things. His

name, his age. If we could get him to speak. If he was receiving any treatment, and for *what*, exactly. *How* I wanted to know that. It burned in me, my heart hammered, I was braised in racing waves of adrenalin.

But I asked her nothing like that.

You could not ask her these things, or I couldn't. And he was there, perhaps understanding, the ultimate constraint.

"It's very cosy here," I said. She grunted. "But I keep wondering why you can't hear the sea. Surely—"

"Yes," she said, "I don't get much time to go into the town centre. What with one thing and another."

That came over as weird. She belonged to the category of person who would do just that—skip an idea that had no interest for her and pass straight on to something that did. And yet, what was it? She'd been a fraction too fast. But I was well out of my depth, and had been from the start.

"Surely," I said, "couldn't the council provide some sort of assistance—a home-help—"

"Don't want anything like that."

"But you'd be entitled—"

"I'm entitled to my peace and quiet."

"Well, yes—"

"Daniel" she said sharply, "drink your tea. Drink it. It'll get cold."

I jumped internally again, and again violently. She'd said his name. Not alliterative after all. Daniel...! She'd also demonstrated he could hear, and respond to a direct order, for he was raising the mug again, drinking again.

"Now," she said to me, "if you've finished your tea, I'll have to ask you to go. I've his bath to see to, you understand."

I sat petrified, blurting some sort of apology. My brief brush with the bizarre was over and done. I tried not to visualise, irresistibly, his slim, pale, probably flawless male body, naked in water. He would be utterly helpless, passive, and it frightened me.

I got up.

"Thank you," I said.

"No, it was good of you to bring the dressing gown."

I couldn't meet her eyes, and had not been able to do so at any time.

I wanted at least to say his name, before I went away. But I couldn't get it to my lips, my tongue wouldn't form it.

I was out of the room, in my coat, the door was opening. The rain had stopped. There wasn't even an excuse to linger. I stepped on to the path.

"Oh, well. Goodbye, Mrs. Besmouth."

Her face stayed shut, and then she shut the door too.

I walked quickly along Sea View Terrace, walking without having yet caught up to myself, an automaton. This was naturally an act, to convince Mrs. Antacid, and the unseen watchers in their houses, and the huge dark watcher of the night itself, that I knew precisely where I wanted to go now, and had no more time to squander. After about half a minute, self-awareness put me wise, and I stopped dead. Then I did what I really felt compelled to do, still without understanding why. I reversed my direction, walked back along the terrace, and into the curling alley that ran down between Number 19, and the shoulder of the cliff.

I didn't have to go very far to see the truth of the amorphous thing I had somehow deductively fashioned already, in my mind. The back of Number 19, which would normally have looked towards the sea, was enclosed by an enormous brick wall. It was at least fourteen feet high—the topmost windows of the house were barely visible above it. I wandered how the council had been persuaded to permit such a wall. Maybe some consideration of sea-gales had come into it.... The next door house, I now noticed for the first time, appeared empty, touched by mild dereliction. A humped black tree that looked like a deformed cypress grew in the garden there, a further barrier against open vistas. No lights were visible in either house, even where the preposterous wall allowed a glimpse of them.

I thought about prisons, while the excluded sea roared ferociously at the bottom of the alley.

I walked along the terrace again, and caught the bus home.

Sunday was cold and clear, and I went out with my camera, because there was too much pure-ice wind to sketch. The water was like mercury under colourless sunlight. That evening, Angela had a party to which I had been invited. I drank too much, and a good-looking oaf called Ray mauled me about. I woke on Monday morning with the intense moral shame that results from the knowledge of truly wasted time.

Monday was my free day, or the day on which I performed my personal chores. I was loading the bag ready for the launderette when I remembered—the connection is elusive, but possibly Freudian—that I hadn't got the pre-paid receipt back from Mrs. Besmouth. Not that it would matter too much. Such records tended to be scrappy in Angela's department. I could leave it, and no one would die.

At eleven-thirty, I was standing by the door of Number 19, the knocker knocked and my heart was in my mouth.

I've always been obsessive. It's brought me some success, and quite a lot of disillusion, not to mention definite hurt. But I'm used to the excitement and trauma of it, and even then I was; used to my heart in my mouth, the trembling in my hands, the deep breath I must take before I could speak.

The door opened on this occasion quite quickly. She stood in the pale hard sunlight. I was beginning to learn her face, and its recalcitrant, seldom-varying expression. But she had on a different apron.

"Oh," she said, "It's you."

She'd expected me. She didn't exactly show it, she hadn't guessed what my excuse would be. But she'd known, just as I had, that I would come back.

"Look, I'm sorry to bother you," I said, "I forgot to ask you for the receipt."

"What receipt?"

"When you paid for the garment, they gave you a receipt. That one."

"I threw it away," she said.

"Oh. Oh well, never mind."

"I don't want to get you in trouble."

"No, it's all right. Really." I pulled air down into me like the drag of a cigarette, or a reefer. "How's Daniel today?"

She looked at me, her face unchanging.

"He's all right."

"I hoped I hadn't—well—upset him. By being there," I said.

"He doesn't notice," she said. "He didn't notice you."

There was a tiny flash of spite when she said that. It really was there. Because of it, I knew she had fathomed me, perhaps from the beginning. Now was therefore the moment to retreat in good order.

"I was wondering," I said, "What you told me, that you find it difficult to make the time to get to the town centre."

"I do," she said.

"I have to go shopping there today. If there's anything you need I could get you."

"Oh no," she said swiftly. "There's local shops on The Rise."

"I don't mind," I said.

"I can manage."

"I'd really like to. It's no bother. For one thing," I added, "the local shops are all daylight robbers round here, aren't they?"

She faltered. Part of her wanted to slam the door in my face. The other part was nudging her: Go on, let this stupid girl fetch and carry for you, if she wants to.

"If you want to, there are a few things. I'll make you a list."

"Yes, do."

"You'd better come in," she said, just like last time.

I followed her, and she left me to close the door, a sign of submission indeed. As we went into the back room, the adrenalin stopped coming, and I knew he wasn't there. There was something else, though. The lights were on, and the curtains were drawn across the windows. She saw me looking, but she said nothing. She began to write on a piece of paper.

I wandered to the red chair, and rested my hands on the back of it.

"Daniel's upstairs," I said.

"That's right."

"But he's—he's well?"

"He's all right. I don't get him up until dinner time. He just has to sit anyway, when he's up."

"It must be difficult for you, lifting him."

"I manage. I have to."

"But—"

"It's no use going on about home-helps again," she said. "It's none of their business."

She meant mine, of course. I swallowed, and said, "Was it an accident?" I'm rarely so blunt, and when I am, it somehow comes out rougher from disuse. She reacted obscurely, staring at me across the table.

"No, it wasn't. He's always been that way. He's got no strength in his lower limbs, he doesn't talk, and he doesn't understand much. His father was at sea, and he went off and left me before Daniel was born. He didn't marry me, either. So now you know everything, don't you?"

I took my hand off the chair.

"But somebody should—"

"No they shouldn't."

"Couldn't he be helped—?" I blurted.

"Oh, no," she said. "So if that's what you're after, you can get out now."

I was beginning to be terrified of her. I couldn't work it out if Daniel was officially beyond aid, and that's where her hatred sprang from, or if she had never attempted to have him aided, if she liked or needed or had just reasonlessly decided (God's will, My Cross) to let him rot alive. I didn't ask.

"I think you've got a lot to cope with," I said. "I can

give you a hand, if you want it. I'd like to."

She nodded.

"Here's the list."

It was a long list, and after my boast, I'd have to make sure I saved her money on the local shops. She walked into the kitchen and took a box out of a drawer. The kitchen windows were also curtained. She came back with a five-pound note I wasn't sure would be enough.

When I got out of the house, I was coldly sweating. If I had any sense I would now, having stuck myself with it, honourably do her shopping, hand it to her at the door, and get on my way. I wasn't any kind of a crusader, and, as one of life's more accomplished actors, even I could see I had blundered into the wrong play.

It was one o'clock before I'd finished her shopping. My own excursion to the launderette had been passed over, but her fiver had just lasted. The list was quite commonplace; washing powder, jam, flour, kitchen towels... I went into the pub opposite the store and had a gin and tonic. Nevertheless, I was shaking with nerves by the time I got back to Number 19. This was the last visit. This was it.

Gusts of white sunlight were blowing over the cliff. It was getting up rough in the bay, and the no-swimming notices had gone up.

She was a long while opening the door. When she did, she looked very odd, yellow-pale and tottery. Not as I'd come to anticipate. She was in her fifties, and suddenly childlike, insubstantial.

"Come in," she said, and wandered away down the passage.

There's something unnerving about a big strong

persona that abruptly shrinks pale and frail. It duly unnerved me, literally in fact, and my nerves went away. Whatever had happened, I was in command.

I shut the door and followed her into the room. She was on the settee, sitting forward. Daniel still wasn't there. For the first time it occurred to me Daniel might be involved in this collapse, and I said quickly: "Something's wrong. What is it? Is it Daniel? Is he OK?"

She gave a feeble contemptuous little laugh.

"Daniel's all right. I just had a bit of an accident. Silly thing, really, but it gave me a bit of a turn for a minute."

She lifted her left hand in which she was clutching a red and white handkerchief. Then I saw the red pattern was drying blood. I put the shopping on the table and approached cautiously.

"What have you done?"

"Just cut myself. Stupid. I was chopping up some veg for our dinner. Haven't done a thing like this since I was a girl."

I winced. Had she sliced her finger off and left it lying among the carrots? No, don't be a fool. Even she wouldn't be so acquiescent if she had. Or would she?

"Let me see," I said, putting on my firm and knowledgeable act, which has once or twice kept people from the brink of panic when I was in a worse panic than they were. To my dismay, she let go the handkerchief, and offered me her wound unresistingly.

It wasn't a pretty cut, but a cut was all it was, though deep enough almost to have touched the bone. I could see from her digital movements that nothing vital had been severed, and fingers will bleed profusely if you hit one of the blood vessels at the top.

"It's not too bad," I said. "I can bandage it up for you.

Have you got some TCP?"

She told me where the things were in the kitchen, and I went to get them. The lights were still on, the curtains were still drawn. Through the thin plastic of the kitchen drapes I could detect only flat darkness. Maybe the prison wall around the garden kept daylight at bay.

I did a good amateur job on her finger. The bleeding had slackened off.

"I should get a doctor to have a look at it, if you're worried."

"I never use doctors," she predictably said.

"Well, a chemist, then."

"It'll be all right. You've done it nicely. Just a bit of a shock." Her colour was coming back, what she had of it.

"Shall I make you a cup of tea?"

"That'd be nice."

I returned to the kitchen and put on the kettle. The tea apparatus sat all together on a tray, as if waiting. I looked at her fawn fizzy head over the settee back, and the soft coal-fire glows disturbing the room. It was always night time here, and always nineteen-thirty.

The psychological aspect of her accident hadn't been lost on me. I supposed, always looking after someone, always independently alone, she'd abruptly given way to the subconscious urge to be in her turn looked after. She'd given me control. It frightened me.

The kettle started to boil, and I arranged the pot. I knew how she'd want her tea, nigrescently stewed and violently sweet. Her head elevated. She was on her feet.

"I'll just go and check Daniel."

"I can do that, if you like," I said before I could hold my tongue.

"That's all right," she said. She went out and I heard

her go slowly up the stairs. Big and strong, how did she, even so, carry him down them?

I made the tea. I could hear nothing from upstairs. The vegetables lay scattered where she had left them, though the dangerous knife had been put from sight. On an impulse, I pulled aside a handful of kitchen curtain.

I wasn't surprised at what I saw. Somehow I must have worked it out, though not been aware I had. I let the curtain coil again into place, then carried the tea tray into the room. I set it down, and went to the room's back window, and methodically inspected that, too. It was identical to the windows of the kitchen. Both had been boarded over outside with planks of wood behind the glass. Not a chink of light showed. It must have been one terrific gale that smashed these windows and necessitated such a barricade. Strange the boarding was still there, after she'd had the glass replaced.

I heard her coming down again, but she had given me control, however briefly. I'd caught the unmistakable scent of something that wants to lean, to confess. I was curious, or maybe it was the double gin catching up on me. Curiosity was going to master fear. I stayed looking at the boarding, and let her discover me at it when she came in.

I turned when she didn't say anything. She simply looked blankly at me, and went to sit on the settee.

"Daniel's fine," she said. "He's got some of his books. Picture books. He can see the pictures, though he can't read the stories. You can go up and look at him, if you like."

That was a bribe. I went to the tea and started to pour it, spooning a mountain of sugar in her cup.

"You must be expecting a lot of bad weather, Mrs

Besmouth."

"Oh yes?"

"Yes. The windows."

I didn't think she was going to say anything. Then she said, "They're boarded over upstairs too, on the one side."

"The side facing out to sea."

"That's right."

"Did you build the wall up, too?"

She said, without a trace of humour, "Oh no. I got a man in to do that."

I gave her the tea, and she took it, and drank it straight down, and held the cup out to me.

"I could fancy another."

I repeated the actions with the tea. She took the second cup, but looked at it, not drinking. The clock ticked somnolently. The room felt hot and heavy and peculiarly still, out of place and time and light of sun or moon.

"You don't like the sea, do you?" I said. I sat on the arm of the red chair, and watched her.

"Not much. Never did. This was my dad's house. When he died, I kept on here. Nowhere else to go." She raised her elastoplasted hand and stared at it. She looked very tired, very flaccid, as if she'd given up. "You know," she said, "I'd like a drop of something in this. Open that cupboard, will you? There's a bottle just inside."

I wondered if she were the proverbial secret drinker, but the bottle was alone, and three quarters full, quite a good whisky.

She drank some of the tea and held the cup so I could ruin the whisky by pouring it in. I poured, to the cup's brim.

"You have one," she said. She drank, and smacked her

lips softly. "You've earned it. You've been a good little girl."

I poured the whisky neat into the other tealess cup and drank some, imagining it smiting the gin below with a clash of swords.

"I'll get merry," she said desolately. "I didn't have my dinner. The pie'll be spoiled. I turned the oven out."

"Shall I get you a sandwich?"

"No. But you can make one for Daniel, if you like."

"Yes," I said.

I got up and went into the kitchen. It was a relief to move away from her. Something was happening to Daniel's mother, something insidious and profound. She was accepting me, drawing me in. I could feel myself sinking in the quagmire.

As I made the sandwich from ingredients I came on more or less at random, she started to talk to me. It was a ramble of things, brought on by the relaxations of spilled blood and liquor, and the fact that there had seldom been anyone to talk *to*. As I buttered bread, sliced cheese and green cucumber, I learned how she had waited on and borne with a cantankerous father, nursed him, finally seen him off through the door in a box. I learned how she weighed meat behind the butcher's counter and did home-sewing, and how she had been courted by a plain stodgy young man, a plumber's assistant, and all she could come by in an era when it was essential to come by something. And how eventually he jilted her.

The whisky lay in a little warm pool across the floor of my mind. I began irresistibly to withdraw inside myself, comparing her hopeless life with mine, the deadly job leading nowhere, the loneliness. And all at once I saw a horrid thing, the horrid thing I had brought upon myself.

Her position was not hereditary, and might be bestowed. By speaking freely, she was making the first moves. She was offering me, slyly, her mantle. The role of protectress, nurse and mother, to Daniel—

I arranged the sandwich slowly on a plate. There was still time to run away. Lots of time.

"Just walking," I heard her say. "You didn't think about it then. Not like now. The sea was right out, and it was dark. I never saw him properly. They'd make a fuss about it now, all right. Rape. You didn't, then. I was that innocent, I didn't really know what he was doing. And then he let go and left me. He crawled off. I think he must have run along the edge of the sea, because I heard a splashing. And when the tide started to come in again, I got up and I tidied myself, and I walked home."

I stood quite still in the kitchen, the sandwich on its plate in my hands, wide-eyed, listening.

"I didn't know I was pregnant, thought I'd eaten something. The doctor put me right. He told me what he thought of me, too. Not in words, exactly, just his manner. Rotten old bugger. I went away to have the baby. Everybody knew, of course. When he was the way he was, they thought it was a punishment. They were like that round here, then. I lived off the allowance, and what I had put by, and I couldn't manage. And then, I used to steal things, what do you think of that? I never got found out. Just once, this woman stopped me. She said: I think you have a tin of beans in your bag. I had, too, and the bill. What a red face she got. She didn't tumble the other things I'd taken and hadn't paid for. Then I had a windfall. The old man I used to work for, the butcher, he died, and he left me something. That was a real surprise. A few thousand it was. And I put it in the Society, and I draw the interest."

I walked through into the room. She had had a refill from the bottle and was stirring sugar into it.

"Do you mean Daniel's father raped you?"

"Course that's what I mean."

"And you didn't know who it was?"

"No." She drank. She was smiling slightly and licked the sugar off her lips.

"I thought you said he was a sailor."

"I never. I said he was at sea. That's what I told people. My husband's at sea. I bought myself a ring, and gave myself a different name. Besmouth. I saw it on an advertisement. Besmouth's Cheese Crackers." She laughed. "At sea," she repeated. "Or out of it. He was mother naked, and wringing wet. I don't know where he'd left his clothes. Who'd believe you if you told them that?"

"Shall I take this up to Daniel?" I said.

She looked at me, and I didn't like her look, all whisky smile.

"Why not?" she said. She swallowed a belch primly. "That's where you've wanted to go all along, isn't it? 'How's Daniel?'" She mimicked me in an awful high soppy voice that was supposed to be mine, or mine the way she heard it. "'Is Daniel Ookay?' Couldn't stop looking at him, could you? Eyes all over him. But you won't get far. You can strip off and do the dance of the seven veils, and he won't notice."

My eyes started to water, a sure sign of revulsion. I felt I couldn't keep quiet, though my voice (high and soppy?) would tremble when I spoke.

"You're being very rude. I wanted to help."

"*Ohhh* yes," she said.

"The thing that worries me," I said, "is the way you coop him up. Don't you ever try to interest him in anything?" She laughed dirtily, and then did belch, patting her mouth as if in congratulation. "I think Daniel should be seen by a doctor. I'm sure there's some kind of therapy—"

She drank greedily, not taking any apparent notice of me.

I hurried out, clutching the sandwich plate, and went along the corridor and up the stairs, perching on two wobbly sticks. If I'd stayed with her much longer, I, too, might have lost the use of my lower limbs.

Light came into the hall from the glass in the door, but going up, it grew progressively murkier.

It was a small house, and the landing, when I got to it, was barely wide enough to turn round on. There was the sort of afterthought of a cramped bathroom old houses have put in—it was to the back, and through the open door, I could see curtains across the windows. They, too, must be boarded, as she had said. And in the bedroom which faced the back. A pathological hatred of the sea, ever since she had been raped into unwanted pregnancy beside it. If it were even true.... Did she hate Daniel, as well? Was that why she kept him as she did, clean, neat, fed, cared for and deliberately devoid of joy, of soul—?

There was a crisp little flick of paper, the virtually unmistakable sound of a page turning. It came from the room to my right: the front bedroom. There was a pane of light there too, falling past the angle of the half-closed door. I crossed to the door and pushed it wide.

He didn't glance up, just went on poring over the big slim book spread before him. He was sitting up in bed in spotless blue and white pyjamas. I had been beginning to visualise him as a child, but he was a man. He looked like some incredible convalescent prince, or an angel. The cold light from the window made glissandos over his hair. Outside, through the net, was the opposite side of the street, the houses, and the slope of the hill going up with other houses burgeoning on it. You couldn't even see the cliff. Perhaps this view might be more interesting to him than the sea. People would come and go, cars, dogs. But there was only weather in the street today, shards of it blowing about, The weather over the sea must be getting quite spectacular.

When she went out, how did she avoid the sea? She couldn't then, could she? I suddenly had an idea that somehow she had kept Daniel at all times from the sight of the water. I imagined him, a sad, sub-normal, beautiful little boy, sitting with his discarded toys—if he ever had any—on the floor of this house. And outside, five minutes' walk away, the sand, the waves, the wind.

The room was warm, from a small electric heater fixed up in the wall, above his reach. Not even weather in this room.

He hadn't glanced up at me, though I'd come to the bedside, he just continued gazing at the book. It was a child's book, of course. It showed a princess leaning down from a tower with a pointed roof, and a knight below, not half so handsome as Daniel.

"I've brought you some lunch," I said. I felt self-conscious, vaguely ashamed, his mother drunk in the room downstairs and her secrets in my possession. How wonderful to look at the rapist must have been. Crawled away, she had said. Maybe he too—

"Daniel," I said. I removed the book gently from his

grasp, and put the plate there instead.

How much of what she said to me about my own motives was actually the truth? There were just about a million things I wouldn't want to do for him, my aversion amounting to a phobia, to a state not of wouldn't but couldn't. Nor could I cope with this endless silent non-reaction. I'd try to make him react, I was trying to now. And maybe that was wrong, unkind—

Maybe I disliked and feared men so much I'd carried the theories of de Beauvoir and her like to an ultimate conclusion. I could only love what was male if it was also powerless, impotent, virtually inanimate. Not even love it. Be perversely aroused by it. The rape principle in reverse.

He wasn't eating, so I bent down, and peered into his face, and for the first time, I think he saw me. His luminous eyes moved, and fixed on mine. They didn't seem completely focussed, even so. But meeting them, I was conscious of a strange irony. Those eyes, which perhaps had never looked at the sea, held the sea inside them. *Were* the sea.

I shook myself mentally, remembering the whisky plummeting on the gin.

"Eat, Daniel," I said softly.

He grasped the sandwich plate with great serenity. He went on meeting my eyes, and mine, of course, filled abruptly and painfully with tears. Psychological symbolism: salt water.

I sat on the edge of the bed and stroked his hair. It felt like silk, as I'd known it would. His skin was so clear, the pores so astringently closed, that it was like a sort of silk, too. It didn't appear as if he had ever, so far, had to be shaved. Thank God. I didn't like the thought of her round him with a razor blade. I could even picture her producing her father's old cutthroat from somewhere, and doing just that with it, another accident, with Daniel's neck.

You see my impulse, however. I didn't even attempt to deal with the hard practicality of supporting such a person as Daniel really was. I should have persuaded or coerced him to eat. Instead I sat and held him. He didn't respond, but he was quite relaxed. Something was going through my brain about supplying him with emotional food, affection, physical security, something she'd consistently omitted from his diet. I was trying to make life and human passion soak into him. To that height I aspired, and, viewed another way, to that depth I'd sunk.

I don't know when I'd have grown embarrassed, or bored, or merely too tired and cramped to go on perching there, maintaining my sentimental contact with him, I didn't have to make the decision. She walked in through the door and made it for me.

"Eat your sandwich, Daniel," she said as she entered. I hadn't heard her approach on this occasion, and I jerked away. Guilt, presumably. Some kind of guilt. But she ignored me and bore down on him from the bed's other side. She took his hand and put it down smack on the bread. "Eat up," she said. It was macabrely funny, somehow pure slapstick. But he immediately lifted the sandwich to his mouth. Presumably he'd recognised it as food by touch, but not sight.

She wasn't tight anymore. It had gone through her and away, like her dark tea through its strainer.

"I expect you want to get along," she said.

She was her old self, indeed. Graceless courtesies, platitudes.

She might have told me nothing, accused me of nothing. We had been rifling each other's ids, but now it was done, and might never have been. I didn't have enough fight left in me to try to rip the renewed facade away again. And besides, I doubt if I could have.

So I got along. What else?

Before I went back to my room, I stood on the promenade awhile, looking out to sea. It was in vast upheaval, coming in against the cliffs like breaking glasses, and with a sound of torn atmosphere. Like a monstrous beast it ravened on the shore. A stupendous force seemed trying to burst from it, like anger, or love; or grief, orchestrated by Shostakovich, and cunningly lit by an obscured blind sun.

I wished Daniel could have seen it. I couldn't imagine he would remain unmoved, though all about me people were scurrying to and fro, not sparing a glance.

When I reached my nominative aunt's, the voice of a dismal news broadcast drummed through the house, and the odour of fried fish lurked like a ghost on the stairs.

The next day was Tuesday, and I went to work.

I dreamed about Daniel a lot during the next week. I could never quite recapture the substance of the dreams, their plot, except they were to do with him, and they felt bad. I think they had boarded windows. Perhaps I dreamed she'd killed him, or I had, and the boards became a coffin.

Obviously, I'd come to my senses, or come to avoid my senses. I had told myself the episode was finished with. Brooding about it, I detected only some perverted desire on my side, and a trap from hers. There was no one

I could have discussed any of it with.

On Wednesday, a woman in a wheelchair rolled through lingerie on her way to the china department. Dizzy with fright, if it was fright, I watched the omen pass. She, Mrs. Besmouth, could get to me any time. Here I was, vulnerably pinned to my counter like a butterfly on a board. But she didn't come in. Of course she didn't.

"Here," said Jill-sans-bra, "look what you've gone and dunn. You've priced all these eight-pound slips at six-forty-five."

I'd sold one at six-forty-five, too.

Thursday arrived, cinema day. A single customer came and went like a breeze from the cold wet street. There was a storm that night. A little ship, beating its way in from Calais, was swept over in the troughs, and there were three men missing, feared drowned. On Friday, a calm dove-grey weather bloomed, and bubbles of lemonade sun lit the bay.

I thought about that window looking on the street. He should have seen the water, oh, he should have seen it, those bars of shining lead, and the great cool topaz master bar that fell across them. That restless mass where men died and fish sprang. That other land that glowed and moved.

Saturday was pandemonium, as usual. Angela was cheerful. Her husband was in Scotland, and this evening the extra-marital relationship was meeting her. Rather than yearn for aloneness together, they apparently deemed two no company at all.

"Come over the pub with us. Jill and Terry'll be there. And I know Ray will. He asked me if you were coming."

Viewed sober, a night of drinking followed by the inevitable Chinese nosh-up and the attentions of the writhing Ray, was uninviting. But I, as all pariahs must be, was vaguely grateful for their toleration, vaguely pleased my act of participant was acceptable to them. It was also better than nothing, which was the only alternative.

"It's nice here," said Jill, sipping her Bacardi and coke.

They'd decided to go to a different pub, and I'd suggested the place on The Rise. It had a log fire, and they liked that, and horse brasses, and they liked sneering at those. Number 19. Sea View Terrace was less than a quarter of a mile away, but they didn't know about that, and wouldn't have cared if they had.

Lean, lithe Ray, far too tall for me, turned into a snake every time he flowed down towards me.

It was eight o'clock, and we were on the fourth round. I couldn't remember the extra-marital relationship's name. Angela apparently couldn't either; to her he was 'darling', 'love', or in spritely yielding moments, 'Sir'.

"Where we going to eat then?" said Ray.

"The Hwong Pews's ever so nice," said Jill.

Terry was whispering a dirty joke to Angela, who screamed with laughter. "Listen to this—"

Very occasionally, between the spasms of noise from the bar, you could just hear the soft shattering boom of the ocean.

Angela said the punch line and we all laughed.

We got to the fifth round.

"If you put a bell on," Ray said to me, "I'll give you a ring sometime."

I was starting to withdraw rather than expand, the alternate phase of tipsyness. Drifting back into myself, away from the five people I was with. Out of the crowded public house. Astral projection almost. Now I was on the street.

"You know, I could really fancy you," said Ray.

"You want to watch our Ray," said Angela.

Jill giggled and her jelly chest wobbled.

It was almost nine, and the sixth round. Jill had had an argument with Terry, and her eyes were damp. Terry, uneasy, stared into his beer.

"I think we should go and eat now," said the extra-marital relationship.

"Yes, sir," said Angela.

"Have a good time," I said. My voice was slightly slurred. I was surprised by it, and by what it had just vocalised.

"Good time," joked Angela. "You're coming, too."

"Oh, no—didn't I say? I have to be somewhere else by nine."

"She just wants an excuse to be alone with me," said Ray. But he looked as amazed as the rest of them. Did I look amazed, too?

"But where are you going?" Angela demanded. "You said—-"

"I'm sorry. I thought I told you. It's something I have to go to with the woman where I stay. I can't get out of it. We're sort of related."

"Oh, Jesus," said Ray.

"Oh well, if you can't get out of it." Angela stared hard at me through her mascara.

I might be forfeiting my rights to their friendship, which was all I had. And why? To stagger, cross-eyed with vodka, to Daniel's house. To do and say what? Whatever it was, it was pointless. This had more point. Even Ray could be more use to me than Daniel.

But I couldn't hold myself in check any longer. I'd had five days of restraint. Vile liquor had let my personal animal out of its cage. What an animal it was. Burning, confident, exhilarated and sure. If I didn't know exactly what its plans were, I still knew they would be glorious and great.

"Great," said Ray. "Well, if she's going, let's have another."

"I think I'll have a cream sherry," said Angela. "I feel like a change."

They had already excluded me, demonstrating I would not be missed. I stood on my feet, which no longer felt like mine.

"Thanks for the drinks," I said. I tried to look reluctant to be going, and they smiled at me, hardly trying at all, as if seeing me through panes of tinted glass.

It was black outside; where the street lights hadn't stained it, the sky looked clear beyond the glare, a vast roof. I walked on water.

Daniel's mother had been drunk when she told me about the rape. Truth in wine. So this maniac was presumably the true me.

The walk down the slope in the cold brittle air neither sobered me nor increased my inebriation. I simply began to learn how to move without a proper centre of balance. When I arrived, I hung on her gate a moment. The hall light mildly suffused the door panels. The upstairs room, which was his, looked dark.

I knocked. I seemed to have knocked that door thirty times. Fifty. A hundred. Each time, like a clockwork mechanism, Mrs. Besmouth opened it. Hallo, I've come to see Daniel. Hallo, I'm drunk, and I've come to scare you. I've spoken to the police about your son, I've said you neglect him. I've come to tell you what I think of you. I've booked two seats on a plane and I'm taking Daniel to Lourdes. I phoned the Pope, and he's meeting us there.

The door didn't open. I knocked twice more, and leaned in the porch, practising my introductory gambits.

I'm really a famous artist in disguise, and all I want is to paint Daniel. As the young Apollo, I think. Only I couldn't find a lyre. (Liar.)

Only gradually did it came to me that the door stayed shut, and gave every sign of remaining so. With the inebriate's hidebound immobility, I found this hard to assimilate. But presently it occurred to me that she might be inside, have guessed the identity of the caller, and was refusing to let me enter.

How long would the vodka stave off the cold? Ages, surely. I saw fur-clad Russians tossing it back neat amid snowdrifts, wolves howling in the background. I laughed sullenly, and knocked once more. I'd just keep on and on, at intervals, until she gave in. Or would she? She had over fifty years of fighting, standing firm, being harassed and disappointed. She'd congealed into it, vitrified. I was comparatively new at the game.

After ten minutes, I had a wild and terrifying notion that she might have left a spare key, cliché-fashion, under a flower pot. I was crouching over my boots, feeling about on the paving round the step for the phantom flower pot, when I heard a sound I scarcely know, but instantly identified. Glancing up, I beheld Mrs. Besmouth pushing the wheelchair into position outside her gate.

She had paused, looking at me, as blank as I had ever seen her. Daniel sat in the chair like a wonderful waxwork, or a strangely handsome Guy Fawkes dummy she had been out collecting money with for Firework

Night.

She didn't comment on my posture, neither did I. I rose and confronted her. From a purely primitive viewpoint, I was between her and refuge.

"I didn't think I'd be seeing you again," she said.

"I didn't think you would, either."

"What do you want?"

It was, after all, more difficult to dispense with all constraint than the vodka had told me it would be.

"I happened to be up here," I said.

"You bloody little do-gooder, poking your nose in."

Her tone was flat. It was another sort of platitude and delivered without any feeling, or spirit.

"I don't think," I said, enunciating pedantically, "I've ever done any good particularly. And last time, you decided my interest was solely prurient."

She pushed the gate, leaning over the chair, and I went forward and helped her. I held the gate and she came through, Daniel floating by below.

"You take him out at night," I said.

"He needs some fresh air."

"At night, so he won't see the water properly, if at all. How do you cope when you have to go out in daylight?"

As I said these preposterous things, I was already busy detecting, the local geography fresh in my mind, how such an evasion might be possible. Leave the house, backs to the sea, go up The Rise away from it, come around only at the top of the town where the houses and the blocks of flats exclude any street-level view. Then down into the town centre, where the ocean was only a distant surreal smudge in the valley between sky and promenade.

"The sea isn't anything," she said, wheeling him along

the path, her way to the door clear now. "What's there to look at?"

"I thought he might like the sea."

"He doesn't."

"Has he ever been shown it?"

She came to the door, and was taking a purse out of her coat pocket. As she fumbled for the key, the wheelchair rested by her, a little to one side of the porch. The brake was off.

The vodka shouted at me to do something. I was slow. It took me five whole seconds before I darted forward, thrust by her, grabbed the handles of the wheelchair, careered it around, and wheeled it madly back up the path and through the gate. She didn't try to stop me, or even shout, she simply stood there, staring, the key in her hand. She didn't look nonplussed either—I somehow saw that. *I* was the startled one. Then I was going fast around the side of Number 19, driving the chair like a cart or a doll's pram, into the curl of the alley that ran between cliff and wall to the beach. I'm not absolutely certain I remembered a live thing was in the chair. He was so still, so withdrawn. He really could have been same kind of doll.

But the alley was steep, steeper with the pendulum of man and chair and alcohol swinging ahead of me. As I braced against the momentum, I listened. I couldn't hear her coming after me. When I looked back, the top of the slope stayed empty. How odd. Instinctively I'd guessed she wouldn't lunge immediately into pursuit. I think she could have overcome me easily if she'd wanted to. As before, she had given over control of everything to me.

This time, I wasn't afraid.

Somewhere in the alley, my head suddenly cleared, and all my senses, like a window going up. All that was left of my insanity was a grim, anguished determination not to be prevented. I must achieve the ocean, and that seemed very simple. The waves roared and hummed at me out of the invisible, unlit dark ahead. Walking down the alley was like walking into the primeval mouth of Noah's Flood.

The cliff rounded off like a castle bastion. The road on the left rose away. A concrete platform and steps went up, then just raw rock, where a hut stood sentinel, purpose unknown. The beach appeared suddenly, a dull gleam of sand. The sea was all part of a black sky, until a soft white bomb of spray exploded out of it.

The street lamps didn't reach so far, and there were no fun-fair electrics to snag on the water. The sky was fairly clear, but with a thin intermittent race of clouds, and the nearest brightest stars and planets flashed on and off, pale grey and sapphire blue. A young crescent moon, too delicate to be out on such a cold fleeting night, tilted in the air, the only neon, but not even bleaching the sea.

"Look, Daniel," I murmured. "Look at the water."

All I could make out was the silken back of his head, the outline of his knees under the rug, the loosely lying artist's hands.

I'd reached the sand, and it was getting difficult to manoeuvre the wheelchair. The wheels were sinking. The long heels of my boots were sinking too. A reasonable symbol, maybe.

I thrust the chair on by main force, and heard things grinding as the moist sand became clotted in them.

All at once, the only way I could free my left foot was to pull my boot and leg up with both hands. When I tried the chair again, it wouldn't move anymore. I shoved a couple of times, wrenched a couple, but nothing happened and I let go.

We were about ten feet from the ocean's edge, but the tide was going out, and soon the distance would be greater.

Walking on tiptoe to keep the sink-weight off my boot heels, I went around the chair to investigate Daniel's reaction. I don't know what I'd predicted. Something, patently.

But I wasn't prepared.

You've heard the words: Sea-change.

Daniel was changing. I don't mean in any supernatural way. Although it almost was, almost seemed so. Because he was coming alive.

The change had probably happened in the eyes first of all. Now they were focussed. He was looking—really looking, and seeing—at the water. His lips had parted, just slightly. The sea wind was blowing the hair back from his face, and this, too, lent it an aura of movement, animation, as though he was in the bow of a huge ship, her bladed prow cleaving the open sea, far from shore, no land in sight.... His hands had changed their shape. They were curiously flexed, arched, as if for the galvanic effort of lifting himself.

I crouched beside him, as I had crouched in front of the house searching for the make-believe spare key. I said phrases to him, quite meaningless, about the beauty of the ocean and how he must observe it. Meaningless, because he saw, he knew, he comprehended. There was genius in his face. But that's an interpretation. I think I'm trying to say possession, or atavism.

And all the while the astounding change want on,

insidious now, barely explicable, yet continuing, mounting, like a series of waves running in through his blood, dazzling behind his eyes. He was alive—and with something. Yes, I think I do mean atavism. The gods of the sea were rising up in the void and empty spaces of Daniel, as maybe such gods are capable of rising in all of us, if terrified intellect didn't slam the door.

I knelt in the sand, growing silent, sharing it merely by being there beside him.

Then slowly, like a cinematic camera shot, my gaze detected something in the corner of vision. Automatically, I adjusted the magical camera lens of the eye, the foreground blurring, the distant object springing into its dimensions. Mrs. Besmouth stood several yards off, at the limit of the beach. She seemed to be watching us, engrossed, yet not moving. Her hands were pressed together, rigidly—it resembled that exercise one can perform to tighten the pectoral muscles.

I got to my feet a second time. This time I ran towards her, floundering in the sand, deserting the wheelchair and its occupant, their backs to the shore, facing out to sea.

I panted as I ran, from more than the exertion. Her eyes also readjusted themselves as I blundered towards her, following me, but she gave no corresponding movement: a spectator only. As I came right up to her, I lost my footing and grabbed out to steady myself, and it was her arm I almost inadvertently caught. The frantic gesture—the same one I might have used to detain her if she had been running forward—triggered in me a whole series of responses suited to an act of aggression that had not in fact materialised.

"No!" I shouted. "Leave him alone! Don't you dare

take him away. I won't let you—" and I raised my other hand, slapping at her shoulder ineffectually. I'm no fighter; I respect—or fear—the human body too much. To strike her breast or face would have appalled me. If we had really tussled I think she could have killed me long before my survival reflexes dispensed with my inhibitions.

But she didn't kill me. She shook me off; I stumbled and I fell on the thick cold cushion of the sand.

"I don't care what he does," she said. "Let him do what he wants." She smiled at me, a knowing scornful smile. "You adopt him. You take care of him. I'll let you."

I felt panic, even though I disbelieved her. To this pass we had come, I had brought us, that she could threaten me with such things. Before I could find any words—they would have been inane violent ones—her face lifted, and her eyes went over my head, over the beach, back to the place where I'd left the chair.

She said: "I think I always expected it'd come. I think I always waited for it to happen. I'm sick and tired of it. I get no thanks. All the rest of them. They don't know when they're well off. When did I ever have anything? Go on, then. Go on."

I sat on the ground, for she'd knocked the strength from me. She didn't care, and I didn't care.

Someone ought to be with Daniel. Oh God, how were we going to get the wheelchair back across the sand? Perhaps we'd have to abandon it, carry him back between us. I'd have to pay for a new chair. I couldn't afford it, I—

I had been turning, just my head, and now I could see the wheelchair poised, an incongruous black cut-out against the retreating breakers which still swam in and splintered on the lengthening beach. It was like a

Surrealist painting, I remember thinking that, the lost artefact, sigil of stasis, set by the wild night ocean, sigil of all things metamorphic. If the chair had been on fire, it could have been a Magritte.

Initially the movement didn't register. It seemed part of the insurge and retraction of the waves. A sort of pale glimmer, a gliding. Then the *weirdness* of it registered with me, and I realised it was Daniel. Somehow he had slipped from the chair, collapsed forward into the water, and, incredibly, the water was pulling him away with itself, away into the darkness.

I lurched up. I screamed something, a curse or a prayer or his name or nothing at all. I took two riotous running steps before she grasped me. It was a fierce hold, undeniable, made of iron. Oh she was so strong. I should have guessed. She had been lifting and carrying a near grown man for several years. But I tried to go on rushing to the ocean, like those cartoon characters you see, held back by some article of elastic. And like them, when she wouldn't let me go, I think I ran on the spot a moment, the sand cascading from under me.

"Daniel—" I cried, "he's fallen in the water—the tide's dragging him out—can't you see—?"

"I can see," she said. "You look, and you'll see, too."

And her voice stopped me from moving, just as her grip had stopped my progression. All I could do then was look, so I looked.

We remained there, breathing, our bodies slotted together, like lovers, speechless, watching. We watched until the last pastel glimmer was extinguished. We watched until the sea had run far away into the throat of night. And after that we watched the ribbed sands, the plaster cast the waves forever leave behind them. A few things had been stranded there, pebbles, weed, a broken battle. But Daniel was gone, gone with the sea. Gone away into the throat of night and water.

"Best move the chair," she said at last, and let me go.

We walked together and hoisted the vacant wheelchair from the sand. We took it back across the beach, and at the foot of the alley we rested.

"I always knew," she said then. "I tried to stop it, but then I thought: Why try? What good is it?" Finally she said to me: "Frightened, are you?"

"Yes," I said, but it was a reflex.

"I'm glad," she said. "You silly little cow."

After that we hoisted the chair up the alley, to the gate of Number 19. She took it to the house, and inside, and shut the door without another word.

I walked to the bus stop, and when the lighted golden bus flew like a spaceship from the shadows, I got on it. I went home, or to the place where I lived. I recall I looked at everything with vague astonishment, but that was all. I didn't feel what had occurred, didn't recognise or accept it. That came days later, and when it did I put my fist through one of my nominative aunt's windows. The impulse came and was gone in a second. It was quite extraordinary. I didn't know I was going to, I simply did. My right hand, my painter's hand. I managed to say I'd tripped and fallen, and everything was a mistake. After the stitches came out, I packed my bags and went inland for a year. It was so physically painful for a while to manipulate a brush or palette knife, it became a discipline, a penance to do it. So I learned. So I became what now I am.

I never saw Mrs. Besmouth again. And no one, of course, ever again saw Daniel.

You see, a secret agent is one who masquerades, one who pretends to be what he or she is not. And, if successful, is indistinguishable from the society or group or affiliation into which he or she has been infiltrated. In the Magritte painting, you're shown the disguise, which is that of a human girl, but the actuality also, the creature within. And oddly, while she's more like a chess-piece horse than any human girl, her essence is of a girl, sheer girl, or rather, the sheer feminine principle, don't you think? Maybe I imagine it.

I heard some rumour or other at the time, just before the window incident. The atrocious Ray was supposed to have laced my drink. With what I don't know, nor do I truly credit it. It's too neat. It accounts for everything too well. But my own explanations then were exotic, to say the least. I became convinced at one point that Daniel had communicated with me telepathically, pleaded, coerced, engineered everything. I'd merely been a tool of his escape, like a file hidden in a cake. His mother had wanted it too. Afraid to let go, trying to let go. Letting go.

Obviously, you think we murdered him, she and I. A helpless, retarded, crippled young man, drowned in Ship Bay one late autumn night, two women standing by in a horrific complicity, watching his satin head go under the black waters, not stirring to save him.

Now I ask myself, I often ask myself, if that's what took place. Maybe it did. Shall I tell you what I saw? I kept it till the end—coup de grâce, or cherry, whichever you prefer.

It was a dark clear night, with not much illumination, that slender moon, those pulsing stars, a glint of phosphorous, perhaps, gilding the sea. But naked, and so pale, so flawless, his body glowed with its own incandescence, and his hair was water-fire, colourless, and brilliant.

I don't know how he got free of his clothes. They *were* in the chair with the rug—jeans, trunks, pullover, shirt— no socks, I remember, and no shoes. I truly don't think he could walk, but somehow, as he slid forward those three or four yards into the sea, the sight of the waves must have aided him, their hypnotism drawing off his garments, sloughing them like a dead skin.

I saw him, just for a moment. His Apollo's head, modelled sleek with brine, shone from the breakers. He made a strong swimmer's movement. Naturally, many victims of paralysis find sudden coordination of their limbs in the weightless medium of fluid.... Certainly Daniel was swimming, and certainly his movements were both spontaneous and voluntary.

And now I have the choice as to whether I tell you this or not. It's not that I'm afraid, or nervous of telling you. I'm not even anxious as to whether or not you believe me. Perhaps I should be. But I shan't try to convince you. I'll state it, once. Recollect, the story about Ray and the drinks may be true, or possibly the quirk was only in me, the desire for miracles in my world of Then, where nothing happened, nothing was rich, or strange.

For half a minute I saw the shape of a man, spearing fishlike through the water. And then came one of those deep lacunas, when the outgoing tide abruptly collects itself, seems to swallow, pauses. And there in the trough, the beautiful leaping of something, white as salt crystal, smoky green as glass. The hair rose on my head, just as they say it does. Not terror, but a feeling so close to it as it be untranslatable—a terror, yet without fear. I saw a shining horse, a stallion, with a mane like opals and unravelling foam, his forefeet raised, heraldic, his belly a carven bow, the curve of the moon, the rest a silken fish, a great greenish sheen of fish, like the tail of a dolphin, but scaled over in a waterfall of liquid armour, like a shower of silver coins. I saw it, and I knew it. And then it was gone.

The woman with me said nothing. She had barricaded her windows, built up her wall against such an advent. And I said nothing because it is a dream we have, haven't we, the grossest of us, something that with childhood begins to perish. To tear the veil, to see. Just for a moment, a split second in all of life. And the split second was all I had, and it was enough. How could one bear more?

But I sometimes wonder if Magritte, whose pictures are so full of those clear moments of terror, but not fear, moment on moment on moment—I sometimes wonder—

Then again, when you look at the sea, or when I look at it, especially at night, anything at all seems possible.

PAPER BOAT

The summer heat had come. It burned the hills to blocks of standing smoke. It filled the bowl of the shore and the spoon of the bay with its opium, it painted the terracotta of the house in progressively darkening washes of red and umber. The sea, a throbbing indigo, pulled itself to the beach and tumbled there as if drugged. The island lay dumb, half conscious, scarcely breathing, vanquished.

It seemed to the poet he was made of some form of clockwork and the clock had stopped. He stood by the narrow window, looking at the blue-black sea, the distant shadow of a dreamlike mainland chalked in haze. Perhaps this was how the island itself felt, the sea; the rock... this lifeless, numb, internal silence, devoid of anything, even questioning or fear.

This was where they had planned to spend the summer. This island and this house. This house, like a doll's house. If you opened the side of it you would see all the pretty dolls in their doll-like attitudes of occupation. Laura, scribbling bitter witty prose, with the yellow blind shielding her window from the sun, turning her to amber, a fierce amber hand, the scorched ember-coloured pages. Farther down, Sibbi bending like an Egyptian over a bowl of osiers and sun-mummified flowers, Sibbi with her magical face and her bright shallow brain, and her husband, Arthur, a bear, at the eternal business of his pipe, knocking out dottle, refilling it, that rank black tobacco odour woven by now into the scalding incense of every room. And somewhere, Albertine, like a tall, white goddess from a frieze, moving silently and gently about, being careful to tread on the paws of none of them, this moody tribe of cats who inhabited her domestic landscape.

And he, the black cat at the top of the house, the black cat in the symbolic tower with a door up to the roof where, under the golden awning, the metallic telescope was pointing like a tongue at the sea. The black cat was a poet and scholar. So, if you had opened the doll's house you should see him seated in the brown shadow at the desk, lost in some elegy or epic, among the open paper mouths of Plato, Virgil and Homer. And instead you saw him at the narrow window, the doll poet with the clockwork stopped inside him.

Below, the silver hammers of the piano began to strike each other, and a girl's lovely singing winged up, yet the sounds had an undersea quality, stifled by the leaden air. Sibbi, her flowers meticulously imprisoned in their bowl, singing her siren's song to the poet in the tower. She sang to disturb him as he worked, to get her image between the pen and the paper. If he should say to her as they ate dinner: "I heard you sing", she would answer: "Oh, I am so sorry. Did I disturb you? I never thought you could hear me." Her eyes were the colour of blue irises; they gave an impression of great depth simply because a world of vacuity opened behind them. She was a claw delicately scratching at him. All three women, the priestesses presumably of his shrine, were claws in his body—Sibbi clawed at his loins, very softly and with her own curious art, promising and never quite giving, giving, and promising more, like all empty vessels offering an illusion of hidden things. Laura clawed at his conscience; sharp-tongued and clever Laura, reminding him of her rights to him by means of a past neither wished to recapture.

Only Albertine clawed at his heart. Albertine, who was sad and travailed not to show it, who was brave and good and adored him, Albertine the best of women, whom he no longer loved. They had metamorphosed into different people from the two impassioned children who met in a graveyard in order to be secret, embraced on graves, and finally, hero and heroine of their own romance, had fled security with a wild hymn of abandon. Now they had grown up, security had gathered on them after all, like barnacles. The dismal shadow of reality overlay them both. They had found out they were not gods and they were not suited.

The light from the sea, so darkly bright, made him shut his eyes. Sibbi sang below. No one else responded to the heat as he had done with this anaesthetic languor. There was a timelessness around him now. No past, no present, nothing to come. He could sense the mechanism stilled, the unheard drone of the sun. A perpetual, well-known knowledge of loneliness gnawed somewhere inside him, yet he scarcely felt it. Only the sullen noise of the sea ran up the beaches of his mind and swooned like an indigo woman against him, and slipped away through his fingers, sighing when he tried to hold her, while down below Arthur Merton knocked the dottle from his pipe, refilled it, lit it, and leaned back in his chair, and considered it was very hot.

"Damned hot," he said.

Through the smoke of the pipe, and through the embalmed-looking stalks and scarlet rose-heads in the Indian bowl, Merton could see Sibbi at the piano in the next room, playing and singing prettily, sometimes glancing towards the open veranda doors with the sly, half-excited, half-evaluating look she reserved for Ashburn. Inadvertently Merton's eyes slid up towards the weary stucco of the ceiling. Above them all, Robert Ashburn would be writing in the tower room, working in this infernal heat. If he was. Too hot to do much now. Even the boat, Ashburn's love, lay neglected by the quay. The sailing days had been good. When it was cooler...

Merton sensed, as if through the steam or fog of his thoughts, the glamour of the girl at the piano, the witchery of that curious straying glance, once turned to advantage on himself. He felt no resentment. He also, in an improbable, asexual way, stirred at the thought of the dark young man above, the anguished poet—anguished by everything or nothing. The moods of the poet lit up dim glares of unrealised fire in Merton himself. Sonnets he did not properly understand, written perfectly obviously to his wife Sibbi, nevertheless pierced Merton's wooden soul like splinters of glass with a painful, inexplicable delight.

Sibbi finished her song. Notes and voice ebbed from the room, and the heat seemed to flood into the empty spaces. Presently she came to the doorway and stood looking at him, like a cat with a canary dead in its mouth, contemptuous, cruel and affectionate, knowing it will be forgiven simply because it is as it is.

"That was very nice," Merton observed.

Sibbi smiled.

"How would you know? You don't care for music."

"Well, I care for yours, you know."

"Actually, I was playing for Robert, but I'm glad you enjoyed it, Arthur dear." She leaned her hand with its wedding ring on the upright of the door, admiring it, her eyes a little glazed with heat and excitement. "How bad of him to be in the garden at this hour, when he should be working. Laura will scold him, I expect. He hasn't completed anything this summer."

Merton laughed.

"We shall have to visit the eye specialist after all," he remarked. A year ago she had been threatened with the nemesis of spectacles, now some little spark of intransigent animosity made him refer to the terror whenever possible, in the form of a joke. "Robert was never in the garden."

"Don't be absurd. I saw him quite clearly. I see better than you do."

"But you don't hear better, Sibbi. I heard him upstairs, walking about while you were at the piano. You know how he walks, like an animal in a cage, up and down."

"I think you must have sunstroke. You had better lie down. I saw Robert absolutely distinctly, by the stone urn at the end of the walk, listening while I played."

Merton got up with a reluctant irritating air of investigation and went slowly across the room, past Sibbi, to the veranda doors. The garden, stripped of shadow by the two o'clock sun, offered a vista of lank and blistered green with clumps of statuary, like unhealthy fungus or sores, pushed up at intervals. The local gardener was trudging complainingly beside Albertine along the walk. The old sunburned islander and the tall, fair girl advanced in a desultory slow motion; nothing else stirred except for an inflammatory scatter of crickets, crackling as if trying to set the grass on fire.

"I spy with my short-sighted eye Albertine and that old devil from the village."

Sibbi came to his side.

"Well, no doubt Robert's come indoors. He was just there a moment ago."

"Then he'd come through these doors here, wouldn't he? The only other way is to jump off the wall and, since the tide's in, swim round to the front, which seems", he knocked dottle from his pipe to stress the point, "unnecessary."

"Then he's still in the garden. What a fuss you're making."

"You, my dear, are the one making the fuss."

Merton went out on to the terrace and waved to Albertine. The girl lifted her head; the gardener picked his fangs, disdaining the mad people of the house, recounting whose debaucheries and insanities kept him in free liquor at the village.

"Did you pass Robert on the walk?"

"Why, no, he's upstairs in the tower room."

"You see," Merton exulted.

Sibbi shook her head. Her teeth snapped on canary bones. "I distinctly saw him, I tell you."

Albertine crossed the lawn, glancing up anxiously at the shuttered landward window of the little tower and at the yellow awning above.

"Now you've made Albertine uneasy," Sibbi said crossly. She glanced at the girl with the same mixture of contempt and liking she had displayed for her husband. She had enchanted the poet, and could afford to be generous to his dull, pleasant handmaiden. Laura, the serpent-tongued, was the one she feared. Albertine called in a high light voice:

"Robert," and then again: "Robert!"

They all stared up as if mesmerised at the closed shutters, even the mahogany gardener, his thumbnail worrying at his canines, added an oil-black stare to theirs.

"Robert," Sibbi suddenly sang out, as if certain her magic would conjure him where Albertine's could not. The heat swirled sulkily and reformed. The gardener muttered ominously:

"He write. He deaf to you."

Abruptly, for no particular reason, each one of them shouted at the masked window.

"Here I am," Ashburn said.

They looked down and saw him coming between the veranda doors.

Albertine and Sibbi exclaimed; the gardener turned and spat disgustedly.

Merton said, "Well, well. Just down from the tower."

"That's right."

"But you were in the garden," Sibbi asserted almost angrily. "I saw you standing on the walk while I played."

The poet looked at her and seemed not quite to see her. His eyes, also glazed by the heat, and very dark, appeared to gaze inwards, backwards into the shadows of his brain. He gave one of his absent, charming, half-apologetic smiles. "Yes, I heard you singing upstairs."

Sibbi failed to take up her cue. She looked feverish, annoyed; she went to him and touched his hand and gave a little hard silver laugh like piano notes.

They went in arm in arm to dinner. Merton trailed after. "Perhaps, you know, we have a ghost."

The food was served and partly eaten. It was too hot for food. Merton, watching Albertine's gentle cameo face, the barley-coloured hair, visualised all the paraphernalia of a saint, fashioned for crucifixion. She ate little. If Ashburn looked at her she might eat something, pathetically attempting to deceive him. Merton passed her rolls reverently and helped her to wine. She was a fine woman, a sweet girl. Her devotion to the poet moved Merton, for perhaps, in some obscure way, it justified his own devotion to his blue-eyed cat wife.

Now, striving to cheer everyone up after the labour of eating, he revived his little piece and filled his pipe.

"Do you think we might have a ghost?"

"Such fun," Laura observed acidly.

Albertine lowered her eyes and played with a piece of bread. "I'd far rather we hadn't."

Sibbi, quickened, seated next to Ashburn, caught his eye. "But how romantic—to think I supposed it was you, and all the time it was a spirit. How edifying!" The wine had gone to her head, and her appetite was unimpaired.

"These old houses, you know," Merton went on, "though I don't really believe in such stuff myself. Rather wish I did, you know."

"Of course," Sibbi said, "you'd frighten any ghost to death."

Laura said; "Does it also write poetry, I wonder? Though, of course, Robert doesn't write anything at present."

"Don't chide me, dear Laura," he said.

"I shall always chide you," Laura said. "No one else dares to do it, and without chiding you would perish."

Albertine rose. "I wish it weren't so hot," she said.

She drifted towards the windows. Merton stared at his plate. Albertine's eyes were full of tears, a nakedness which thrilled and embarrassed him.

"Just think," Laura said, also rising, "if there were a ghost, we should have to call one of those village priests to exorcise it." She crossed to stand behind Ashburn's chair, and set one hand very lightly on his shoulder. "Do you know," she said, "they are praying for rain—actually praying. And never in my life did I hear such pagan screaming as emanates from the Catholic church. Come now, Robert, we will take a walk in the garden, you and I, and you shall tell me what you are writing."

Sibbi said: "Yes, the garden, I think I shall come with you—"

Laura smiled at her. "I have a much better idea. I heard you playing earlier. You have such a delicate touch and yet, I believe, that latest piece would benefit from practice—why not practice now, Sibbi? It's a little cooler, I think."

Sibbi narrowed her cat's eyes as Laura and Ashburn strolled into the garden. She stalked to the piano and began to play very loudly and brilliantly. "How do you stand that woman, Albertine?" she demanded. "Does she suppose she owns everything?"

Albertine sat in the wicker chair by the veranda doors. Her dress spilled about her feet like a pool of milk. "Never mind," she said soothingly, as if to a child. She watched Ashburn and Laura go up and down the walks among the burning green with its little filigree flickers of shade. The brazen clangour of heat was mulling, darkening, lying down like lions under the trees. Albertine could imagine Laura saying to Ashburn:

"Yes, I know what I am to you. Albertine is your heart, and this silly little Sibbi your appetite. And I am your brain. Do you think you can relinquish me?"

Albertine imagined she saw how the poet became animated, speaking of what he wrote to Laura. She sat very still in the wicker chair, watching them. A whole procession with its banners travelled through her mind, the first meeting, the first dream, the first embrace, the green graves, the seascapes, the hot gipsy summers with, superimposed upon it all, Laura, with her sharp dark gown slashing at the grass.

Suddenly Sibbi jumped up. "Why didn't I think of it before? We must hold a séance. There is an ideal little table, and I recall there is something one does with a wineglass—" She ran to the veranda doors and called out. Ashburn turned at once. Sibbi stood, like a slender flower stalk, holding out her hand to him across the lawn.

And shortly they all sat round a table, like figures inscribed on a clock.

They held hands, the obdurate glass discarded. Nothing had happened, but it was too hot to move. Merton, seated between Sibbi and Laura, fell suddenly asleep and woke as suddenly with a wild grunt. As it had mummified the flowers, the earth, the island, the heat mummified the two men and three women at the table.

Only the eyes of the women sometimes darted, like needles stabbing between their lashes, observing the poet. Sibbi held one of his hands, Albertine the other. Ashburn, blinded by the heat, shut his eyes and experienced the sensation of two leeches, one on either palm, sucking his blood from him. He thought he had fallen asleep for a moment as Merton had done; he could not resist looking down at his hands. Albertine's hand was cold as ice, Sibbi's warm and dry. A peculiar stasis had fallen over them all. The poet glanced up and saw the clock had fittingly stopped on the mantelshelf. The eyes of the three women and of the man, as always, were on him.

"This is very irksome," Laura said. "Really, Sibbi, can't you use some blandishment to persuade your ghostie to appear? I have three letters to write—"

"I could sing," Sibbi said; her hand moved in his. "If

Robert thinks I should."

"That should charm any ghost, I'm sure," stung Laura. They had drawn the blinds; the room was drowned in a bloody shadow. The poet stared at the silent clock.

"What would you like me to sing?" Sibbi murmured, offering the sting so that he could draw the poison from it.

"Anything," he said. *What does it matter*, he thought, *what she sings?* Desire ran through her hand into his body, yet he scarcely felt it, sex, like an absent limb lost in some war, castrated by some mental battle... His eyes unfocused on the face of the clock. He did not want to go back to the room in the tower, to the unfinished work, the spell which evaded him, urgent once, now meaningless. He had put it off. The girl began softly to sing; she sang as if far away over some hill of the mind, words he had written to an old tune of the island:

> *"Stream, from the black cold sun of night,*
> *Phantoms in robes of darkest light,*
> *To muddy the clear waters of our lives*
> *With dreams."*

And after this dream, what? The room began to breathe about him, or else it was the sea. Nothing achieved or to come, and if achieved what did it signify? Ants crawling in ant cities... He felt the floor tilt a little beneath his chair and thought distantly: *Now, an earthquake.*

But it was the sea, the sea cool and green, washing in across the floor.

"By George, we're flooded," Merton observed jovially, without rancour or alarm. "And the roof's come down."

The house was gone. In a paper boat they rocked

gently over an ocean glaucous and slippery as the backs of seals.

"Look at this," Merton said, prodding the paper. "Soon sink. Dear chap, I said the shipwright should look at her. Not sea-worthy, you know."

The ship was composed of manuscripts. The ink ran and darkened the water.

"You have had my wife, of course," Merton said, "but it's all for the best. Ballast, you-know. Jettison extra cargo."

The poet looked down and saw that Laura and Sibbi floated under the glass-green runnels of waves with wide eyes and fish swimming in their hair and in and out of their open mouths. With his right hand he was holding Albertine beneath the water, while her garments floated out like Ophelia's, and she smiled at him sadly, encouraging him to do whatever was necessary to save himself.

Ashburn leapt to his feet and the bottom gave way in the paper boat and, as the water closed over his head like salty fire, he saw Merton knock the dottle from his pipe—

Albertine still lay against his arm, he was trying to lift her above the sea and she was calling to him and struggling with him and suddenly he found himself in the blood-red room with fragments of glass on the table, Sibbi cowering in her chair, and no hands visible except Albertine's, both holding on to him, as if he and she were drowning indeed.

But it was night which drowned everything, all confusion and outcry.

It swooped on the island. The sea turned red then black, the sky opened itself to an ochre moon. A serpent of lights wound out of the village at sunset and settled upon the beach below the house with the hoarse screeches of predatory bats.

"Our favourite pagan-Christians are restive again," Laura said. "Dear God, who would believe such ceremonies could still exist. Are they sacrificing maidens to the sea?"

"Praying for rain," Merton said. "Poor beggars. They get little enough from the land in a good year, but this drought—well, there's no telling."

"Their hovels are empty of food, clothing and furniture," Laura said, "and in the church are three gold candlesticks. How can such fools hope to survive?"

Merton lit his pipe and relapsed in his shadowy chair. Sibbi sat slapping down cards before the lamp; Laura, her wormwood letters written, stood at the window gazing out at the firefly glare on the foreshore. And above? From time to time each of the three looked up at the ceiling. The poet and his pale woman were locked in some curious, stilted, yet private and unsharing communion.

My satisfaction lies only in observing my fellow exiles, Laura thought, and glanced at Sibbi with a dark little smile. "Really, dear Sibbi, you did get such a scare, didn't you?"

Sibbi slapped down the coloured cards, commonly, as Laura had seen the market women do with fish. "I don't know what you mean. Anyone might be taken ill in this weather."

"Yes, of course," Laura smiled, "and scream at the top of his lungs, and frighten little Miss Muffet into a flawless fit. Did you imagine only women are permitted to have hysterics? You will have to get accustomed to such things in this house."

"Some sort of—of nightmare," Merton ventured.

"Dropped off myself."

Laura showed her teeth, as sharp, predatory and feline as Sibbi's and with no pretence. "What does Sibbi see in the cards? Good fortune, health and happiness? Or is it a soupçon of undying love?"

She leaned back against the window frame. The torches were guttering out, the howling voices blown to cindery shreds on the wind. A melancholy hollowness yawned inside her, a disembowelling ache, She suffered it, waiting, as if for a spasm of pain, until it passed. *Does nothing die?* she thought, her heart squeezing its bitterness like a lemon into her veins.

The shore was all darkness now. The foxy moon meanly described only the edges of the sand, the ribs of the water. Above on the tower, the awning gave a single despotic flap like the wing of a huge bird. Laura looked upward, then down, and made out a figure walking along beneath the garden wall, towards the beach and the sea. For a moment she did not question it, saw only some fragment of the night, a metaphysical shape without reference. Then, from the turn of the head, the manner of moving, she recognised Ashburn.

"Merton—look—" Merton came rumbling to the window. His pipe smoke enveloped Laura; she thrust it from her eyes. "Do you see? What can he be doing?"

"Good lord," Merton muttered, "Good lord."

"For heaven's sake, go after him," Laura cried. "In this state, he'll walk into the sea and never realise it."

They ran together towards the front of the house and burst out wildly onto the beach, Merton stumbling, Sibbi erupting in a frenzy of curiosity, demand and fright after them. The dreadful, enormous intimacy of the darkness swept over them, the hot dim essence of the night, which still faintly carried the arcane noises of the islanders and the smell of torch smoke.

"Oh, where is he?" Laura cried. She could not reason why she was so afraid, yet all three had caught the fear, like sickness.

"There, I see him. You stay here—" Merton set off across the sand, a blundering, great, bear-like form, shouting now: "Ashburn! Robert!"

"Oh, the unsubtle fool," Laura moaned.

Sibbi half lay against the door biting her wedding ring, hissing over and over: "I can't bear it, I simply won't bear it."

Merton plunged towards the sea, waving his arms, yelling; then abruptly stopped. Simultaneously, the seaward window of the tower opened, and the wind snatched pale handfuls of hair out upon itself as if unravelling silver wool from the head of Albertine.

"What's wrong?" she called down, in a soft, panic-stricken voice.

"Don't you know?" Laura screamed at her.

"Oh, please be quiet," Albertine implored. "Don't wake him, for God's sake."

Laura ran out onto the shore, stared up at the window, then towards the bone-yellow breakers of the sea smashing at Merton's feet.

"I saw Robert walking towards the water," Laura said. "So did Arthur."

"But he's sleeping," Albertine protested. She glanced over her shoulder into the tower room. Her normally calm face betrayed itself when she looked again downwards at Laura. It was convulsed in horrified accusation and loathing and white as the face of a clock. She shrank back and closed the window after her with violent noiselessness.

Merton came up the beach, sweat ran down his cheeks. He looked at Laura silently and passed on. Sibbi giggled wildly in the doorway. "I didn't see," she cried. The breakers clashed on the shore and raked the sand with their black fingers.

They had expressions suitable for everything.

They breathed closely, at midnight, like a woman on the poet's pillow, her ocean voice sounding in the seashell of his ear. He woke and searched for her, a woman with any number of faces. But no woman lay on the narrow bed in the tower, only a girl sat asleep in a chair near the window.

He got up quietly and went to look at her, yet somehow had no fear that she would wake. Her profile, her defenceless hands and alabaster torrent of hair, all these touched him with a listless tenderness. He wanted to stroke the tired lines away from her mouth which, even in sleep, had a touch of the hungry recalcitrant childishness that generally moulds only the mouths of old women. He wanted to soothe her, go back with her to the green shades of the past. Yet he had no energy, no true impulse. He stood penitently before her, as if she were dead. He desired nothing from her, really desired nothing from any of them, and they clamoured to load him with their gifts, to fetter him with their kindness.

What do you want, then? Undying fame, the glory of the king whose monument is made of steel and lasts forever? Or does any monument last, or any hope? And does any wish of a man matter?

He left her slumped there and went down the stair from the tower. In her wasp-cell Laura would be sleeping, curled like a foetus around her hate and pain. And pretty

Sibbi, probably quite content in the arms of her bear. He crossed the room where the piano stood like a beast of black mirror. He opened the veranda doors yet the garden seemed more enclosed even than the house, full of heat and shadows like lace, and the huddled leper colony of statues. He went out on to the terrace nevertheless and stood there, and the noise of the sea poured around him and on the beaches inside his brain.

He felt nothing.

He wanted nothing, expected nothing.

He did not quite expect the man who came from the side of the house, along the terrace.

A slight dark man, walking, looking out of dark eyes, carrying with him the primaeval green odour of the sea. The poet turned and looked at the man. A little white-hot shock passed through his heart, but he felt it only remotely. The man was himself.

Ashburn said quietly: "Well?"

The man who was himself gazed back at him, without recognition, without dislike, without love. His clothes, Ashburn's clothes, were soaked, as if he had been swimming in the sea. Incredible black and purple weeds had attached themselves to his shoulders.

"How long", the man said to him, "will you make me wait for you?"

Ashburn leaned back against the wall of the house. All the strength had gone out of him; it seemed as if his body had fainted yet left his mind conscious and alert. He laughed and shut his eyes. "I have called up my own ghost," he said, and looked again, and the man had gone. The poet rubbed his head against the hot, hard wall and discovered, with little interest, that he was weeping. The tears tasted of the sea, teaching him.

Yet, "Don't go," Albertine said in the morning, as she stood on the shallow step by the royal blue water. Her eyes were fixed, not on him, but on the little boat, the young brown islander arrogantly at work on her rigging, fixed on Merton standing on the beach, smoking his pipe, nodding at the waves.

"The sea's as calm as glass, look at it," Ashburn said. He smiled at her, took her hand. "Do you think Merton would risk the trip otherwise, or the island boy?"

Albertine reached out and took his face fiercely between her hands.

"Don't go, don't leave me."

"There are things we need from the mainland, my love, beside Laura's vitriolic letters to be posted."

"No," she said. Her eyes were wide and desolate as grey marshes; her cold hands burned.

Merton came up, patted her arm. "Come now, it's just what we all need." He winked anxiously, indicating to her that Ashburn would benefit from an hour or so in the boat. "Sea's like blue lead, and it's hot enough to fry fish in that water."

Albertine suddenly relinquished her hold on the poet. Her eyes clouded over and went blank as if she had lost her sight. "Good-bye," she said. She turned and went back into the house.

Merton, glancing up, saw her emerge presently on the flat roof of the tower, and wait by the black telescope beneath the awning.

The two men walked towards the boat together. The village boy nodded sneeringly and let them, as a particular favour, get in, packing his brown bony limbs in position as he took the tiller. They cast off. The silken arms of the water drew them in.

The ship clove the waves gracefully, with a gull-like motion, her sails opening like flowers to the wind. The island and the red house dwindled behind them, and the smoking hills.

"Cooler here," Merton said. He knocked the dottle from his pipe as if relieved to be rid of it. "Feel better now, I expect, old chap?"

The poet smiled as he lay against the side of the boat, ineffably relaxed. The sea and sky seemed all one colour, one ebony blue. He was aware of a lightness within himself, an inner silence. All the busy organs of the body had ceased, the ticking clocks, all unwound, all at peace, no heart beat, no beat in the belly or loins, no chatter in the brain. The sky appeared to thread itself between sail and mast like sapphire cotton through a needle. The heat was almost comforting, a soporific laudanum summer breath sighed into the motionless bellows of his lungs. He smiled at Merton, he smiled compassionately. He felt himself regarding a man who is unaware that in his flesh the advanced symptoms of an incurable illness have manifested themselves. *Should I tell him? No, poor creature, let him be. Let him go on in impossible hope.*

"Do you swim?" Ashburn asked.

"Swim? Why yes, you know I do, unlike yourself."

The poet turned to the brown boy with the same smiling compassion. "And you?"

"I? I swim like dolphin." He glared at them, however, with the kingly eyes of a shark.

"What's all this worry about swimming?" Merton said, lighting the pipe. "Afraid we'll capsise or something?"

"Look," Ashburn said, softly.

Merton looked. He saw a strange, mysterious phenomenon, a bank of nacreous fog, afloat like a great galleon and bearing down on them.

"Good God."

"Yes," Ashburn said, "a good God, who sends his people rain."

With an abrupt entirety as if a grey glove had seized the ship, the fog closed over them and they lost each other in it.

"Turn back for shore!" Merton shouted. No one apparently heard him. The boat swung drunkenly sideways. The drums of his ears seemed to stretch tight; there was a growling in the air. The sky and sea tilted to meet each other, and slammed together as thunder shattered the ocean into a broken plate. A lightning appeared to strike to the vitals of the boat itself: wood splintered, a terrifying unreasonable sound. Merton fell to his knees; he could hear the boy screaming about a rock in the sea.

"Ashburn, where are you?" he cried, groping with his hands through the greyness, but the wind rushed into his throat, and the world leaned sideways and flung him into its salty mouth, and gulped him down.

Albertine was still waiting at the telescope. She had watched the ship bob on the leaden sea, she had watched the fog rise like a hand from the floor of the ocean and gather the vessel into itself.

Soon the sky broke up. Explosions of thunder and dazzling lightnings divided the landscape between them. Viscous rain began to fall, at first like great gems, opals or diamonds, then in a boiling sheet of white fire that flamed across the house, the shore, the sea in impenetrable gusts. From the village the islanders came running, shouting, opening their arms to the storm. Albertine, her hair flattened to her skull and shoulders, the colour of the rain itself, stared through the one-eyed thing towards the abstracted ocean.

The storm was brief; it failed and fled away shrieking over the land trailing its torn plumes. The sky cleared, the sea, the shore, even the distant coast became visible. Nothing stood between the island and the coast. The ship had vanished.

The black tongue of the telescope licked to left and right, probing with its cold cyclopean glass, but not for long.

Soon, Albertine drew away from it. Her clothes and her hair ran water as if she had come from the sea. Yellow water dripped from the slag-bellied awning. As if across miles of desert, she could hear the voice of a frenzied woman in the house below her feet. "Poor Sibbi," she whispered, as if comforting herself. "Poor Laura." She did not cry, only frowned a little, striving to comprehend the perfection of her knowledge, the completeness of the event which had befallen her. She rocked her grief in her arms like a sleeping child.

When she turned down the stairway into the tower room, she saw the poet at his desk, the manuscripts, the open books set out before him. He looked up at her, not with a lover's face or the face even of an enemy, but merely with the soulless look of something which is only spirit. She held her grief in her arms and watched the poet's ghost fade like water in the air of the room, until only the room, the shadows remained, and the unfinished poem, spread like the white wings of a dead pigeon on the desk.

This peculiar account of the last days and night of the poet,

Shelley is closely based on actual of what took place. Most biographies concerning him carry references, and many of them much more than that.

My choice of (fictional) name for him comes phonetically from the story by Henry James:

<u>*The Aspern Papers.*</u>

To meet oneself is, apparently, usually Bad News. You are either dead, or soon will be.

LACE-MAKER BLADE-TAKER GRAVE-BREAKER PRIEST

From an idea dreamed by John Kaiine during an afternoon catnap.

The sea! The sea!
Xenophon: Anabasis. IV vii.

1

It seemed as if only one second after the double blow was struck, the storm came up in answer out of the ocean. Of course, it did not happen quite in that way. But Ymil, who had briefly turned his back on the argument and was staring out to starboard, said and believed that, directly following the sound of the leather glove slapping the fine blond cheeks, a bubble of sable cloud rose there on the horizon's curve. And the first kick of the sea unbalanced the ship.

Until then the voyage had been tranquil and pleasant, in itself. They were bound for the Levant. Blue skies canopied blue water with emerald margins and frills of lacy foam. Suns were born and died in splendour. Scents of oleanders and olive trees drifted from the edges of the land. The nights dripped heavily with stars.

But from the very first, those two had formed a dislike for each other.

Surely any intelligent man realised it was unsensible to take, let alone so overtly, against a fellow passenger on a voyage of more than two or three days. Apparently, neither could help it. And both, one saw, were arrogant.

Vendrei was the worst, however, and he had seemed to be the one to start the feud openly. It was he also, in those last moments before the tempest arrived, who offered the duellist's invitation. He had been idly slapping one of his elegant gloves against his sumptuous boot. Then, rising suddenly, he had slapped the glove instead once, twice, across Zephyrin's face. "Do you know what that means, you damned gutter-rat?"

And pale fair Zephyrin, now with two cheeks pink as a Paris fondant, smiled thinly and replied, "Oh yes. Do *you*?"

After which, Ymil insisted, the ship rumbled and arched her spine, and storm-breath coughed vulgarly in the sails .

What had been carelessly noted before—that no land was by then visible anywhere—now seemed of consequence. And so it was to be.

For in less than five minutes more, the sky turned black, the vessel was racing sidelong, masts and yards leaning and cracking and screeching, things crashing below-decks, the groans, bellows and shouts of crew and passengers already lost in tumult.

Less than *twenty* minutes more and the ship, partly dismasted and having struck some unseen and unseeable obstacle, reeled headlong in the maelstrom and began to go down.

All on deck had been swept off into the water. Here they whirled and spilled about among the terrible, smothering sheets of the waves.

Ymil lost consciousness, expecting to awaken dead. But when he did regain his senses he found that he, with a small group of others, had fetched up alive on an unidentified shore.

Whether this was the hem of mainland or isle he did not know, as nor did any of them.

They huddled on the sand as the storm dissolved in distance, its mission fulfilled. There was no sign of the foundered ship, not even so much as a broken spar, barrel or shred of canvas. Only the repaired lace of the foam followed them to the beach.

Sunset had gone by in a mask of weather.

Night was constructing itself brick by brick.

2

Prince Mhikal Vendrei had come aboard at the Mediterranean port with the seamless modesty of a flamboyant man. His luggage was meagre and soon stowed in the better part of the passengers' quarters. He was a very beautiful picture, tall and slim, with a sunburst of dark gold hair, and everything augmented by silk, leather and clean linen. At his side, in a satin-cased sheath, rested the true gentleman's final accessory, a sword of damascened steel, with a lynx engraved under the hilt. He spoke like a gentleman too, and in many languages. French he had, and several of the coiled tongues of the Eastern Steppes; it seemed from his few immaculate books he could read Latin and Greek. The local patois he had no trouble with, nor even the slangy argot of the sailors. He did not keep to himself, graciously appearing at meal-times, or to walk the upper deck and sea- or stargaze with the others. He flirted nicely with the rich elderly lady from Tint, as with the younger, less wealthy ladies from Athens. He played cards where desired, prayed calmly with the rest on the three saints' days that fell during the voyage, and was virtually faultless. He even consented to being sketched by the motherless son of the merchant from Chabbit.

They learned a little about the prince.

He was a landowner's son from the north-east, schooled in Paris, and at the great University in Petragrava. But he had been leading a dissolute life lately, until deciding to change his ways and to become, as he put it with a flippant, rueful smile, *"Virtuous"* for his father's sake.

On the other hand no one ever did quite learn *where* precisely he had been born or raised, where he had carried on his dissolution, nor what made him give it up (assuming he had for he still gambled for money and drank quite an amount before, during and after supper).

The general consensus was that he was likeable and liked. A pleasure to the eye, the ear, and—for he often good-naturedly lost at cards—the pocket of many aboard.

Some five days into the voyage the ship called at the port of Ghuzel. Here a handful more passengers joined her. Only one was notable, for this male figure too was a glamorous creation quite out of the ordinary.

Zephyrin—if Zephyrin owned another name nobody had discovered it during the trip—looked a very young man, who seemed at least some ten years the junior of Prince Vendrei, sixteen perhaps or at most eighteen. Unusual in one so immature, however, was Zephyrin's knowledge, poise, and ability to charm and to contend with everyone and thing—saving, of course, the prince himself.

For it was evident by the end of Zephyrin's first day on board, that the young one and the elder one had fallen into an immediate hatred of each other.

Could it be they were jealous? Unlikely as it seemed, some of the passengers suggested this to each other. Two men, they said, of such wonderful looks and such otherwise incompatible aspects, could well find causes for resentment. For example, Vendrei *was* the elder, might not approve a rival with so much extra youth to spare. Formerly, after all, Vendrei had been the voyage's sole magician, particularly among the women passengers. But it seemed they liked the newcomer just as much. Or more...

As for Zephyrin: clearly not well-off, and occupying quarters in the ship's belly, an airless stern area below-decks, private enough but dark, dank and rat-nipped. Zephyrin meanwhile was clad only in an old black cavalry uniform from an unrecognisable battalion of Europe. (Some said too this might even be a mercenary band). The attached sword, for as an army officer, which Zephyrin claimed to be, the young person had one, was plain steel in a drab sheath and showed no crest.

There was another odd thing.

Zephyrin's thick almost white hair—was a wig. That was not so uncommon among the gentry, but for an impoverished army captain it could have seemed an odd affectation, if Zephyrin had not swiftly made allusion to it in an off-hand way. It turned out: "In infancy I fell deathly ill and almost died. Though a clever physician saved my life, my hair dropped out and never fully regrew, save, as you see, for my brows and lashes." For this reason Zephyrin wore the realistic wig, a moon-blond mane, on which was clapped a protective hat when anything more than a faint breeze blew. The captain was beardless also for the same past cause; not even the long strong fingers gave any evidence of hair. These facts seemed neither to embarrass or inconvenience Zephyrin. Yet the shade of the wig, chosen presumably to compliment the soldier's own pale colouring, might hint at vanity? The brows too—were they perhaps a little darkened? The eyes needed no help at all. They were large and of a sombre green, more malachite than jade.

Eyes notwithstanding, did this interloper loathe the luxuriantly-locked Vendrei? Covet his good birth, education and money? Zephyrin had revealed nothing of parentage or natal country, and spoke, albeit in a musical tenor, only the language of the ship - and that with an army accent. Probably such a life as his had been perilous and disgraceful. All of which might be a cause for discontent.

Whatever did touch the spark to the powder, each of the drama's actors was quickly a foe to the other.

Ymil had seen their quarrel begin.

He himself was nothing, was a writer. He had neither excess cash nor fame, no property, no clout, had been born in a backstreet of Petragrava itself, but to a street-girl who knew less of Ymil's father than Ymil knew of the kingdom of God. Dragged up as through a thorn-hedge backwards, (as he himself had sometimes said), Ymil travelled about on the business of others who paid him, and wrote when he had a moment on paper, with a series of leaky ink-pencils. But *always* he was writing in his mind.

Frankly, he thought, he might have devised and written the first abridgement between Ven and Zeph himself. For, if unacknowledged, Ymil was more arrogant than either of these slender, be-sworded, masculined beauties, and had a brain like a thirsty sponge.

That first day then, starting off from the port of Ghuzel, with the sea skilfully hooking and knotting together its delicate lace of foam...

"And so, sir. I seem to interest you?"

This from golden-mane Vendrei, to the soldier they did not yet know as Zephyrin.

"Your pardon. *You*? And... *I*?"

"Just so. Ever since you came aboard this vessel. Not a great while, I admit. But sufficient time, it appears, to learn to stare."

"You must excuse me," said the shabby, beautiful, *young*, flaxen captain. "I failed to see you at all. How remiss, as you seem to require to be looked at. And I, so rudely, did not notice you and looked—directly, er—*through* you. "

Ymil, at the scene's perimeter, raised mental ears as high as a hare's.

"Truly? Through me. How quaint. But I suppose you're not accustomed to mixing with my sort."

"Your... sort?" questioned the captain, gently.

"Oh, an aristocrat, an educated man who travels a great amount—"

"I see. In the travelling way of a merchant, do you mean? One who sells things?" asked the captain, raising an eyebrow.

"Not in that way at all, *sir*. In the way of a man of leisure, who may *please himself*."

"Ah," said the fair captain. Then paused as if admiringly impressed. Before adding, with mildest interest, "And do you find you do, sir? I mean, please *yourself*? Or ... anyone ?"

For a heartbeat Gold-hair looked as if he might laugh. But then he checked and coldly said, "Your impertinence is evidently due to your lack both of breeding and grasp of any language you are attempting to converse in. I'll leave you to compose yourself. Good morning. Yet perchance, a word of advice from one a little older than yourself. Don't *stare*."

The captain curtly bowed. And replied, "I shall attempt to benefit from your estimable warning. *Perchance* I can return the favour by exhorting *you*, sir, to avoid giving such cause."

Thus, their first exchange.

Certainly, a very childish way of going on. Fascinated, nevertheless Ymil thought so. But being as he was, and doing what he did, human things intrigued and captivated him, and to a greater extent in their displays of extremis.

He had already been watching all and everyone, constant to his normal formula. Then when the boyish captain came aboard Ymil was instantly prepared to watch especially hard. But anyone might think Zephyrin a curiosity.

Unlike Zephyrin, Ymil's close but cunning scrutiny had not been noted.

And indeed, as Ymil had seen, Zephyrin *had* stared on and on at Vendrei. Spoiling for a fight from the start, seemingly.

Their duel stayed verbal, however, for eight further days and nights.

But they would not keep a minute in each other's vicinity without some quip or carp. Even once Zephyrin, passing Vendrei, who was strolling with the two Athenians, simply whistled a snatch of song. It was the ballad from a popular play, concerning a stupid fop who

fancied he was a king among women, while at his back all
females scorned him. Leaving the ladies, Vendrei walked
over to Zephyrin. "It's unlucky to whistle at sea."

"Oh, is it? Why?"

"Because, captain, you may summon something to you
that may prove unwelcome."

At this Zephyrin shrugged, and smilingly asked,
"Yourself?"

But it was a fact, they could not even hand each other
the salt at table in the saloon, not even blow their noses or
look at the stars, without one would make unfavourable
comment on it in the hearing of the other.

On the eighth day, as the ship bore north-easterly
under peerless skies, Zephyrin came up on deck,
apparently, one might have thought, *searching* for
Vendrei. Instead the searcher found a seat the older man
had occupied, where lay one of Vendrei's Latin books,
which contained some of the writings of Catullus.

To Ymil's surprise—could Zeph decipher Latin? —the
slender captain began to read, or pretend to read, the
book.

Back came Vendrei.

"What do you think you're at, sir, in God's name? Put
that down. It is my property. It was my father's—I won't
have your unclean paws on it—*down*, I say!" he almost
shouted, as if to some unruly hound.

Not before had Ymil witnessed Vendrei quite so out of
his coolth.

Zephyrin though looked up calmly, and recited from
the book, in excellent Latin: "*Miser Vendre, desinas ineptire
et quot vides perisse perditum ducas.*"

Ymil's not unlessoned brain bounded after the words.
They came, he thought, from the lyric poems, but

Zephyrin had replaced Catullus' own name with a version of *Vendrei*. The meaning? Approximately — "Piteable Vendrei, leave off your clowning, and relinquish as lost what you can see is lost."

The prince had gone white.

"And what do you suppose, you *dog*, I have lost? What can *you* know of loss, *dog*, that never possessed a single thing of worth, nor would know one now if ever it should lie before you? "

"Ah," said Zephyrin, getting up and replacing the book neatly on the seat. "But I *do* know a thing of worth when it is before, me. Even if it lies there dead on its back."

And so saying the younger antagonist walked off, leaving the elder one in a definite state of ire and discomfort.

Dead on its back?

What could *that* mean?

The Athenian ladies, (with both of whom, Ymil believed, Vendrei had a romantic nocturnal understanding), were whispering nervously. Prince Vendrei went to them, gracefully flirting and soothing, apologising for his annoyance, saying the other fellow was scum, and not to be thought of anymore.

Gradually Vendrei's colour returned to normal. The 'other fellow', Ymil had thought, had flushed in equal amounts to Vendrei's pallor. As if they were a balance of heat and cold.

There must then be more to all this than mere jealous antipathy, must there not? Of course, Ymil was already quite informed that madness motivated Zephyrin. But in this matter the cause stayed unsure.

Zephyrin in any case did not ornament the saloon with

personal presence that evening. And the following afternoon, which was on the ninth day of the voyage, they were far out on the crossing, not even the hint of an island yet on the horizon, and a card game was started up.

The gaming table had been set out on deck, under the sail aft, for at that point the light was mellow and the weather slow and honey-sweet. Vendrei was playing, losing as so often he did and with his usual good manners, to the old merchant from Chabbit and the wily widow from Tint, plus two or three more that Ymil later could not quite remember, a thing for which, in the wake of the shipwreck and their vanishment, he chid himself.

About three o'clock by the sun, Zephyrin appeared like an early moon. What a beautiful creature, all that ivory blondness, and such a face—nearly, Ymil judged, fine-carved as a woman's—and those black-green eyes, level as two silver spoons full-drawn from the deeps of the sea.

Never before had this rogue officer deigned to join in with the gambling. Now a chair was selected and the figure sat itself, directly facing Vendrei across the painted oblongs of the cards.

"The stakes are high," said Vendrei flatly.

Zephyrin did something that chilled Ymil through; drawing the dull notched blade of cavalry sword, that pale hand laid it along the table's edge. "The sword's all I possess of any value. Will it do?"

The table was silent as the inside of a lead box.

Much later, Ymil believed that this, in actuality, was the initial moment when the temper of sea and sky might be felt to change.

"Young sir," said the Tintian widow, in hesitant Greek,

"are thee so desperate thee does risk the weapon of thy trade?"

Zephyrin bowed. "I've risked it in battle, madam. Now I do so again. For here's *another* battle."

"Come, lad," said the Chabbit merchant. "You're hardly older than my boy, my last born by my dear wife, now in Heaven's garden. Put up the sword. I'll lend you coins –"

"No, sir, with my thanks. My fight, not yours."

"What fight is this, then?" asked another man.

But obviously they knew, having assumed it was the eternal feud between the captain and the prince.

Zephyrin stretched out long legs. Despite that slender frame, they had all seen, Zephyrin was strong, and only three or four inches less in height than tall Vendrei himself.

"*He* cheats," now said Zephyrin casually, and nodding at Vendrei almost companionably. "I wish to prove it."

Few jaws that did not drop. A buzz of astonishment next. Then the Chabbitese, not illogically exclaimed, "*Cheats*, boy! You're cracked. His honour *loses* nine times out of ten""

"Yes, such is his cleverness, gentlemen and lady. For he lulls you all. Then, during the last days, when we near the wine-red shore of Taurus, he'll win the hoard back by his tricks, and fleece you of the rest down to the very skin, like shorn goats. I've met his sort before. A prince? You only have his word for that. I'd not put it past the devil to search your luggage and filch your wallets too."

All this while, a steady background syncopation, there had been the *slap-slap* of Vendrei's glove on his boot; Vendrei merely keeping time.

But now that ceased, for Vendrei got to his feet. And it

was exactly then that Ymil swung about and glared away to starboard, dazzled, his mind leaping and crying to him, *Of course, you idiot Ymil! It's THAT! What else can it be? All bloody lies—*

After which he heard the duellist's challenge, the blow of the glove to each of Zephyrin's cheeks. And the sky filled as if from one of Ymil's leaky ink-pencils, and the storm rose from the belly of the deep.

3

Above the sands of the rock-strewn beach, the land lifted into wild green woods of feathery poplar and giant freckled laurel, shadowed by pine and fir and other conifers.

Beyond, nothing was visible that any of them could make out. Although the Chabbitese merchant's son had said at dawn he had seen something vague and far away that might be either a mountain—or a cloud. An hour after, this had disappeared.

Conversely, to either side of the landfall, the shore tapered gradually into high, grainy cliffs, perhaps impassable.

Their party was small. It comprised a pair of sailors named Dakos and Crazt, the merchant and his son, (said son having helped his father ashore, since the merchant could not swim), the old Tintian widow, who claimed God and her skirts had borne her up, and Ymil. There were just two others. Vendrei. Zephyrin.

It transpired they both could swim very well. And even Zephyrin's precious wig had been spared by the sea, for it had somehow been kept clamped on under the hat.

thing else of moment, or use, however, was lost,
⌐₁unk down by the greedy water.

Not a single gun had been saved. The flintlocks from
Ymil's, Vendrei's and the widow's baggage lay in the
ocean's basement. Not even the ancient explosive
matchlock Dakos had prided himself on remained. The
sailors and the widow — she had been commendably well-
armed — had retained a variety of small knives. But they
would be effective for no more, as the merchant
remarked, than picking one's nails or teeth. The
merchant's son had his pocket catapult, but the string had
snapped.

As for Vendrei and Zephyrin's blades — they were
gone.

The latter's sword, as everyone well recalled, had been
taken off minutes before the storm, and laid on the card
table as surety. While Vendrei's sword-belt, blade
included, had been ripped from around his waist by the
violence of the waves. Gone too were his coat and
waistcoat. Most of the survivors were tattered and bereft
also of certain items of clothing. The widow had suffered
the least, had lost only hairpins, allowing her magnificent
silver and ebony tresses to tumble free around her. Ymil,
even in this extremity, noticed the merchant abruptly
taking her in. Though not young, a little older than he,
she was comely, and had shown herself a woman of
character.

Despite losses, the new day was warm when once the
sun rose. The previous night they had lit a fire, which was
made easily possible by driftwood and shed branches in
the wood. They had no problem with fresh water either.
A small freshet ran from the wood into a pool adjacent to
the beach. They must only therefore get their bearings,

organise a look-out for shipping, and for helpful or harmful visitors—persons, animals. A search must be made too for eatable food.

These duties were now undeniably prime targets.

Not one among them could disagree.

Vendrei stood in the morning light and scowled in fury at them all.

"Be damned to that. The lying filth there owes me his life. We are sworn to a duel. For me, nothing else shall count till I have settled it in his blood."

And Zephyrin, who had been sitting on a rock, inspecting the salt damage to his boots, glanced up and said, "For once, he and I are in some agreement. I can give my mind to nothing until the matter's seen to, in blood certainly, but his, of course, not mine."

Vendrei swore inventively and at some length. The widow and the merchant's son looked on in envy. The others, Ymil included, were slightly shocked by the terms and the words in several languages.

"But where in the name of God—" rounded off Vendrei in a roar, "are we to find two swords?"

A writer's life, unless he be not only talented but also blessed by fortune, can turn out a scrabbly affair. So it had for Ymil. An educated untypical patron of his mother, the street-girl's night-time acquaintance, had taken pity on the dishevelled child, and taught him to read and write, and even enough of figures he could add two and two and not make seven. Otherwise Ymil's existence was uncouth, and by the age of twelve he was acting as both runner for a gambling den and an occasional thief. By inevitable stages, equally he ascended and failed in these unchosen careers. The ascent was due to his knack with literacy as well as his nimbleness and gift of observation. The failure came from his total dislike of brutality. He had seen enough of that in the hovel with his mother. Meanwhile, by the cliché of a solitary candle, he often wrote down stories, political reflections, and now and then even a song or two. Intermittently then he would have the tiny success of selling them, seeing them in print in popular pamphlets, or on the sort of rough paper sheets that circulated among the poor but readerly, and were subsequently often put to use during less erudite functions.

By the year of his majority, Ymil could count thirty-one bits and pieces published, most by then long since destroyed, and none of them having paid him more than the price of a meal that would excite only a mouse.

He kept body and soul in tandem another way.

On the day he boarded the ill-fated ship, Ymil, for almost ten years, had earned his bread by providing his services as a reliable blood-hound. He had discovered, watched and followed, persuaded, tricked and delivered up countless strays, runaways, villains and madmen, to those who wished to have them back, did not know where or how to search, but could pay well one who did.

And it was on just such an errand that Ymil had taken ship at all.

He had been in eastern Europe the winter before, on other business. Then a rich aristocrat summoned him to his palace. It was a grand one, with marbles, silk drapes, gold candlesticks. But Ymil was respectfully unimpressed. By that time he had seen such stuff frequently. "I hear you can find anyone on earth, providing he lives," had stated the aristocrat, a big man in his middle years who, they said, possessed three houses here, another in Petragrava, and a clutch of estates in the country. In demeanour he was an odd combination of expansive and guarded, but when Ymil modestly suggested tales of his wisdom were exaggerated, the aristocrat ignored that like a hiccup, and told Ymil straight out what he required.

It seemed this man had a son, a very handsome, unusually sensitive and charming son who, four years ago, had been shamelessly jilted by his intended marriage partner. "Less than a day after this shock, my son fell deathly ill—a fever, such as had once struck him in childhood. His hair dropped out as it had then. We believed he must die. Yet he turned the corner that very night, and hopes were high he should recover. Then— horror! Next day he had vanished from the house. Of course instantly I attempted to have him found. It was obvious enough, his mind had been disturbed by sickness. One whole year they took to find him. And then—though by now we knew where he must have gone, and the insane mode of life he had adopted—even achieving unlikely success in it—once again he gave my men the slip. Since that time, any I hire to find him have only detected his whereabouts stupidly to lose him again. Yet he lives still, this I know. I have heard, only yesterday, he is somewhere in the Mediterranean area, having given up at last, it seems, his totally unsuitable and unseemly post in the army."

The father then described his son in detail. He was slender, white-blond, green-eyed, nearly feminine in appearance, the father added with some embarrassment. "Though doubtless less so now," bitterly. "Dressed as a soldier and hardened by God knows what adventures. And with a sword at his side with which," now in distaste, "he has done, I am told, a great deal of damage."

The name this absconding youth had assumed—which was not his true one—was Zephyrin.

Ymil accepted the assignment. Among the cypress, orange and lemon trees of the Mediterranean sink, he uncovered and set out on Zephyrin's track. And hence the ship, which Ymil had learned Zeph meant to board at Ghuzel.

Prepared for the assorted results other such cases had presented, Ymil had only *not* anticipated the instantaneous hatred that sprang to life between Zeph and Mhikal Vendrei.

And not until those last pre-tempest minutes did Ymil figure out that, on *this* occasion, two and two *indeed* added up to seven.

In the end it was Ymil, with Dakos and Jacenth, the merchant's son, who went up into the woods to cast about for provender.

Crazt meantime had rigged a line from various debris—boot laces, one of the widow's two saved hairpins—and baited it with some small dead sea beast found further along the beach. The old widow and elderly merchant, (who by now were on the first name terms of Maressa and Frokash), stayed as sentries of fire and sea.

Ven and Zeph however, stuck to their prior plan.

Ignoring everyone else, seeming careless at the lack of breakfast, they swore a sort of pact, publically, watched by the rest in mixtures of admiration, irritation, contempt and disbelief.

Both enemies were to walk in an opposite direction along the two arms of the beach, searching there for two suitable weapons, preferably long blades. "Do they think they will find such hung up on the rocks?" pondered Frokash.

"Both are deranged." said Maressa, not without some enjoyment.

But the two gallants, still splendid even after total immersion, and lacking portions or entireties of certain garments, faced each other, white and adamantine.

"Until this evening then, sir," said Zephyrin. "When, let us hope, I can curtail your futile life, and thus spare the world further boredom from it."

"Till this evening, wretch. Delight in your last day upon earth. You'll find Hell much less pleasant."

Which said, each of them marched off along the sands, Vendrei to the west, a vision of ruined linen, lace, and icy rage; salt-stained Zephyrin heading east, face set like a mask, wig-saving hat crammed down on head.

4

Vendrei discovered the fishing village with startled abruptness, as if Fate were jesting, playing games.

By then he had gone about ten miles down the shore. The cliffs stood high on his right, and the sand was mostly covered by smooth, round, sea-greened boulders—as if thousands of tortoises had congregated, and been heartlessly turned to stone by some passing gorgon. The precarious walkway had also narrowed to the width only of three or four feet, in places less. Then, slithering and sliding around a bulge in the cliff wall, Vendrei beheld a hitherto hidden bay, a long apron of glassy blue water, a broad amble of sand, where distant fisher-craft were drawn up, and small cranky houses had fixed themselves to the cliff like barnacles.

That the village might be very good news for his fellow survivors did not immediately cross Vendrei's mind.

He took the village personally to be, not only the joke of Fate, but the provider of swords. Why else was it there in his path at this fraught hour, unless to give most desperately—not sustenance or rescue, but a means to murder his dearest foe.

It was not that the golden prince was a solipsistic dunce, exactly. More that life, and other people, had made him sometimes resemble one.

He had fled from his father's house in panic at the strictures of a stern parent determined to have his way. This man had treated his only son Mhikal as a possession merely. Very much, let it be said, as he treated also wife and daughters. Yet worse, he valued Mhikal more highly, thought him *worth* more. What the father ultimately wished from his son nevertheless was, for Mhikal, intolerable. It was horrible, coercive, *obscene*. It would have meant for him an end to all he valued at that time, or held dear.

But then, Mhikal Vendrei's resultant resistant act, so he himself came to believe, was not only dishonourable and vile, but in its effect worthy of damnation. He had brooded on it, too. On nothing else.

Ever since he had spent his life, (truly spent, like cash or blood), in deliberate dissolution and itinerancy. He had been afraid for years to put down any root, to form any lasting attachment. He journeyed, he thought, with less baggage than a herder of camels, and now of course the sea itself had robbed him of all, even of the books he had stolen from his father's library. And even of his sword which here, of all times, he *wanted* as a lover wants the beloved—passionately and obsessively.

From the initial instant he had loathed Zephyrin, not knowing why. For Vendrei was neither a snob nor physically unconfidant. Probably, he presently decided, it had been an instinctive forewarning. Zephyrin's stares and jibes had soon cut deep beneath his skin, long before the final calumny—the lie that he was a cheat and thief— propelled him to claim the satisfaction of a duel.

The worst irony of all, however, was that he had taken ship for the express purpose of going home, to face his demon and pay its price.

The people in the hidden village spoke some sort of oriental Greek that, for all his knowledge of languages, Vendrei could barely fathom. He struggled to grasp their words. To make them understand *his*. But they gave him a glass of wine with milk curdled in it, and then sat him down on a stone in the narrow street that rambled round the houses up the cliff. After a while an older man came along, garlanded with a vast grey beard.

"Is you to be look for," so Vendrei *guessed* the greybeard said, "the drownwards lost off ship-thing?"

"Ah—no—but—are men from the ship here?"

"Some is to be have washed up always into us place, if ship sunken. We have two man-things since of yester here. They am drownward. We have of bury them, as is our way with the drown-made dead."

"Commendable," said Vendrei. Repressing an hysterical urge to bellow with laughter.

Did these villagers think no one else ever buried the lifeless? This was a primitive place, but surely—

The wine had gone to Vendreils head, straight into his brain. He felt dizzy, and thought of his own near drowning, and that he might have ended by being swept in too, and buried by one of these strangers. He *thought* that two men, now beyond his help, might well have been, each of them, equipped with a useable blade. Which now lay in the grave with them.

"I should wish—I should like," he faltered, "to visit the graves." And then blushed with shame, (a thing he had not done for several years), at his own appalling behaviour. For he meant to investigate the graves, *undo* them, *borrow*—oh, borrow of course only, he would return his theft, (cheat, thief), replace their swords. Maybe two gentlemen would not grudge this, in order to settle one like Zephyrin? No, they would be seated in the best seats in Paradise, applauding.

I'm drunk.

But the bearded man was assisting him to his feet.

"You come, and I to you show buried. But a long climb."

To Heaven?

Yes, for me, now.

Up the wandering street they went and so reached another treacherous path that teetered on up the cliff. Wild blue and topaz flowers, and stunted oleanders, grew along the sides of it. And here and there he saw a shell.

They climbed high above the village, and then the path snagged down. A rough carving appeared beside the track. It was of a long-bearded man with the tail of a fish, who held regally in his left hand the three-pronged trident of the pagan marine god, Poseidon.

An idea of what might be going on attempted to invest

the brain of Vendrei. He wrestled with it, then gave up as the greybeard drew him aside into a cool tunnel.

"Below," said the man. "Step careful. Tall sea come at sun-die. Then go they."

"They go, do they. Very well. Tall sea."

The tunnel plainly ran down through the inside of the cliff. Where it led to must be the village burial ground. That was strange enough, for at the edge of the village there had stood the usual church, a ramshackle little stone building with a saint painted above the door. Normally the graveyard would lie handy. Not here, it seemed.

Turning to ask another unwieldy question of his guide, Vendrei saw the man had gone, slipped away slick as a shadow.

Vendrei shook his head to clear it. Which did nothing but make him laugh.

Then he stepped through into the tunnel, stooping a little for the rocky roof was uneven and low. The route had been, most likely, a natural one, but hacked out to a greater space by men. Soon he came to a ledge where rested tapers, flint and tinder. Vendrei had already begun to see he would need light, for as the tunnel descended it grew inevitably darker. He struck flame and ignited a taper. And in that moment a profound sense of the supernormal washed in on him. How long had this death-road existed? It felt to him old as the cliff. How many unquiet ghosts, then, flitted through the shade, attracted to a light like moths but, being already dead, unable to burn. . .

"Steady, you fool," he said to himself aloud, and the rock surged with a low, humming echo. "Bloody Zephyrin," Vendrei whispered. "I shall—" Yet here was not a spot to utter maledictions. And Vendrei suddenly remembered the youth of his adversary, his paleness and handsomeness, and felt a terrible pity at what he meant to do to him. But Vendrei reckoned himself damned anyway, what did one more young life matter? What did anything matter. *Come on, fool, find the dead and rob them, take their swords, go back and kill the wretch and have done.*

Ymil, Jacenth and Dakos returned to the beach in the late afternoon with meat, three plump conies, slain quick and clean by the boy, who was apt with a stone even lacking his catapult. They had plucked red grapes from a wild vine, green figs, and mint and sage for flavouring.

Crazt meanwhile had caught a whole heap of fish, which were now enticingly toasting on sticks across the fire. Maressa and Frokash were playing a game with differently marked pebbles. They had seen no shipping; did not seem to mind.

Of the other pair there was no sign.

"Fell off the land's edge into the ocean," said Crazt under his breath. "To both, our fondest farewell."

This opining was proved valueless however when, as the sun itself reached the brink of the sea, scalding it to carmine, Zephyrin appeared, tramping back along the eastern stretch of sand.

Zephyrin's hat was off, there was no breeze at all and the fine white wig hung limply. Hollows smudged beneath the green eyes. The captain seemed tired out, tired in the manner of an almost grown-up child. Looking at this, Ymil thought, one might know Zephyrin had been recently ill, or very ill some years ago, and was left weakened by it.

Coming near the fire, the slender figure slumped down a short distance from the others.

"I found this," Zephyrin said, and rolled a small barrel towards them, "up the beach."

"French Brandy!" approvingly exclaimed Dakos and the merchant as one.

"Just so," said Zephyrin. "There was flotsam from the ship, or from some other casualty, all over. I expect you'll like to go and look, tomorrow."

And that was all the captain said. In fact all the captain *was* to say for some while.

Obviously too this one showed no interest in food or brandy, nor in any of *them*, only in the missing Vendrei. Also obviously, Zeph had *not* discovered the one (or two) items searched for. No swords,

The sun went down. Lavender flooded the sky, swiftly chased away in turn by the indigo of night. Stars spangled. The company feasted on grilled fish and roast meat, herbs and fruit, and passed the little brandy barrel, and were glad. Only Zephyrin did not join in, ate only a morsel of fish, one grape, went off again and drank sips of water from the freshet pool. Then stayed up by the pool too, sitting there silhouetted against the deep blue and bright silver of the sky.

"How he misses the prince. You'd think he was in love with him," said Crazt.

"He longs for Mhikal Vendrei's death," said Dakos. "Hate is always worse than love, whatever the wise men say."

"Oh, *love* is somewhat strong," said the merchant Frokash. "And sometimes begins unexpectedly." (Ymil noted he glanced at the widow when he said it).

Ymil was pleased to see that two people might be made happy from this muddle, perhaps even three, for Jacenth appeared to like the idea of the widow as a future addition to his father's life.

Mostly though, with a sort of curious dread, Ymil kept one of his observant eyes peeled for Vendrei, walking out of the west like Death himself in the old pictures. Ymil had no doubts the prince would return. None at all.

He arrived about an hour before midnight.

Most of them were asleep. These he woke up, for Vendrei was incandescent with fury, nearly insane it seemed, as he lurched into the firelight.

"*God's stars—*" he shouted. "Damnable black foulness!"

He looked dampened more physically than in optimism.

His hair was wet and dripping, the remains of his shirt plastered to his body. Had he been for a swim?

He towered over the six seated or prone persons, and then irresistibly raised his wide and flaming eyes to the figure that now sprang towards him from the pool.

"Oh, can it be," Zephyrin asked in a silken voice, "the wondrously clever Prince Mhikal has *failed* to find a sword?" Where there had been no energy to Zephyrin, now there was nothing but. Zephyrin *glowed* in the darkness, galvanic, a lightning made flesh.

Vendrei snarled.

"There you're wrong, you sty-rat. I found a sword, by God's might—"

And here indeed was the blade, flashing fire and starlight as he flung it point down into the sand. Where it waited, quivering also with energy, *readiness.*

"Then, Vendrei, tomorrow we shall fight."

"*Ha!*" bawled Vendrei. What a splendid melodramatic the stage had lost in him, Ymil thought. But already he had reasoned, and was not amazed, when Vendrei added, in a guttural hiss, "No."

5

Soon after he lit the taper, the tunnel had plunged unnervingly in a series of steep and sloping steps.

At any rate, this scoured the last tipsiness out of Vendrei.

With extreme care he descended, and after about five minutes the tunnel floor levelled somewhat, and he heard, instead of his own hurried pulse, the slow heartbeat of the sea.

A vague luminous quality began. Then the taper became obsolete. He blew it out to save it for going back.

The rock curved, and next opened out into a wide low cave, where Vendrei must first stoop double, and then get down on his knees and crawl.

Full afternoon light now came in from the cave mouth. It displayed for him a jumble of rocks and slabs, mossed due to moisture, some clung with pallid ocean weeds. Shells were littered about, and the tiny delicate bones of fish. There was a matured fishy smell, but no note of human decay. For a burial vault it was, that way, an odourless place. Empty also. No grave or tomb of any sort that Vendrei could see. All there was—

All there was were two heaps of broken twigs and branches, small stones, sand, this strewn with wild flowers. The heaps lay side by side right up against the opening in the cliff that showed the sea. They were each about the size and length one might expect of an average man's body, lying flat.

Vendrei now, despite his former superstitious unease, swore colourfully.

He had, he believed, heard of such customs among some of the primal fisher communities of the region. Although devoutly orthodox in religion, sometimes antique rites of conception, birth, marriage or death were celebrated, that went back to the sunrise of time, and the ancient gods who had then supposedly ruled the world. Just as a newborn babe might be baptised by such people in the sea, before ever it felt holy water, just so those the sea had drowned but then cast up on land, were blessed in the names of saints before being returned into the waters. They were the sea god's, Neptune, Poseidon. He sent them home to say goodbye; thereafter they must be restored to him.

It was true luck for Vendrei. *Meant* for him. Now he would not have to unearth some deep-dug grave, but need only lift off the branches and the flowers, to find the pair of swords his destiny demanded.

Carefully, being as respectful as he could, he removed the covering of the first man.

Yes, he recalled the poor fellow from the voyage. Wealthy and young, his sad face battered, bloated by the water. And yes, *yes*—here in the spoiled scabbard, the blade of good steel, nearly the right weight too, just a touch light, but that would not matter. Cursed thin Zephyrin should have this one.

With less respect, for he was in haste now, Vendrei pulled the piecemeal carapace from the second man.

And froze. Froze there, and let his arms fall loose, leaning, staring, not crediting what he saw.

For the second dead man, one Vendrei did not even recollect, was a drowned sailor, handsome and oddly unmarked, but most of his clothes and accoutrements taken by the waves. Decidedly he had no blade of any type, not even a knife to whittle sea-ivory.

Two men, two swords. But it was two men and one sword. Only one.

Vendrei kneeled there like the fool he had called himself, almost blind and half-dead himself with leaden disappointment .

One. Only one.

Fate's joke.

The greybeard had tried to explain the method of burial, that was the giving back to the god. Vendrei had forgotten the mention of the "tall sea".

In the Mediterranean sink, as a rule tides were mild and sluggish. Here and there, due to some eccentricity of rock or sea-floor, another rogue tide might come to be, such as that, it seemed, which had flushed the survivors of the wrecked ship out on to this coast, and brought in too some of her dead.

At sunfall, here in the hidden bay, an even more sprightly element of this rogue tide would, at certain seasons, leap upward to the cliff, missing the village, but bursting into the cave. Swirling then like a giant spoon, it would set down fish and weeds and shells, and gather up in payment any unfastened thing left for it. Such as two dead men in easily broken 'graves' of twigs.

The sun went, carmine red, and Vendrei was still in the cave, nursing the single sword, stunned as a child promised a horse and given only saddle and bridle.

And as the sun went, the sea came.

It crashed up and washed the cave from end to end, poured out and came ploughing back, smashing off the remains of the burial covers, picking up the two dead without difficulty, trying to pick up as well a third, living man.

He resisted, having woken to himself at the last instant.

But by dint of youth, strength and fright, Vendrei expelled himself from Poseidon's hungry sea, which pursued him, growling like green dogs, back along the tunnel to the awful steps. Even *up* the first steps the sea chased him. But perhaps it was simply chasing him off.

Only stars saw him finally drag himself out of the tunnel above the village. He was again soaked through, demented, clutching the useless uniqueness of the sword. Below, lamps were lighting in the little houses. But Vendrei did not go there. He turned from the village as from a cruel mocker, and getting down the cliff by another track, to the interest of five or six goats stationed there, he regained the shore and staggered away towards the survivors' camp. And his enemy.

6

"Heaven pardon me," Vendrei would murmur, much later. "I should have begged their forgiveness too. Should have prayed for them, those drowned men in the cave. Have I lost my human heart? What have I become through all this?"

But *much later* was not yet, certainly not that night.

Having heard of the village, and that therefore some form of civilisation was near—food, shelter, a small boat that might ferry them to larger settlements—Frokash and Jacenth, with the help of Dakos and Crazt, had created a second smaller fire in the lea of the cliffs, and settled there for the night, with the widow Maressa.

Vendrei and Zephyrin were left at the larger fire, to their own devices, they and the single sword. Ymil also remained. "Someone should stay," Ymil answered the merchant quietly, when asked to the second, calmer fireside.

"Not to leave them to their madness, eh?"

"Merely to watch," Ymil replied, with abnormal truth.

Nevertheless, he sat back, some feet away from them.

No one spoke. From the other fire drifted faint talk, silences, presently the low snores of Crazt. The moon had come and gone long before.

When the big fire sank, Vendrei or Ymil replenished it from the store of driftwood and branches. Once Vendrei went up to the pool, then came back and sat down again. He had eaten nothing and refused the brandy. Although he was so quiet the smoulder of his rage was on him. His hair had dried, shone like guineas in the firelight, and the sword shone too, planted there, presiding, deriding the two unarmed men and their mortal dream of a duel.

Ymil, watching, saw how Zeph watched also only Ven. Those dark green eyes scarcely blinked, so fixed they were, But Ven watched nothing, or else only the angry blank his thoughts had become.

Well past midnight, Ymil began quietly but audibly to talk, almost as if to himself.

"How bizarre it is, that just the few of us were saved. Is our rescue then for a purpose? I mean, some purpose we have yet to fulfil? What can it be? Maybe, in my own life... I once did a cruel and stupid thing. There was a young lady I was set to marry. But I changed my mind. And—I abandoned her." Under his watchful eyelids, (for Ymil sometimes watched even with his eyes *shut*), he studied Zeph's finely chiselled profile. True to the aristocratic father's embarrassed words, this young captain did look delicate enough to be taken for a woman, if one ignored the clothes. But that would be most unwise, for the core of Zephyrin, it seemed, was made of purest steel. Did the invented story Ymil now told touch any nerve? (Admittedly, in the father's account, the genders were reversed, it was the son who had been abandoned by a girl.) No reaction? It was impossible to be sure. "I regretted my actions afterwards. I heard she had fallen very ill—my fault, I must assume. I wonder if I can atone for my crime against her. Or am I too late?"

Vendrei said nothing, did not even look up. Had he even heard? Why should he besides have any response to the tale, either the father of Zephyrin's tale, or Ymil's altered one ?

But now Zephyrin turned that pale wonderfully-wigged head and stared full at Ymil, so for an instant Ymil reckoned his role as tracker and spy had been sussed.

Zephyrin however said, "She sounds a spineless simpleton, your *lady*. Some dolt deserts her. She falls into a sickness. You're better, sir, well shot of the ninny."

And that was that again. At least upon the subject of desertion.

For about another hour after, as the stars wheeled ever over and on into the west, Zephyrin announced:

"Well. Vendrei, it appears you're content to sulk and do nothing else to conclude our quarrel. Why am I not astonished?" (Vendrei offered no word). "Yet as I said, quantities of stuff from the doomed ship are scattered over the beaches further east. Where the cliffs close down upon the sea there, I thought I saw too some wreckage far out on the water. It seems to me now there's a chance there could be weapons in with it, if only the weapons of dead men that you, Vendrei, naturally, would never mind thieving and employing."

Vendrei spoke. "Tomorrow I shall go and see."

"Such a hero. I gasp at you."

"Go to Hell, Zephyrin. Once I find a second sword, whatever its calibre, I'll send you there with it. You may as well familiarise yourself with the country first."

Of all things, possibly Ymil did not expect to do more than doze.

Sleep accordingly took him by surprise.

As also it must have done Vendrei who, exhausted by water, shocks, walking, but mostly by the hundred conflicting emotions in his mind, had slumped over like a boy, with his cheek pillowed on his hand.

The sun blew out of the sea, the colour of Vendrei's golden-guinea hair.

The people at the two fires woke up, or were woken by the wakening of others. They were in number seven, and should have been counted eight. Zephyrin had left them.

They went down the shore, striding eastward, Mhikal Vendrei and Ymil. On Ymil's apparent personal involvement in searching for and locating Zephyrin, Vendrei made no comment. No doubt he was so obsessed with the captain, Ymil's dissimilar yet total obsession seemed only inevitable.

"He's swum out to that wreckage he claimed to see," Vendrei had shouted, rather illogically—for if the wreckage were not real, why swim out to it? "The currents here, the tides, are crazed—he'll drown himself, the devil—anything to deny me the satisfaction of killing him myself."

Not long after, unbreakfasted, their toilette consisting of hand-rubbed faces, finger-combed hair, and brandy-moistened mouths, the two men set off.

Both barely kept themselves from running.

The day, however, ran. Forward, upward.

Eventually, in the solar light that was like smashed crystal, they reached a stretch of whiter sand. Where, gleaming and sparkled by sun, lay the spars and barrels of the shipwreck, a torn sail spread like dirty washing, a handful of iron bits, bolts and nails, the dreadful inefficacious irony of a holy medallion.

Here and there along the route the booted footfalls of Zephyrin had been discernible in softer sand. Now, these narrow markers led, infallible clue, to the water's edge.

The sea had drawn out some way from the beach. This in itself showed a variant tide, since from what Zephyrin had said, one deduced that yesterday the margin had been consistently far more slender here.

"Look! There they are, his bloody boots thrown off—and the uniform jacket too, the better to swim."

They scanned across sunlit splinters of ocean.

Nothing obvious was to be made out. Neither the alluring wreckage, nor any mortal form.

"If anything was here, the sea's moved it. And the fool's gone after."

They stood between earth and water, under air and fire, dumbfounded.

"Oh God," Vendrei said then, softly, "why do I hate him so? Why? What did he ever do to me but gaze and jeer, and what's that, to a grown man? What have I done to myself these past years of my escape, to bring me down to this baseness and idiocy? I was never happy in all that time. I was never free. I drank and gamed and made love and played at living, and look where it's carried me. And—carried this young man who so enraged me— Have I gone mad for certain, Ymil, do you think?"

"It is," said Ymil, cautious and quite gentle, "a *kind* of madness."

"Yes, mad. The mad-house is the vile hell in which I must leave myself next." He gazed blindly across the bright water. "You talked last night, Ymil, of something you called a crime—that you'd deserted a young woman to whom you had promised marriage. You seemed to want to go back to her, to make it right. You said, I think, she fell ill... Oh, Ymil, We have almost the same story. If not exactly. My father sought to force me into an arranged marriage, with the daughter of a princely neighbour. I was already reluctant, yet took care I caught a glimpse of her before any formalities allowed me to meet her. Base as I was, and am, I think if I had been struck in admiration, I might have gone on with the fiasco. But no such thing occurred. Oh, she was not unpleasant, a little gawky, brown-haired, busying herself with some silly woman's pretence of gardening. Seventeen years of age. An uneducated, ignorant, skinny child. With a whole ten yards, and most of a thick hedge between us, I grew incensed. I rebelled. Because besides I thought myself at that time in love with another woman, the clever, elegant wife of an acquaintance, let it be said, and I planned to seduce this person and steal her from her husband. I'll tell you straight, when I proposed this to her, she laughed in my face. She said she was '*greatly tempted*' but liked her house too well to desert it and go '*adventuring*'. So then I went off alone, and wasted four years of my life. And what became of the little girl of seventeen with the brown hair? She too fell sick, Ymil. And so I heard later, she died. I had this from a man who had known the family. I beat him at cards and he took it out on me by telling me this. He said it was well known, she had died of shame, and her own father had called me her murderer. I might as well have cut her in half with a sword. And now. Now I'll kill a man for laughing at me. Am I so friendly with death, I yearn to *feed* him?"

Vendrei breathed a moment.

"Heaven pardon me, I should have begged their forgiveness too. Should have prayed for them, those drowned men in the cave. Have I lost my human heart? What have I become through all this? Mind lost, heart lost, inhuman, a monster—" And that said, Vendrei sat down and pulled off with some labour his own well-made boots. "I'll swim out too, Ymil. Try to find that boy, save him—"

Ymil had no words to give. He was aware Vendrei would no more hear them now than he would have listened to his own contrition, earlier.

As the prince launched himself into the water, graceful and muscular, assured in this even in his sudden lack of all other assurances, Ymil squinted away along the beach, attempting to gauge what the sea did there.

They were difficult to divine, the moods, the schemes of the sea.

In the end, once Vendrei had vanished entirely into the distance, Ymil moved on along the beach.

There was for some way still a trail of objects tossed on the sand. Then the heavy masonry of the cliff put its foot down and ended the beach entire. Here one jagged rock stuck up in the water, and draped artistically across the rock was what Ymil, briefly, took to be a perfectly white garment. Until he saw that it had long green hair.

Ymil had met nothing in his life that conclusively established things supernatural did not exist. Ghosts, vampires, feys, all sorts were conceivable. Thus, so might this be. For plainly, a white-skinned, naked, lovely woman lay over the arm of the rock, emerald-haired, her flat smooth belly finalizing in a coiled black tail.

He was staring at the mermaid when he heard Vendrei call from behind him, and the prince trudged up again out of the ocean, his own arms empty as his distraught face. All his shirt was gone now. How much of his soul?

Then they stared together at her, the lady from the sea.

It was Ymil who said at last, "She's human after all. It's weed caught in her hair, that greenness—and see, the tail's just the effect of some dark torn material wrapped around her legs."

Vendrei, who had been more still than the rock, started violently and said, "She isn't dead. I thought she was. But she's breathing."

At that second the woman who was not a mermaid stirred, coughed, and leaning sidelong, quickly voided her lungs of water. After which she sat up, glanced at them in angry dismay, and put one slim arm across her very beautiful breasts.

Ymil identified her. Or, recognised her. For he had secretly known her from those minutes before the tempest struck.

But "Is she from the ship?" asked Vendrei, as if in a sort of stupor. "Madam," he added, "allow me to assist you—"

"Keep your damned hands off me, you cur," replied the woman, in the tenor voice of Captain Zephyrin.

Those years before, Zophyra, at seventeen, had been ill-at-ease, and it was true also she had been poorly educated. She could read and write, sing and sew. Aside from that she was continually instructed in a single lesson, being that she must be feminine, obedient, and ready to marry whichever suitor her father chose her.

One day the father did choose. Zophyra was consumed by utter terror. She had heard—and read—plenty of tales of young maidens wedded to evil and frequently elderly men. Despite her condition not uninventive, she found a means therefore, at a time when the proposed bridegroom was visiting the estate, to see him, herself unseen. Her notion was that if he were foul she would slay herself—or, perhaps, run away.

What she saw, on that amber harvest morning, when the scent of wheat and hay, apples and white alcohol was buzzing in the air, was Mhikal Vendrei, then just twenty-two years of age, marvellous as a young god.

She fell in love with him at once.

A favour, alas, he did not return on the subsequent occasion that, unbeknownst to Zophyra, *he* had spied on *her*.

A trio of months following he jilted her, (unmet), and was gone into the wide world.

Her father and his vied with each other to make each other recompense. She meanwhile felt fragments of her shattered heart rattling in her breast, piercing her, and she succumbed to a recurrence of the dangerous fever, which seemingly still lay dormant in her blood. In infancy this malady had almost finished her. Now it made a worse assault. She had been, unknowing in delirium, given the last rites, when that very midnight the febrility cracked like a burning-glass and spilled her forth. As before, all her hair had fallen out. (In childhood the first attack of fever had turned it nearly white on its return, and ever since her father had seen to it that this albino tendency was corrected with a brown dye. He had not wanted to scare off possible swains with her almost-uncanny pallor). In adulthood once again the hair grew back, if anything whiter than before, only her brows and lashes retaining their darker shade. But by then her father never saw this. For as soon as she was able, still perhaps slightly unhinged from heartbreak and sickness, Zophyra fled the parental home.

She rushed out into the unknown and extraordinary world, which she had had the sense, (having also read a few rather ridiculous stories of such things), to approach in male attire and the assertive pretence of masculinity. Or masculinity as she perceived it: arrogant, overbearing, unkind, elusive. All this only worked because, despite her naivety, she had the cunning instincts of a genius.

She passed herself off as fourteen. As a lad she appeared much younger than her actual span. She joined one of the roving armies of the Steppes, more because it presented itself before her than for any concrete reason. She had been so scorched by passion and its rejection, (someone had told her Vendrei had seen her and been unimpressed), she was by then fearless, generally reckless. Among the men she would pass for a boy. The vagaries of Fate had aided her too, for her feminine monthly courses, traumatised by the fever, ceased for the time being to occur. By the time they did, she was well able to protect herself from any scrutiny.

She learned early on to fight. She was skilful and daring. She had begun to have a goal. She took proper lessons too whenever she could, from such scholars as she encountered, on many subjects, including the Latin and ancient Greek languages, literature and philosophy. (The one she hated was, she had been told, a paragon in this area). She paid for tuition with her army pay and was otherwise abstemious in all things. (When men advised her to visit the brothels, she told them she had a sweetheart at home she would not betray. As in much else they found her, or the youth she acted, weird but not unlikeable. And she was, they also knew, a demon with the drawn blade).

When she was nineteen, had grown taller, beautiful if she had known it, and must bind her breasts to protect and prevent discovery, she shaved her head and told those who commented on her lack of facial hair that a fever had depilated her almost entirely. Later, leaving the battalion, she *grew* her hair, told the same tale and claimed the real hair to be a wig. It was unusually thick and lustrous enough, added to its paleness, that she was believed.

Her goal, needless to say, remained constant.

She had, too, heard rumours of her own 'death' at home on the old estate. Nothing if not quirky, it seemed to her *that* Zophyra *had* died, had indeed been murdered by the callous suitor who had not wanted her.

She intended now to find this man. Firstly she would demonstrate to him she was his equal, or superior. Next she would make a mock of him, present him to others as shoddily as she could. Lastly, so well able to fight, not to mention tutored in the mental symmetry of poetic revenge, she would run him through the heartless heart with a steel blade. For had he not, metaphysically, spiritually, *carnally*, done as much to her?

Like Ymil, then, Zophyra—for a while known by the name of Zephyrin—tracked Vendrei. Just as presently, Ymil, hired and misled in embarrassment by her father, tracked *her*. (Him).

Learning the passenger list on the ship, Zophyra-Zephyrin took passage. As Ymil, knowing she-he would, had likewise done.

Ymil alone had seen to the bottom of her relentless vendetta—and that not until almost the last moment.

The rest was—uproar.

As detailed here.

7

Even the most diligent observer will sometimes deliberately turn away.

Ymil did so on the beach below the cliffs.

He took himself off along the shore, and began to examine some of the flotsam broadcast there, quite studiously.

Half naked the pair of them, Vendrei and Zeph-Zophyra glared at each other. After a second, however, the young woman pulled herself to her feet, and took a couple of angry baleful strides towards him. Her gait was not steady, needless to say, and gave way abruptly. The instant she staggered Vendrei leapt to her like lion at gazelle, and seized her in both arms. His grip was fierce, yet gentled. And Zophyra, while her head spun, could make no proper resistance.

The weed was still tangled in her hair. Vendrei therefore found himself kissing both her pale hair and the pale weed. Each tasted of ocean, but her hair also of her youngness and female flavour. Her skin more so.

"When I am better," she whispered, "I shall kill you for this."

"Already you kill me. One look from your eyes— who—what—who *are* you?"

"You know me."

"Do I?" Vendrei paused, his mouth against her cheek—that his duellist's glove had slapped, this skin like silk. "I seem—to have seen you. But that was in your male disguise. I should have guessed. Nothing so delicious, so rare, could be anything but a woman—"

"Oh, but it can, sir. Even dead on your back, with my sword so nicely planted in your heart, you would be worth all this world to me."

Both of them sighed then. They were worn out, and leaned on each other, in a while sitting down on the sand.

The sun warmed them. Their hair was drying, mingled in long strands of gold and cream.

Eventually he said, in a low, penitent voice, "Are you the girl from the other estate? *That* girl? But you can read Latin—"

Then she laughed. "What shall I do?" she asked the sky and the water. "It's no use, Mhikal Vendrei."

"No use at all. You've won the duel," he said. "You won it when I saw you and thought you half dead on the rock. I knew you then, somehow. But somehow I knew you anyway, and *that* was the cause of my hatred perhaps—that I'd refused something so—fine. Worth ten of me. A thousand. You have won the duel."

"No. *You* won it. From the moment I first saw you, four years ago, on the harvest morning. Then."

The watcher Ymil did glance, just once, back over the sand. A precaution perhaps. But they were embraced by then of course, mouth on mouth, their hands in the other's hair, yearning and almost crying aloud. Like two shipwrecked survivors who, after years of tempest, crashing waves and tumult, reach the kind arms of the land alive.

It is the sea, Ymil thinks, weeks later, when he is safe in the port of Pharos. The sea is so versatile, has so many trades. It makes itself adornments of lacy foam, disarms aggressive humans of their swords, rises to undo the graves of mankind and claim back the dead it has already destroyed, in its priestly role of sacrificer. But also the sea is the benign priest, joining in the marriage of love old widows and aging wifeless merchants, and young men and women who have lost what they can never see they have lost, which is simply their way. Brief dusk lies on Pharos, and the stars come out in crowds to gape at the nightlife below. The waters of the Mediterranean uncurl against this Egyptian strand. The sea, the priest, Ymil thinks, is also singing orisons above the depths, to honour them, those that never do reach the land, those forever lost; the drowned, the lonely. The watchers far from shore.

Under Fog
(The Wreckers)

Oh burning God,
Each of our crimes is numbered upon
The nacre of your eternal carapace,
Like scars upon the endless sky.

'Prayer of the Damned'
(Found scratched behind the altar in the ruined church at Hampp.)

We lured them in. It was how we lived, at Hampp. After all, the means had been put into our grip, and we had never been given much else.

It is a rocky ugly place, the village, though worse now. Just above the sea behind the cliff-line, and the cliffs are dark as sharks, but eaten away beneath to a whitish-green that sometimes, in the sunlight, luridly shines. The drop is what? Three hundred feet or more. There was the old church standing there once, but as the cliff crumbled through the years, bits and then all the church fell down on the stones below, mingling with them. You can still, I should think, now and then find part of the pitted face of a rough-carved gargoyle or angel staring up at you from deep in the shale, or a bit of its broken wing. The graveyard had gone, of course, too. The graves came open as the cliff gave, and there had been bodies strewn along the shore, or what was left of them, all bones, until the sea swam in and out and washed them away. Always a place, this, for the fallen then, and the discarded dead.

By day of my boyhood, the new church was right back behind the village, up hill for safety. The new church had been there for two hundred years. But we, the folk of Hampp, we had been there since before the Doomsday Book. And sometimes I used to wonder if they did it then too, our forebears, seeing how the tide ran and the rocks and the cliff-line.

Maybe they did. It seemed to be in our blood. Until now. Until that night of the fog.

My first time, I was about nine years. It had gone on before, that goes without saying, and I had known it did, but not properly what it was or meant. My nine-year-old self had memories of sitting by our winter fire, and the storm raging outside, and then a shout from the watch, or some other man banging on our door: "Stir up, Jom. One's there." And father would rise with a grunt, somewhere between annoyance and strange eagerness. And when he was gone out into the wind and rain, I must have asked why and Ma would say, "Don't you fret, Haro. It's just the Night Work they're to."

But later, maybe even next day, useful things would have come into our house, and to all the impoverished houses up and down the cranky village street. Casks of wine or even rum, a bolt of cloth, perhaps, or a box of good china; once a sewing machine, and more than once a whole side of beef. And other stuff came that we threw on the fire, papers and books, and a broken doll one time, and another a ripped little dress that might have been for a doll, but was not.

On the evening I was nine and a storm was brewing, I knew I might be in on the Work, but after I thought not and slept. The Work was what we all called it, you see. The Work, or the Night Work, although every so often it had happened by day, when the weather was very bad. Still, Night Work, even so.

My father said, "Get up, Haro." It was the middle of the night and I in bed. And behind the curtain in my parents' bed, my mother was already moving and awake. My father was dressed.

"What is it, Da?" I whispered.

"Only the usual," said my father, "but you're of an age now. It's time you saw and played your part."

So I scrambled out and pulled on my outdoor clothes over the underthings I slept in. I was, like my father, between two emotions, but mine were different. With me that first time, they were excitement, and fear. Truly fear, like as when we boys played see-a-ghost in the churchyard at dusk. But in this case still not even really knowing why, or of what.

Out on the cliff the gale was blowing fit to crack the world. There were lanterns, but muffled blind, as they had to be, which I had heard of but not yet properly seen.

Leant against the wind, we stared out into the lash of the rain. "Do you spot it, Jom?"

"Oh ah. I sees it."

But I craned and could *not* see, only the ocean itself roughing and spurging, gushing up in great belches and tirades, like boiling milk that was mostly black. But there was something there, was there? Oh yes, could I just make it out? Something like three thin trees massed with cloud and all torn and rolling yet caught together.

"You stay put, Haro," said my father. "Here's a light.

You shine that. You remember when and what to do? As I told you?"

"Yes, Da," I said, afraid with a new affright I should do it wrong and fail him. But he patted my shoulder as if I were full-grown, and went away down the cliff path with the others. Soon enough I heard them, those three hundred feet below me, voices thin with distance and the unravelling of the wind, there under the curve of the crumbled white-green cheese of the cliff-face. Though I was quite near the edge, I knew not to go too far along to see, but there was a place there, a sort of notch in the crag, whereby I could see the glimmer of the lamps as they uncovered them. And I knew to do the same then, and I uncovered my lantern too.

So we brought it in. The thing with the clouded trees that was adrift on the earthquake of great waters. The thing that was a ship.

She smashed to pieces on the rocks below, where the tallest stones were, just under the surface at high tide, against rock and shale, and the faces of angels and devils, and against their broken wings.

This was our Night Work, then. In tempest or fog we shone our lights to mislead, and so to guide them home, the ships, and wreck them on the fangs of our cliffs. And when they broke and sank, we took what they had had that washed in to shore. Not human cargo, naturally. That counted for nothing. It must be left, and pushed back, and in worse case pushed under. But the stores, the barrels and casks, the ironware and food and, if uncommon lucky, the gold, they were rescued. While they, the human flotsam, might fare as wind and darkness, and their gods—and we—willed for them, which was never well.

I saw a woman that night, just as the great torn creature of the vessel heaved in and struck her breast, with a scream like mortal death, to flinders on our coast.

The woman wore a big fur cloak, and also clutched a child, and in the last minute, in intervals of the storm-roil, I saw her ashen face and agate eyes, and he the same, her son, younger than I, and neither moved nor called, as if they were statues. And then the ship split and the water drank them down. But there was a little dog, too. It swam. It fought the waves, and they let it go by. And when it came to land—by then I craned at the cliff's notch, over the dangerous edge—my father, Jom Abinthorpe, he scooped up the little dog. And my reward for that first night of my Night Work was this little innocent pup, not yet full-grown as neither I was. Because, you will see, a dog can tell no tales, and so may be let live.

But the ship and her crew, and all her people, they went down to the cellars of the sea.

I was always out to the Work with the men after that. By the time I was eleven, I would be down along the shore, wading even in the high savage surf among the rocks, with breakers crashing sometimes high over my head, as I helped haul in the casks, and even the broken bits of spars that we might use, when dried and chopped, for our fires.

Hampp is a lorn and lonely place; even now that is so. And when I was a boy, let alone in my father's boyhood, remote as some legendry isle in the waste of the sea. But unlike the isles of legend, not beautiful, but bony bare. There were but a dozen trees that grew within a ten mile walk of the village, and these bent and crippled by the winter winds. In summer too there were gales and storms, and drought also. What fields were kept behind their low stone walls gave a poor return for great labour. And there was not much bounty given by the ocean, for the fish were often shy. The sea, they said, would as soon eat your boat as give you up a single herring. No, the only true bounty the sea would offer came on those nights of fog or tempest, when it drew a ship toward our coast and seemed to tell us: *Take it then, if you can.* For to do the Work, of course, was not without its perils. And to guide them in too required some skill, hiding the light, then letting out the light, and that just at the proper angle and spot. But finally the sea was our accomplice, was it not, for once drawn into that channel where the teeth of the rocks waited in the tide, and the green skull faces of the outer cliffs trod on into the water and turned their unforgiving cheek to receive another blow, the ocean itself forced and flung each vessel through. It was the water and the rocks smashed them. We did not do it. We had not such power, nor any power ever. And sometimes one of our own was harmed, or perished. Two men died in those years of my boyhood, swept off by the surge. And one young boy also, younger than I was by then, he broken in a second when half a ship's mast came down on him with all its weight of riven sail.

But ten ships gave up their goods in those years between my ninth and fourteenth birthdays, and I was myself by then a man. And the dog had grown too, my rescued puppy. I called him Iron, for his strength. He had blossomed from a little black soft glove of a thing to a tall and long-legged setter, dark as a shadow. He was well-liked in our house, being quiet and mannerly. Also I trained him to catch rabbits, which he killed cleanly and brought me for my mother's cooking. But he hated the sea. Would not go even along the cliff path, let alone to the edge with the notch, or down where the beaches ran when the tide was out. Whenever he saw me set off that way to fish, he would shift once, and stare at me with his great dark eyes that were less full of fear than of disbelief. Next he would turn his back. And here was the thing too; on those nights when the weather was bad, and the watch we posted by roster spied a ship lost and struggling, Iron would vanish entirely, as if he had gone into the very air to hide himself.

I thought after all he did not know what we were at. Certainly, he would eat a bowl of the offal of any beef or bacon or whatever that came to my family's portion out of a wreck. By then, I suppose, it had no savour of the sea.

He had not known either that we let his ship, his own first master likely *on* that ship, be drowned. Iron only knew, I thought, that my father, and next I, had plucked him from the water after all else was gone.

For a while I had recalled the cloaked woman and her son. I said nothing of it, and put it from me. And soon I had seen other sights like that, and many since that time. The worst was when they tried to save each other, or worse yet, comfort each other. Those poor souls. Yet, like my dog, I would start then turn my eyes away. I could not help them. Nor would I have, if I could. We lived by what we took from them, lived by their dying. All men want and will to live. Even a dog does, swimming for the shore.

Iron is here now. He leans on my leg and the leg of the chair. Strange, for there is iron metal there also, but he does not know this. They are kind, compassionate to have let him in. Well then. Let me tell the rest.

I had seen fogs often, and of all sorts. Sea-frets come up like a grey curtain but they melt away at Hampp and are soon gone. The other sort of fog comes in a bank, so thick you think you might carve it off in chunks with your rope-knife. And it will stay days at a time, and the nights with them.

In such a fog sometimes a ship goes by, too far out and never seen, yet such is the weird property of the fog that you will *hear* the ship, hear it creak and the waves slopping on the hull of it, and the stifled breathing of the sails if they are not taken in and furled. It is often worthwhile to go down with extra lanterns then, and range many lamps too along the cliff by the notch, for the ship's people will be looking for landfall and may see the lights, even in the depths of the cloud. But generally they do not. They pass away like ghosts. After they were gone men cursed and shrugged, wasting the lamp-oil as they had and nothing caught. But now and then a ship comes in too far, misled already by the fog, and by the deep water that lies in so near around our fanged rocks. For surely some demon made the coast in this place to send seafarers ill, and Hampp its only luck. These ships we would see, or rather the shine of their own lanterns, and they were heard more clearly, and soon they noticed our lamps too, and sometimes we called to them, through the carrying silence, called lovingly in anxious welcome, as if wanting them safe. And so they turned and came to us and ran against the stones.

That night of the last fog I was seventeen years, and Iron my dog about eight, with a flute of grey on his muzzle.

I had been courting a girl of the village, I will not name her. But really I only wanted to lie with her and sometimes she let me, therefore I knew we would needs be wed. So I was preoccupied, sitting by the fire, and then came the knock on the door. "Stir up, Jom Abinthorpe. Haro—waked already? That's good. There is a grey drisk on the sea like blindness, come on in the hour. And one's out there in it, seen her lamps. Well lit she is, some occasion she must have for it. But sailing near, the watch say."

So out we went, and all the village street was full of the men, shouldering their hooks and pikes and hammers, and the lanterns in their muffle giving off only a pale slatey blue. By now I did not even look for my dog Iron, though a few of the men had their dogs with them, the low-slung local breed of Hampp, with snub noses and big shoulders, that might help too pulling the flotsam to shore.

We went along the cliff, near the edge now all of us, but for the youngest boys, three of them, that we posted up by the notch. Then the rest of us went down to the beach.

It was a curious thing. The fog that night was positioned like a fret, one that stayed only on the sea, and just the faintest tendrils and wisps of it drifted along the beach, like thin ribbons of smoke from off a fire.

The water was well in, creaming clear on the shale, the tide high enough, and not the tips of the fangs below showing even if the vessel could have made them out. But the ship was anyway held out there, inside the box of the fog, under the fog's lid, like a fly in thick grey amber.

It was a large one, too, and as our neighbour had said, very well lit. In fact crazily much-lit, as if for some festival being held on the decks. We all spoke of it, talking low in case our words might carry, as eerily they did through these fogs. The watchman came and said he reckoned at first the ship had caught fire, to be so lighted up. For she did seem to burn, a ripe, rich, flickering gold. How many lamps? A hundred? More? Or torches maybe, flaming on the rails —?

A dog began barking then behind us, a loud strong bell of a bark. Some of the men swore, but my father said, "It's good. Let them know out there land is here. Let them hear and come on. Let's show the lanterns, boys. I'll bet this slut is loaded down with cash and kickshaws — we'll live by it a year and more."

And just then the vessel slewed, and the line of it, all shown in light, altered shape. We knew it had entered the channel and was ready to run to us.

Something came rushing from the other way though, and slammed hard against my legs, so I staggered and almost fell. And turning I saw my dog there. He was standing four-square on the shale, panting and staring full at me with eyes like green coals. Brighter than our uncovered lamps they seemed.

I said, Iron would never come to the sea, nor anywhere near it.

"Wonders don't cease," said my father. "The dog wants to help us with it too. Good lad. Stay close now —"

But Iron turned his eyes of green fire on my father, and barked and belled, iron notes indeed that split the skin off the darkness. And then he howled as if in agony.

"*Quiet*! Quiet, you devil, for the sake of Christ! Do he want to sour our luck?" And next my father shouted at me. I had never seen him afraid, but then I did. And I did not know why. Yet my whole body had fathomed it out, and my heart.

And I grabbed Iron and tried to push him back. "Not now, boy. Go back if you don't care for it. Go home and wait. Ask Ma for a bit of crackling. She knows when you ask. She'll give it you. Go on home, Iron."

And Iron fell silent, but now he sank his teeth in my trouser and began to tug and pull at me. He was a muscular dog, though no longer young, and tall, as I said.

The other men were surly and restless. They did not like this uncanny scene, the flaming ship that drove now full toward us and cast its flame-light on the shore, so the cliffs were shining up like gilt, and the opened lanterns paled to nothing—and the dog, possessed by some horrible fiend, gnawing and pulling, his spit pouring on the wet ground in a silver rain, as if he had the madness.

And then there came the strangest interval. I cannot properly describe how it was. It was as if time stuck fast for a moment, and the moment grew another way, swelling on and on. Even Iron, not letting go of me, stopped his tugging and slavering. And in the hell of his eyes I saw the wild reflection of the gold fire of the ship growing and moving as nothing else, for that moment, might.

"By the Lord," said my father softly, "it's a big one, this crate." It was such a foolish, stupid thing to say. And the last words I ever did hear from my father.

They call them she; that is, the seafarers call each ship *she*. As if she were a woman. But we did not. We could not, maybe, seeing as how we killed them in the Night Work. Just as we ignored the women who died with the ships, and the children who died.

But now I must call it she. The ship, the golden ship.

Believe this or not, as you will.

I do not believe it, and I saw it happen. I never will believe it, not till my last breath is wrung from me. And then, I think, I shall have to.

The moment which had stuck came free and fled. We felt time move, felt it one and all. It was as if the two hands of a clock had stuck, and then unstuck, and the ticking of it and the moving of it began again.

But as time moved, and we with it, it was the *ship* instead that froze. Out there at the edge of the grey slab of the fog, under it, yet visible now as if only through the flimsiest veil. She was well in on the last stretch. She could not stay her course. No vessel, even a mighty and huge one, could have stayed itself now. So far she had driven in, she must hurl on towards her finish against the rocks, and on the faces of the cliffs around, those that crowded out into the sea to meet her. Yet—she did not move. Our clock ran, hers had halted. But oh, something about her there was that moved.

I behold her still in my mind's eye. So tall, six or seven decks she seemed, and so many masts, and all full laden with her sheets. There was not a man on her that I could see. None. Nor any lamps or torches to light her up so bright that now, almost free of the fog, half she blinded me. No, she blazed from something else, as if she had been coated, every inch of her, in foil of gold, her timbers, her ropes, her sails—coated in gold and then lit up from within by some vast and different fire that never could burn upon this world, but maybe under it—or high above. Like the sun. A sun on fire at her core, and flaming outward. Lampless. *She* was the lantern. How she burned.

Not a sound. No voice, no motion. Even the ocean, quiet as if it too had congealed—but it moved, and the waves came in and lapped our boots, and they made, the waves, no sound at all.

And then the dog, my Iron, he began to worry at me, hard, hard, and I felt his teeth go through the trouser and he fastened them in my very leg. I shouted out in pain and turned, not knowing what I did, as if to cuff him or thrust him away. And by that the spell on me was rent.

I found I was running. I ran and sobbed and called out to God, and Iron ran by me and then just ahead of me. It seemed to me he had me fast by an invisible cord. I had no choice but to fly after him. And yet, oddly, a part of me did not want to. I wanted only to go back and stand at the sea's brink and look at the ship—but Iron dragged me and I could not release myself from the phantom chain.

I was up on the cliff path when I heard them screaming behind me and some one hundred and fifty feet below. This checked me. I fell and my ankle turned and a bone snapped, but I never heard the noise it made, for there was no sound in that place but for the shrieking of the men, and one of them my father.

Of course, I could no longer stir either forward or back. I lay and twisted, feeling no pain in my foot or leg, and stared behind me.

And this is what I saw. Every man upon that shore, every lad, even the youngest of them, ten years old, and the dogs, those too, and those screaming too as if caught in a trap, all these living creatures—they were racing forward, not as I had inland, but out toward the sea, toward the fog, toward the golden glare of the ship— But they howled in terror as they did so, men and beasts, nor did they run on the earth. They ran on *water*. They ran through the *air*. The three children from the cliff-top— they too—off into the air they had been slung, wailing and weeping, and whirling outward like the rest. And up and up they all pelted, as if racing up a cliff, but no land was there under their feet. Only the ship was there ahead of them, and she waited. The thin veil of the outer fog hid nothing. The light of her was too fierce for anything to be hidden. The men and the boys and the dogs ran straight up and forward, unable to stay their course until, one by one, they smashed and splintered on the cliff-face of the golden ship, on the golden fangs and cheek and rock of the ship. I saw so clear their bones break on her, and the scarlet gunshot of their blood that burst and scattered away, not staining her. As they did not either, but fell down like empty sacks into the jet black water. Till all was done.

After which, she turned aside, gently drifting, herself as if weightless and empty, and having moved all round she returned into the fog, under fog, and under night and under silence. She slid away into the darkness. Her glow went soft and melted out. The fog closed over. The night closed fast its door, and only then I heard the waves that sucked the shale, and the pain rose in my leg like molten fire.

They will be hanging me tomorrow. That is fair; it is what I came to the mainland for, and made my confession. At first I never said why I had had to. How I had crawled up the path, with my dog helping me. And in the village of Hampp, all the faces, and seeing that each one knew yet would not speak of it. My mother, she like the others. How I stayed two months there, alone, until I could walk with a stick, and by then almost everyone had left the place, the empty houses like damp caves. And then I left there also. But I came here, and my dog quite willing to cross water, and I found a judge, and was judged.

Men have gone to search the waters off the coast below Hampp. They find nothing of the dead ships. We took all there was to take. As for corpses, bones, theirs and ours are all mingled, like the gargoyles and angels in the stones of the beach.

When I did tell the priest of the ship, he refused to believe me. So I have told you now and let it be written down, since I was never learned to make my letters.

You see there is an iron manacle on my ankle, but it is quite a comfort. It supports the aching bone that snapped. The rope perhaps will support my neck and then that will be crushed, or it will also break, and then I will leave this world to go into the other place, from which golden things issue out.

It is kind they let me say farewell to Iron, my dog. Yes, even though he is no longer mine. They have told me a widow woman, quite wealthy, is eager to have him, since her young son is so taken with Iron, and Iron with him likewise.

I have witnessed it myself, only this morning from this window, how the dog walked with the child along the street, Iron wagging his strong old tail that is only a touch grey to one side. The child is a fair boy too, with dark sad eyes that clear when he looks at Iron. And certainly his mother is wealthy, for her cloak is of heavy fur.

That is all, then. That is all I need to say.

No. I am not sorry for my village. No, I am not afraid to go to the scaffold. Or to die. No, I am not afraid of these things. It is the other place I fear. The place that comes after. The place they are in, the men of Hampp, and my father too. The place where she came from. The Ship. I cannot even tell you how afraid I am, of that.

THE SEA WAS IN HER EYES

This sequel to "Girls in Green Dresses" is also for John Kaiine - who told me something too, of Elaidh

Day by day the great ship swung across the ocean. She was rigged so full she seemed to carry the clouds above her decks. At first, the passengers had looked up, wondering, at these. Then they looked down and about, and most of them saw the young woman, for she was the only human female thing aboard.

"She's a fine-looking girl, she is so," they said. Her hair was brown and piled up heavily on her head.

She was slender and green-eyed. Her clothes were good, but more than those, they noted three ruby rings on her fingers and the long rope of pearls, nearly long as she was tall, that she wore at night to dinner in the saloon.

"She's alone. Such a girl should have some company," said they.

They generously tried to give her company then, the older men and the younger men, the sailors and the passengers both. She was quiet and graceful with them all, but they slid from her surface as fishes slip through water.

"It's a pity she is a tease," they said.

"She's plain as dough," they said, "despite her rubies and pearls."

"She has emeralds for eyes and a cold green heart."

The sea was wide as the sky, but now and then a bit of land appeared, the thin strip of a coast. Here passengers got off and new passengers walked on. At one land-strip, which had an edging of mountains, a young man stepped aboard, with six brass-bound boxes and a chest, and two servants, two white horses and two black dogs, and an owl that would sit on his arm. His hair was dark and his skin fair. He was handsome, too, and like everything else, his looks came aboard with him.

Half the day he would sit reading, and the other half playing the piano in the saloon. He was rich. A prince, they said.

"Prince Cuzarion," they said, bowing to him. And they tried to win his money off him at cards, or by means of bets and wagers, inviting him to race his dogs against other dogs on board, or to set the owl on some passing gull. But they never won a penny, and the dogs did not race, and the owl never chased the gull.

Sometimes the passengers would tell stories in the saloon after the dinner.

One night the prince, if so he was, told a marvellous and clever story, about a prince who, on a voyage, was carried down into the deep by a mermaid where he lived with her some while—she having, by then, taught him how to breathe under the sea.

"Is that what you'd like, then?" they asked.

"I am already betrothed,"' said Prince Cuzarion. "Although perhaps I might not mind it, for a month or so."

All this while, the girl had sat in her usual corner, drinking her glass of wine, the rubies burning on her white hands and the pearls weeping down her dress.

Maybe some of them had noticed she would often glance at the prince. Maybe some of them had even seen her gaze at him very long.

So now, one of the other men said to her, "Well, my lady, what do you think of mermaids?"

Although she was so young, she was never discomposed. And now she spoke calmly and clearly, with neither arrogance or shyness.

"I think that they exist," she said, "but they are not as you imagine, being a cruel race, who like to eat men raw and sometimes alive, spitting out the bones to make flutes."

This shocked everyone. The idea itself, and that this young girl should speak of it. So they said no more to her. But Prince Cuzarion, he flipped her one look. It was probably only the second he had ever given her, for she had not taken his fancy, though perhaps he had taken hers.

That night a storm came up out of the sea, boiling and black. It put out the stars and smashed the plate of the moon. That done, it scanned about for something to harm, but though the land was not far off, it did not want the land. Then, it saw a ship dancing along, rigged with clouds, and with lights shining from the port-holes and in the lanterns, and under the howl of the wind fluttered the notes of a piano.

"I'll have you," said the storm, and flung itself forward, kicking the waves from its path.

When the storm hit the vessel buffeting blows, the ship's world went to pieces. Lights and wine glasses and coffee-pots flew one way, and with them the chairs and boxes, and the piano even. And all the passengers. Then everything went another way

There was a great yelling and praying. From the depths of the ship the pair of horses neighed, and above, dogs barked. But in the ship's seams the rats looked philosophically about, for they always knew things might end in tears, and tonight it would be the tears of the sea.

None saw, or if they did they paid no heed, to the slight young girl with her hair blown from its pins, standing on the upper deck, and staring over at the churning waves.

Then the ship split from one end of herself to the other, and everything spilled out into the sea.

That moment, the girl jumped over the side. And if any had spied her, they would have seen she was naked as a knife, but for her ruby rings and the rope of pearls, and her long brown hair.

Cuzarion—and he was a prince—had a great many accomplishments. He had matchlessly waltzed in glittering ballrooms, and faultlessly fought on foot and on horseback; he could play the piano better than most. But swim he could not.

So now, as the cold black water closed over him, he thought with wrathful despair of all he would miss, and gave himself up to darkness.

But in the dark, just as the last light in his brain was going out, he felt a cool warmth pressed all the length of his body, and through the shadow saw a naked woman held him, while her hair swirled round them through the currents like a huge flag. She pressed her lips to his, but all he could taste was salt. Then she blew into his mouth.

"Why have I not died?" Cuzarion presently asked the deeps of the icy sea. But then he thought that probably he had, and just did not know it yet.

Up above, on the surface of the water, which was as tumultuous as the lower reaches were almost still, a curious thing happened.

Among the floating spars and smashed rails, which were all that was left of the ship, amid the turmoil of night and waves, the storm, having successfully broken something, was ebbing away to sleep, but the elements remained all disturbed and out of kilter. Now a lantern bobbed by, still burning in the murk, and you might see two pale horses swimming, led by long brown reins, and it was a girl leading them on, and hair that made the reins. And then several dogs went by, balanced companionable on a piece of stiff sail, and towed along. And an owl perched on a shattered mast, to which twenty men were also clinging, lifting its wings above the brine.

Later, when they had come to shore—and not one of them was lost, although, to be exact, they thought that one of them of them had been—they told this strangest tale. Of a woman in the sea who drew them up from the ocean and hung them out like her washing on the bars and stays and wreckage of the ship. Who bound them there with wet wippy weed from the under-shores of the sea, and pressed, with small slender hands as strong as steel, the water from their lungs, then dragged them in, by a net of weed—and some said of brown hair—to the shores of the land.

There then, in the last of the awful night, men stood by the driftwood fires they had made, wringing out their washing-wet clothes and fear-sodden souls, while the horses stamped and the dogs ran about and the owl dried its feathers. Then rescuers came, with torches and brandy, from the nearby town.

"It is a miracle—is every man here?"

"Every man and every beast. Look, even the bloody rats are saved and brought ashore!"

"No, no," cried one of the servants, "we have lost our prince."

"They have lost their prince."

"And her, we've lost the young lady—" cried another. But when he said this, the rest shushed him.

"She was no girl or maid or lady."

"What then? What?"

"The sea she was."

He woke on a far coast like none he had ever seen, though, being well-read, he had read of such a place, now and then.

Palms like green spiders on stilts swept the sand with their legs. The water was a blue turquoise. Above rose wooded hills, from which blew the scent of orange groves, and the dim ringing of the bells of a monastery on a high rock.

Nearby sat a girl in a satin dress and a rope of pearls, toasting fish over a small fire.

"We're ship-wrecked, then," said the prince. "Only you and I. The other poor devils have all gone down. But I grieve too for my horses and dogs, and the owl. Although perhaps the owl at least may reach land."

"Grieve for none," said the girl, "all have reached the shore, though another shore than this."

"Indeed," said Cuzarion. But a memory was coming back to him, like a remembered dream. "I think you saved me," said he.

"So I did. I saved each and all."

"That is most praise-worthy and talented of you," said Cuzarion, raising his brows. "How, pray, did you do it?"

Then the girl brought him some fish, and he ate this hungrily, and then drank from the bottle of wine she had also set by, which was very nicely aged.

"Did people bring these provisions out of pity for us? And these clothes—this fine shirt and breeches I have on, which are never mine—and your dress, since—I hope you'll forgive me—you seemed without one earlier."

The girl smiled, not looking at him. She put back her mass of hair with one hand.

"I brought the fish and the wine, and the clothes too from chests, out of the deeps of the sea."

"Did you now," said Cuzarion.

"Up from the deeps, out of which I brought you all. It is work I set myself to do."

Cuzarion made no comment. But then he said . "It's a noble thing to be so busy, and at your young age too."

"How old do you make me out to be?" said she, tossing her head a little.

"Oh, a great age—eighteen or so."

"One hundred and eight is nearer the mark."

"Ah."

Then she laughed. "You think I lie, of course. But I tell you true. My name is Elaidh. My mother was a mermaid, and she got me by a human man, and left me in his care, the way the mermaids do, for all that race are female. Then when I was thirteen years old, my mother wanted me, to transform me to her kind, with a long silver tail and hair green as grass. But I loved my da, and so I stayed with him. I thought I should only be a woman, but it seems I have great powers from my mother, though she was cruel, as mermaids are. I am long-lived, and the ocean is familiar to me. I can breathe in water easy as air, and I can give my gift to humankind for a little while, when I blow in their mouths. Also, I can tell the ships that may go down. I walk about the quays, and suss them out.

Then I go sailing on them, and when they sink, save everyone I can. With your ship I had great luck, and saved every living thing."

"I must thank you, then," said Cuzarion, attempting to laugh, but seeming uneasy. He added, "Do your pearls and rubies come from the sea, too?"

"Oh yes. There are great hoards of jewels and other riches that lie there, mermaid-trove, that I steal from them. My da and I were rich, while he yet lived."

"Yet a pity," said Cuzarion, looking under his lids at her, "that you only blew the breath of life into my mouth. All this while I'd been thinking it was a kiss."

Then she sat back and looked quietly at him.

"Oh, do you see me now?" she asked.

Cuzarion, though a prince, had the grace to blush. But then, he was young as a child beside her.

Some while they were on that coast.

Elaidh taught Cuzarion to swim, and sometimes she would whisper the magic air into his mouth so he might swim under the sea, but not very far down. Even so, he saw wonderful sights there. Peculiar creatures that moved about below the rocks, and mysterious plants and corals, and fish of rainbow colours.

By day, he and she would swim then, or walk about the country. Going inland, they went by mustard fields and fields of lavender, and on the hills the bees rose in clouds, just as the fish rose in the sea at their passing. Now and then they met with people, who spoke a language Cuzarion, for all his education, did not know. But Elaidh knew it. She told him frankly she knew by now most of the languages of the earth, for she had jour-neyed nearly everywhere. "There's no land," said she, "the water cannot take me."

In a village under the monastery rock, they went into a cool blue church whose walls were figured with saints. And Cuzarion was amazed Elaidh could do this, and more amazed when she bowed to the cross, for he had heard mermaids, and their kin, could not have one single thing to do with God.

As time went on, Cuzarion began to think less and less of who he was, who he had been, his other life. He thought more and more of Elaidh. And as he thought more of her, he saw her more and more clearly. At first she seemed plain, but very graceful. Then she seemed lovely, and then beautiful. At last she seemed the only living thing, so that if a bird exquisitely sang, somehow it was Elaidh, and when it flew, it was Elaidh. And the dawn was Elaidh, and the evening star, and the moon.

"I should like to stay with you," said Cuzarion, "for ever."

"That is hardly possible," said Elaidh.

"Because you will never die, and I shall?"

"One day I shall die."

She led him into the wood at dusk. The grass was thick with clovers and warm still from the sun. They became lovers with finesse, and ease, for each had been a lover before.

And at first Cuzarion was most happy. But then, he was less happy. He became content, then static, then restless. And Elaidh became again only beautiful.

"Elaidh, I must get home. How long have I been away?"

"One month," said she.

"So long—it seems only a day or so—"

But she knew he lied.

"You'll understand my difficulty," said Prince Cuzarion. "My father is old and gives over much of the running of things to me. Besides—I was to marry."

"She'll be that impatient." said Elaidh. From her face you could tell little, only perhaps that she had spoken in this way before, once, twice.

"Yes, she's a royal girl, and she will be very angry."

"What is her name?"

"Oh—some royal name Sapphyra, that's her name."

"Will you not give her up," said Elaidh, "for me?" But she spoke in a light and mocking manner, and Cuzarion smiled.

"Would that I could," he said. "Kingdoms depend on it."

"Go up to the monastery, " said Elaidh. "Say the sea cast you here, but now you'd be going home. The priests are wealthy and wise and will find you a ship."

"Come with me, Elaidh."

"I? Come with you where, and to what?"

"In my own country—maybe we can make an arrangement, you and I. It's not unknown. I must marry the princess, but even so, there will be times when I can get free of her."

"No, then. I will not be going with you for that."

Cuzarion was sorry. He felt badly about himself. And so he walked off through the fields of mustard and lavender and mint, and among the olive groves where, as the soft wind blew, every leaf flashed, like the silver tails of a thousand fish.

When he came back near evening, Elaidh was not there. He searched a long while, even standing at the edge of the dark blue sea, calling her. But she was gone. She was gone for good. After a day or so, he walked up to the monastery where the priests were gracious to him, for he was a prince, charming, and well-read.

The ocean is not made of tears, though one might think it. No, it is the other way about, for the water of the sea is in us, in our blood, and when we cry, we cry the sea's own salt water.

The princess whose name was Sapphyra, had herself done some crying, but that was now over. She had a fair face of sharp features, and raven-black hair.

"How good it is, to see her cheerful again," said her maids. "A year ago, when she thought him dead, she grieved so." They did not add that while she grieved, she had pinched and slapped them every day.

Now the princess, and her three highest attendants, were gathering flowers, in the palace's wild gardens that ran to the shore. In one more day, Sapphyra would be married to the Prince Cuzarion, and the garlands—which others would weave from the flowers—were for her wedding: A quaint custom.

"Who is that?" said the First Attendant, straightening up with her armful of lilies.

"Some great lady," said the Second Attendant, "standing by to watch."

"She's only a girl, she is," said the Third Attendant.

Then Sapphyra turned and looked.

There the woman stood, under a tamarisk tree. In the sunlight, she shone like a church window. Her gown was silver, there were diamonds in her hair, and on her fingers three red ruby rings of incalculable price.

"Good day, madam," said Sapphyra, feeling quite undressed in her embroidered morning-wear.

The woman nodded. "You are the Princess Sapphyra?"

"I have that joy."

"Long then, may you be joyful," said the woman.

"But let me ask," said the princess, frowning somewhat, "your own name, and your purpose."

"My name is Elaidh, and my mother was a mermaid. I am here to offer you my wedding-gift."

A great silence had fallen in the wild gardens. Even the daylight nightingale had left off her song.

"A gift? Why should I deserve one from you?"

"Ah," said Elaidh, sadly, "you must take my word for that."

The three Attendants were in a fuss.

They bustled about, and everywhere flowers fell from their hands and out of their gilded baskets. But Sapphyra said, "If I should accept your gift, how am I to receive it?"

"You must come down to the shore," said Elaidh.

The Attendants did not wish to. But Sapphyra took hold of them and shook them.

"Do you know nothing? The mermaid-kind are wealthy beyond all thought. And see—the gems all over her—why, even her two shoes are studded with pearls."

"And why should she need shoes," said the Third Attendant pertly, "if her mother was a fish?"

But Elaidh was walking slowly away by now, and Sapphyra soon followed. The Attendants unhappily went after.

The sea came gently to the gardens, it was there an ocean of low tides.

But Elaidh stood, with her pearl shoes in the water. "Now, princess Sapphyra, you must be brave, and trust me. For I'm set to show you an astonishment of this world, which is a treasure-hoard of the mermaids. But to see it, you must come down with me, under the waves."

At this, all three Attendants began to scream, but such silly little screams, like operatic mice.

Besides, Sapphyra turned and slapped them. One! Two! Three! After which there was only snivelling.

"They must come down too," said Sapphyra, spitefully.

"Very well," said Elaidh.

So she stepped up to each of the women, and kissed her on the lips, and as she did so, into each of their mouths she blew her pure salt breath.

This dazed them a touch. So, when she walked out into the sea, they went after her, lifting their skirts foolishly, to keep them dry, until the water closed over their heads.

Down and down sank the princess and her maids, after the swift form of Elaidh—who seemed to fly through the water.

The light left the sea. It grew dark and then black. But everywhere in the black it was lit up by gleaming objects, some of which were stones, or plants, and some of which were glowing fish with eyes like candle-flames.

Huge rock-faces rose about them, and from the ledges of these, bloated shapes sometimes launched themselves, and flapped off like crows. Then they came into an orchard of corals, which were all in razor blossom.

Now and then Elaidh spoke to Sapphyra and her ladies, and through the sorcery of her breath, or her mind, they heard her, although they themselves could not utter at all.

"There is a giant octopus," said Elaidh. "Never fear him, he knows not to be discourteous to me." Or, "Look there, the wreck of an antique galleon." The octopus was a cause of discomfort to the princess and her ladies, though he did no more than blink his eye at them. The galleon filled them with terror, for the bones of men lay over its decks, and even the figurehead had become a skeleton.

But then Elaidh led them through a forest of tall seaweeds, everyone of which was like a long, six-fingered hand. And then they passed through a tunnel of the rock, and coming out, they were in a vast cavern, elsewhere open only at its top. But somehow, through this opening, miles up, the sunlight entered, and came down and illuminated the space, and the floor of fine, moon-white sand.

Sapphyra and her ladies stopped, balanced in the sea, and staring.

"Here," said Elaidh, "as I promised you, is a treasure of the mermaid-kind."

On every side went up heaps and actual towers of riches, such as would surpass the trophy chambers of an emperor. There were caskets and chests of golden coins and silver, and cascades of pearls, emeralds and diamonds. There were statues of solid gold with eyes of opal, and unusual artefacts of gold, one of which was a model of a golden palace, very intricate, and large enough a child could have played in it. It had windows of carnelian, amethyst and chrysoprase, and roofs of polished ivory.

The ladies seemed to forget their terror. They floated to and fro, handling things and exclaiming silently, so crystal bubbles blew out of their mouths like words.

"You may take anything you can carry," said Elaidh.

At this, Sapphyra strove to pick up the gold palace, but Elaidh came to her and pressed her arm. "For you, princess, there is another treasure."

Then Elaidh drew Sapphyra aside into a second cave. And here Sapphyra lost all her composure. For from the floor to the ceiling, the cave was piled with jewels of a shining, heavenly blueness, some set in gold and some strung in ropes, some burnished, and some cut so they had become like stars of the northern pole. And some were larger than a man's hand. They were sapphires.

"For your name," said Elaidh. "Take whatever you want."

Then Sapphyra made an apron of her skirt, and she darted about the cave, until she had gathered everything she could, and rather more. And still she was digging out rings and necklaces and putting them on, and tying others into her corset ribbons and her black hair.

After a time, however, a louring weariness seemed to overtake her. She sat down on the sand, holding the treasure to her. Then she spoke to Elaidh, and though no words were to be heard, Elaidh heard them.

"Madam," said Elaidh, "it is a great disservice I have done you, although I did it without malice, or intent, without thinking. Listen now. Keep these jewels from your husband, the prince. Then, when a time comes that what you wish for most you find you do not have, put on some of these gems, and go to him. Then he will give you back what I have taken from you. And if it is really mine, it is also his, and shall be yours."

Riddles! said the crystal bubbles from the lips of the princess.

But next moment Elaidh raised her up, and gave her a push that sent her spinning, and Sapphyra found, to her indignation, she was rushing out of the cave, and up and up through the light-changing water, with the three

Attendants whirling around her. Until all four broke the skin of the sea, and fell out on the sands of the earth. And there lay the tame wild gardens of the palace, and all around the gold and jewels that had tumbled from their skirts.

Years passed. To the prince and princess they seemed only a few in number. So that, should they add them up, they were startled always. To others, the number of the years was more than twenty-five.

They were not often together, the prince, the princess.

She would be at cards, or at her dressmakers, or she would be lying on her sofa, eating something that had to do with chocolate. Or in the theatre, in a dream.

He would be riding, and then he would be aching from the ride. He would be up all night to drink or gamble. Or, now and then, with one of the scatter of his mistresses. Or he would play the piano in the echoing marble music-room of the palace, surprising himself by how often his fingers stumbled on the keys.

There was a solitary odd story told of the royal couple.

At the start, for a decade, almost, they had been childless. Then one day the princess had given birth—astounding the physicians who had, it seemed, burst in too late to do more than ponder the flawless child—and shake their heads over its largeness and the adjacent slenderness of the princess, which had persisted throughout her term, right up to the morning of the child's unheralded appearance.

Once, at a dinner some months later, the princess had drunk a great deal of champagne. Pointing at a sapphire necklace she had on, she exclaimed, "Do you see this? This is the reason for my child." Which was thought, by the assembly, very daring, perhaps rather too bold, and also most curious.

More curious still was the truth. But there came a night the prince told it to his heir, the son the Princess Sapphyra had shown to him that morning, eighteen years before.

The boy entered the music-room, and found his father, the prince, seated there at the piano.

Cuzarion was no longer young. His hair had turned grey, and though his court, and the mistresses, still lauded him as handsome, it was a sort of handsomeness which might have looked better on a statue than a man.

But the boy—oh, the boy. He was like the morning sun, so young and straight and fair, his hair the light brown of acorns, his eyes the green of apples. In honesty, he resembled neither his father nor his mother, the princess, at all.

In the tradition of the royal household, the prince's son had the same name as his father, just as the prince had had his own father's name. Cuzarion, they were all named that.

"Cuzarion," therefore said Cuzarion, to his son, "I've called you to me to tell you a tale that you will think a lie. Or else you'll think I have gone mad."

But Prince Cuzarion's son, Prince Cuzarion, smiled kindly at his father.

"No, sir. I would never think that."

"Well, then, we'll sit here. Let me tell it through, and then decide, for you have reached a proper age, both to hear it, and to judge."

Then the elder prince spoke of the voyage he had made those few years, more than twenty-five, in his past. Of the storm and the sinking ship, of how Elaidh had saved him and every other living thing aboard. But then he told of how he had loved Elaidh, and lain with Elaidh, and presently left Elaidh to come home and resume his life. To do him credit, the elder Prince Cuzarion did not paint his love for Elaidh as anything more than it had been, the passion of a month, nor himself as any more than he was, a man capable only of a month's fidelity.

And the younger prince listened gravely. Even when his father explained how Elaidh was a magical being, the daughter of a human man and a mermaid of the deeps of the ocean.

Then the elder prince mentioned his marriage to the Princess Sapphyra. That it was pleasant enough. That it went by. And that one day he found her sobbing, and she said, "We have no children, you and I."

"And we had done everything that humans may do," said the elder prince, "to ensure a child between us. Yet none arrived."

"But then I did arrive," said the young prince. "It is most sorry I am, to have kept you and mother waiting."

"My son," said the elder prince, "you were born of a spell. You are my child, it is a fact, but not the child of the princess. The mermaids have their children by another means. It is the father brings them forth, having carried them a while, without knowing it. It seems Elaidh visited the princess before her wedding. Elaidh gave her sapphires, for her name, from the depths of the sea. And one night Sapphyra came to me in a necklace of these jewels. Later, as I slept, I dreamed of Elaidh, and in my sleep I possessed Elaidh as a man possesses a woman. And when I woke, the sheet was damp from my lust." He glanced here at his son, a little afraid to have embarrassed him. But the younger prince was not ashamed. Still he sat gravely, listening, as if in his heart he somehow knew it all.

"Sapphyra too," said the elder prince, "lay in the bed that night. In the dawn, a ray of sun fell on the coverlet. Then she and I woke, for something stirred on the mattress between us. And when she threw off the covers, a baby lay there, white as the sea-foam, and clean as the morning.

"And this was I?"

"And this, my son, my mermaid's son, was you."

"Then," said the young man, "Elaidh is my mother."

"So she must be."

"Shall I ever meet her?"

The eider prince sighed. "Perhaps. I hope you may. But I think it will never be in my lifetime. For I think I shall never meet that lovely girl again, she that was the evening star to me, and the flight of a bird. She that I forgot then, as I forget now how to play my piano, and everything—but her."

But the boy was in a sort of trance, and could only look glad, thinking of his new history. He said, "How shall I know her, if she should come here?"

"Ah," said the elder Cuzarion. "Easily enough. She will look, I think, just as she did. Eighteen she will look, your own age now. For her kind live long but never grow old. And she is in her colouring also like you. Her hair is brown that has a spirit of green in it. Her skin is clear as waters."

"And since she is half mermaid, how will I notice that?"

"As I did, my son, if I'd looked as I should. For though she shed no single tear, the sea was in her eyes."

Because Our Skins Are Finer

In the early winter, when the seas are strong, the grey seals come ashore among the islands. Their coats are like dull silver in the cold sunlight, and for these coats of theirs men kill them. It has always been so, one way and another. There were knives and clubs, now there are the guns, too. A man with his own gun and his own boat does well from the seals, and such a man was Huss Hullas. A grim and taciturn fellow he was, with no kin, and no kindness, living alone in his sea-grey croft on the sea rim of Dula under the dark old hill. Huss Hullas had killed in his time maybe three hundred seals, and then, between one day and the next, he would not go sealing anymore, not for money and surely not for love.

Love had always been a stranger to him, that much was certain. He had no woman, and cared for himself as any man can in the islands. And once a month he would row to the town on the mainland, and drink whisky, and go upstairs with one of the paid girls. And row back to Dula in the sunrise, no change to be seen in him for better or worse. Then one time he went to the town and there was a new girl working at the bar. Morna was her name. Her hair was black as liquorice, and her skin was rosy. As the evening drew to a close, Huss Hullas spoke to Morna, but not to order whisky. And Morna answered him, and he got to his feet and went out and banged the bar door behind him. It seemed she would not go with him as the other girls would. She had heard tell of him, it seemed. Not that he was rough, or anything more than businesslike in bed, but he was no prince either, with no word to say and no laugh to laugh, and not even a grunt to show he had been gladdened. "I will not go upstairs with a lump of rock, then," she said. "There are true men enough who'll pay me."

Now love was a stranger to him, but so was failure. And though this was a small prize to fail at the winning of, yet he did not like to fail. If he would eat a rabbit or bird for his meal, he would find and shoot one. If he baked bread, it would rise. If he broke a bone, he could set it himself, and it would mend. Only the sea had ever beaten him, and that not often, and he is a foolish man will not respect the sea, who lives among her isles. Even the Shealcé, the Seal People, dropped down before Huss Hullas's gun obediently. And since he had never yet asked a free woman to take him, he had never yet been refused, till Morna did it.

When he went again to town, he went before the month was up, and when Morna came by his table, he said she should sit down and drink whisky with him. But Morna stepped sharply away. "I will not do that, neither."

"What will you do, then?" said Huss Hullas. "Will you begot the sack?"

"Not I," said she. "The rest like me. They have cause."

"I will give you a pound more," he said.

Morna smiled. "No."

"How much, then?"

"Nothing, then." And she was gone, and presently so was he.

When he came back the next month, he brought her a red lacquer comb that had been his mother's.

"What now?" she said. "Is it wooing me, you are?"

"Learning your price, then," he said.

"Well, I'll not go with you for an old comb."

"It's worth a bit."

"I have said."

"For what, then?"

Morna frowned at him angrily. It must be made clear, he was not a bad-looking man for all the grim way he had with him, which had not altered, nor his stony face, even as he offered her the comb. And his eyes, dark as the hill of Dula, said only: *You will do it. This is just your game.* And so it was.

It was winter by then, and all along the shore the oil-lamps burned where the electricity had not yet been brought in, and the seals were swimming south like the waves, as they had swum for hundreds of years.

"Well," said Morna, "bring me a sealskin for a coat, and I'll go upstairs with you. That is my promise. It shall keep me warm if you cannot, you cold pig of a man."

"Ah," said Huss Hullas, and he got up and went out of the bar to find another woman for the night, on Fish Street.

The seals came that month and beached on all the islands west of Dula. They lay under the pale winter sun and called to each other, lying on the rocks where the sea could find them. On some of these bleak places it might seem men had never lived yet in the whole world, but still men would come there.

One or another rowed over to Dula and hammered on Huss Hullas's door, and he opened it with a rod and a line he was making in one hand.

"The seals are in. Are you ready, man?"

"I am."

"We shall be out at dawn tomorrow, with the tide to help us."

"I'll be there."

"So you will, and your fine gun. How many will you get this winter?"

"Enough."

"And one for her on the mainland."

"We'll say nothing of that," said Huss Hullas, and the man looked at him and nodded. Grim and hard and black, the eyes in Huss Hullas's head could have put out fires, and his fists could kill a man, as well as a seal.

In the first stealth of the sunrise, Huss Hullas rowed away from Dula with his gun and his bullets by him. He rowed to where the ocean narrows and the rocks rise up to find the air. In the water ever westward, dark buoys bobbed in the blushing water that were the heads of seals. Tarnished by wet they lay, too, on the ledges of the isles, shelf on shelf of them, and sang in their solemn inhuman way, not knowing death approached them.

There was some ice, and here and there a seal lay out on the plates of it. They watched the men in the shadowy boats from their round eyes. The Shealcé is their old name, and still they are named so now and then, the Seal People, who have a great city down under the sea.

When the guns spoke first, the Shealcé looked about them, as if puzzled, those that did not flop and loll and bleed. When the guns spoke again, the rocks themselves seemed to move as shelf upon shelf slid over into the water and dived deep down. The guns shouted as if to call them back, the pink water smoked and blood ran on the ice. Men laughed. It is not the way, anymore, to know that what you kill is a living thing. It was different once, in the old times, very different then, when you would know and honour even the cut-down wheat. Men must live, like any other creatures, and it is not always a sin to kill, but to kill without knowledge may well be a sin, perhaps.

Huss Hullas had shipped his oars, and let the current move him through the channels. He knew the islands and their rocks as he knew his own body, their moods and their treacheries, and the way the water ran. He drifted gently in among the panic of the seals, and slew them as they hastened from the other men towards him, along the ice.

Each one he killed he knew, and would claim after. Every man marked his own.

Then, as Huss Hullas's boat nosed her way between the rocks, the sun stood up on the water. In the rays of it he saw before him, on a patch of ice, one lone seal, but it was larger by far than all the others, something larger than any seal Huss Hullas had ever seen. Plainly, it was a bull, but young, unscarred, and shining in the sunlight. It had a coat on it that, in the dawn, looked for sure more gold than grey. And even Huss Hullas could not resist a little grimace that was his smile, and he raised the gun.

As he did so the seal turned and looked at him with its circular eyes, blacker than his own.

Yes, now, keep still, the man thought. For to blunder in the shot and spoil such fur would be a grave pity.

Huss Hullas was aiming for one of the eyes, but at the last instant the great golden seal lowered its head, and the bullet, as it speared away, struck it in the brain. It seemed to launch itself forward, the seal, in the same instant, and the dull flame of its body hit the water beyond the ice. Huss Hullas cursed aloud and grabbed up one of his oars. Already dead, the seal clove the water in a lovely arching dive—and was dammed against Huss Hullas's wooden rower.

His strong arms cracking and his mouth uttering every blasphemy known among the islands—which is many and varied—Huss Hullas held the seal, first with the oar, next with his hands, and as the boat roiled and skewed and threatened to turn herself over in the freezing sea, he struggled and thrust for the nearest edge of rock. Here, by some miracle, he dragged the dead weight of the seal the boat, himself, aground, his hands full of blood and fur, and the oar splintering.

He stood over the seal, until another boat came through the narrows. Frost had set the seal's dead eyes by then, as he towered over it ranting and cursing it, and the golden fur was like mud.

"That is a rare big beast, Huss Hullas. It should fetch a good price at the sheds."

"This is not for the sheds."

Taking out his knife then, he began to skin the great seal.

When he was done, he tossed the meat and fat and bones away, and took the heavy syrupy skin into the boat with him. After the other seals had been seen to, he left his share with the rest of the men. They saw the oar was ailing, and they knew better than try to cheat him.

He rowed back to Dula with the skin of the one seal piled round him and the oar complaining.

The remainder of that day, with the skin pegged up in the out-house, Huss Hullas sat fishing off Dula, like a man who has no care on earth, and no vast joy in it, either. If he looked forward to his next visit to the town, you could not have said from the manner of him. But he caught a basket of fish and went in as the sun was going out to clean and strip them and set them to cook on the stove.

The croft was like a dozen others, a single room with a fireplace in one wall and a big old bed on another. Aside from the stove there was a cupboard or two, and tackle for the boat or for the fishing stacked about, some carpentry tools, and some books that had been his father's that Huss Hullas never read. A couple of oil-lamps waited handy to be lit. Often he would make do with the light of the fire. What he did there in his loneliness, sitting in his chair all the nights of the months he did not go drinking and whoring, was small enough. He would clean his gun, and mend his clothing and his boots; he would repair the leg of a stool, cook his food and eat it, and throw the plate into a pan of water for the morning. He would brew tea. He would think to himself whatever thoughts came to him, and listen to the hiss and sigh of the sea on the rim of Dula. In the bed he would sleep early, and wake early. While he slept he kept his silence. There rose up no comfortable snoring from Huss Hullas, and if he dreamed at all, he held the dreaming to himself. And two hours before the sun began, or before that, he would be about. He could stride right across Dula in a day, and had often done so and come back in the evening, with the stars and the hares starting over the hill.

This night though, as the fish were seething and the sun going down into the water on a path of blood, he walked back to the out-house, and took a stare at the sealskin drying on its pegs. In the last sunglare, the fur of the pelt was like new copper. It had a beautiful sheen to it, and no mistake. It was too good to be giving away. But there, he had made his bargain—not to the girl, but to himself. Set in his ways, he had not the tactics to go back on his word. So with a shrug, he banged shut the outhouse door, and went to eat his supper in the croft.

It was maybe an hour after the sunset that the wind began to lift along the sea.

In a while, Huss Hullas put aside the sleeve he was darning, and listened. He had lived all his life in sight and sound of the ocean, and the noise of water and weather was known to him. Even the winds had their own voices, but this wind had a voice like no other he had ever heard. At first he paid it heed, and then he went back to his darning. But then again he sat still and listened, and he could not make it out, so much any could tell, if they had seen him. At last, he got to his feet and took the one oil-lamp that was burning on the mantelpiece, and opened the door of the croft. He stood there, gazing out into the darkness, the lamp swinging its lilt of yellow over the sloping rock, and beyond it only the night and the waves. There was nothing to be found out there. The sea was not even rough, only a little choppy as it generally would be at this season of the year. The sky was open and stars hung from it, though the moon would not be over the hill for another hour or more.

So there was no excuse for the wind, or the way it sounded. No excuse at all. And what had caught Huss Hullas's attention in the croft was five times louder in the outer air.

It was full of crying, the wind was, like the keening of women around a grave. And yet, there was nothing human in the noise. It rose and fell and came and went, like breathing, now high and wild and lamenting, now low and choked and dire.

Huss Hullas was not a superstitious man, and he did not believe any of the old tales that get told around the fires on winter nights. He had not enough liking for his own kind to have caught their romancing. Yet he heard the wind, and finding nothing he went inside again and bolted the door.

And next he took a piece of wood and worked on it, sawing and hammering it, while the kettle sang on the hob and the fire spat from a dose of fresh peat. The wind was not so easily heard in this way. Nor anything much outside. Though when the knock came sharp on his bolted door, Huss Hullas heard it well enough.

In all the years he had lived on Dula, there had only been one other time someone had knocked on the door by night. There are some two hundred souls live there, and no phone and not even a vet. One summer dark, with a child of his ailing, a man came to ask Huss Hullas to row him over to the mainland for a doctor. Huss Hullas refused to row, but for three pounds he let the man hire his boat. That was his way. Later that night the doctor was operating for appendicitis over the hill on a scrubbed kitchen table. The child lived; the father said to Huss Hullas: "Three pounds is the worth you set on a child's life."

"Be glad," was the answer, "I set it so cheap."

Money or no, Huss Hullas did not like to be disturbed, and perhaps it was this made him hesitate, now. Then the knocking came and a voice called to him out of the crying of the wind.

"Open your door," it said. "I see your light under it."

And the voice was a woman's.

Maybe he was curious and maybe not, but he went to the door at last and unbolted it and threw it wide.

The thick dull glow of the lamp left on the mantelpiece fell out around him on the rock. But directly where his shadow fell instead, the woman was standing. In this way he could not see her well, but he made a guess she was from one of the inland crofts. She seemed dressed as the women there were dressed, shabby and shawled, and her fashion of talking seemed enough like theirs.

"Well, what is it?" he said to her.

"It's a raw night," she said. "I would come in."

"That's no reason I should let you."

"You are the man hunts the seals," she said.

"I am."

"Then I would come in and speak of that."

"I've nothing to sell. The skins are in the sheds across the water."

"One skin you have here."

"Who told you so?"

"No matter who told me," said the woman. "I heard it was a fine one. Beautiful and strangely coloured, and the size of two seals together."

"Not for sale," said Huss Hullas, supposing sullenly one of the other sealers had jabbered, though how news had got to Dula he was not sure, unless he had been spied on.

"It is a love gift, then?" said the woman. "You are courting, and would give it to her?"

At this, his granite temper began to stir.

"This skin is mine, and no business of yours," he said. "Get home."

When he said this the wind seemed to swell and break on the island like a wave. Startled, he raised his head, and for a moment there seemed to be a kind of mist along the water, a mist that moved, swimming and sinuous, as if it were full of live things.

"*Get home,*" the woman repeated softly. "And where do you think my home to be?"

When he looked back at her, she had turned a little

and come out of his shadow, so the lamp could reach her. She was not young, but neither was she old, and she was handsome, too, but this is not what he saw first. He saw that he had been mistaken in the matter of the shawl, for she was shawled only in her hair, which was very long, streaming round her, and of a pale ashy brown uncommon enough he had never before seen it. Her eyes, catching the lamp, were black and brilliant, but they were odd, too, in a way he could not make out, though he did not like them much. Otherwise she might have seemed normal, except her hair was wet, and her clothing, which was shapeless and looked torn, ran with water. Perhaps it had rained as she walked over the hill.

"Your home is nothing to me," he said. "And the skin is not for sale."

"We will speak of it," she said. And she put out her hand as if to touch him and he sprang backwards before he knew what he did. Next moment she came in after him, and the door fell shut on the night, closing them in the croft together.

In all his life Huss Hullas had never feared anything, save the ocean, which was more common sense than fear. Now he stood and stared at the woman with her wet dress and her wet hair, knowing that in some way fear her he did, but he had not the words or even the emotion in him to explain it to himself, or what else he felt, for fear was not nearly all of it.

He must have stood a long while, staring like that, and she a long while letting him do so. What nudged him at length was another thing altogether. A piece of coal barked on the fire, and in the silence after, he realised the wind had dropped, and its eerie wailing ceased.

"Your name is Huss Hullas," the woman said in the

silence. "Do not ask me how I learned it. My name, so we shall know each other, is Saiuree."

When she told him her name, the hair rose on his neck. It did not sound human, but more like the hiss the spume would make, or the sea through a channel, or some creature of the sea.

"Well," he said harshly. "Well."

"It shall be well," she agreed, "for I'll have the skin from your shed. But I'll pay you fairly for it, whatever price you have set."

He laughed then, shortly and bitterly, for he was not given to laughter, he did it ill and it ill-became him.

"The price is one you would not like to pay, Missus."

"Tell it me, and I shall know."

"The price," he said brutishly, "is to spill between a woman's spread legs."

But she only looked at him.

"If that is what you wish, that is what I can give you."

"Ah," he said. "But you see, it's not you I want."

"So," she said, and she was quiet awhile. He felt an uneasy silly triumph while she was, standing there in his own croft with him, and he unable to show her the door. Then she said, "It is a black-haired girl on the mainland you would have. Her name is Morna."

His triumph went at that.

"Who told you?" he said.

"You," said she.

And he understood it was true. She smiled, slow and still, like a ripple spreading in a tide pool.

"Oh, Huss Hullas," said she, "I might have filled this room up with pearls, and not have missed them, or covered the floor with old green coins from the days before any man lived here. There is a ship sunk, far out, and none knows of it. There are old shields rotting black on the sides of it and a skeleton sits in the prow with a gold ring on his neck, and I might have brought you that ring. Or farther out there is another ship with golden money in boxes. Or I could bring you the stone head with stone snakes for hair, that was cast into the sea for luck, and make you rich. But you will have your bar girl and that is your price."

Huss Hullas sat down in his chair before the fire and wished he had some whisky by him. At the woman who called herself Saiuree, he snarled: "You're mad, then."

"Yes," she said. "Mad with grief. Like those you heard in the wind, crying for the sea they have lost and the bodies they have lost, so they may not swim anymore through the waterworld, or through the towered city under the ocean."

"I've no interest in stories," he said.

"Have you none."

"No. But you'll tell me next you are one of the Shealcé, and the skin you seek is your own."

"So I am," she said. "But the skin is not mine. It is the skin of my only son, Connuh, that you shot on the ice for his beauty and his strength as the dawn stood on the water."

Huss Hullas spat in the fire.

"My mother had a son, too. There's no great joy in sons."

"Ah," she said, "it's that you hate yourself so much you can never come to love another. Well, we are not all of your way. Long before men came here, the Seal People held this water and this land. And when men came they took the fish from us and drove us out. And when, in passing then, we paused to rest here, they killed us, because our skins are finer than their own. How many of this People have you slain, man? Many hundreds, is it not? And today with your gun you slew a prince of this People. For he was of the true Shealcé, from whom all the Shealcé now take their name. But still even we do not give hate for hate, greed for greed, injustice for injustice. I'll pay your price. Look in my eyes and see it."

"I'll not look in your eyes."

"So you will," she said.

She came close. No steam rose from her, nor was she dry. Her dress was seaweed, and nothing else. Her hair was like the sea itself. He saw why he had misliked her eyes. About their round bright blackness there was no white at all. Even so, he looked at them and into them and through them, out into the night.

Above, the night sea was black, but down, far down where the seal dives, it was not black at all. There was a kind of light, but it came from nothing in the sea. It came from the inside of the eyes of the ones who swam there, who had seen the depths of the water in their own way, and now showed it to the man. If Huss Hullas wished to see it, who can say? Probably he did not. A man with so little life-love in him he was like one without blood, to him maybe to see these things he saw was only wasted time. But if he had only walled himself in all these years against his own thought and his own dreams, then maybe there was a strange elation in the seeing, and a cold pain.

At first then, only the darkness through which he saw as he went down in it, like one drowning, but alive and keeping breath, as the seals did, on land or in ocean both. Then there began to be fish, like polished knives without their hafts, flashing this way and that way. And through

the fish, Huss Hullas began to see the currents of the
water, the milky strands like breezes going by. All around
there too, the dim shadows of the Shealcé, each one
graceful and lovely in that gentle shape of theirs, like
dancers at their play, but moving ever down and down,
and ever northwards.

They passed a wreck. It was so old it was like the
skeleton of a leaf and in the prow a human skeleton
leaned. It had a gold torc round its bone throat, while the
shields clung in black bits and flakes to the open sides of
the vessel, just as Saiuree had said. It was a Wicing
longboat of many, many hundred years before.

The seals swam over and about the wreck, and then
away, and Huss Hullas followed them.

And it began to seem to him then that he felt the silk of
the water on his flesh, and the power and grace of the seal
whose body he seemed to have come to inhabit, but he
was not sure.

Shortly beyond the wreck there was a space of sheer
blackness, that might have been a wall of rock. But here
and there were openings in the black, and one by one the
seals ebbed through with the water and Huss Hullas after
them. On the farther side was the city of the Shealcé.

Now there are many tales told of that spot, but this
was how he saw it for himself.

It must in part have been a natural thing, and this is
not to be wondered at, for the Shealcé have no hands in
their water form with which to build, whatever figure
they may conjure on the land. Above would be islets, no
doubt, where they might bask in the sun of summer. But
here the cold-sea coral had grown, pale greyish red and
sombre blueish white, and rose in spines and funnels all
about. It seemed to Huss Hullas like a city of chimneys,

for the curious hollow formations twisted and humped and ascended over each but all went up—in places ten times the height of a man and more—and at their tops they smoked and bubbled, and that was the air brought down into them by the Shealcé themselves, in their chests and in their fur, which gradually went up again and was lost in the water.

So he beheld these pastel spires, softly smoking, and glittering too. For everywhere huge clusters of pearls had been set, or those shells which shine, or other ornaments of the sea, though nothing that had come from men, not silver or gold, nor jewels.

But strangest of all, deep in the city and far away, there were a host of faint lights, for all the world like vague-lit windows high in towers. And these yellow eyes beamed out through the water as if they watched who came and who departed, but if the Shealcé had made and lit them he did not know. Nor did he think of it then, perhaps.

For all the seals swam in amid the chimneyed city and he with them, and suddenly he heard again that dreadful hopeless crying, but this time it was not in the wind he heard it, but in his own brain. And this time, too, he knew what it said. He saw, at last, the shapes about him were shadows for sure, were wraiths, the ghosts only of seals, who swam out this final journey before their lamenting memory should die as their bodies had already died from the bullets of men.

Oh, to be no more, to be no more, the seals were crying. *To be lost, to be lost. The hurt of the death was less, far less, than the hurt of the loss. Where now are we to go?*

If he felt the hurt they cried of, he did not know himself, most likely. But he was close to it as generally no man comes close to anything, and rarely to his own self.

And then one of the yellow-eyed towers was before him, and he swam up into the light and the light enclosed him—

—and he was in the corridor above the mainland bar with Morna opening a door.

Then they were in the bedroom, and she was not sulky or covetous, but smiling and glad. And she took her stockings off her white legs and bared her rosy breasts and combed her liquorice hair with her hands. He forgot the seals that moment, and the water and the crying. "Lie down with me, sweetheart," said Morna, and took him to her like her only love. And he had something with her that hour he never had had with any woman before, and never would have again so long as he lived.

A while before dawn, just as the sky was turning grey under the hill, he woke up alone in his bed in the croft. That he thought he had been dreaming is made nothing of by the fact he came instantly from the covers, flung on his clothes, and went to the door. He meant to go and look in the outhouse, doubtless, but he had no need. What he sought lay on the rocky edge of Dula, less than twenty strides below him.

The whole sky was higher, with the darkness going fast. He had a chance to see what he was staring at.

There by the ocean's brink a woman knelt, mourning over a thing that lay along the rock and across her lap. Her showering hair covered what remained of this thing's face, and maybe Huss Hullas was thankful for it. But from her hair there ran away another stream of hair that was not hers, richer and more golden, even in the 'tween-light. And beyond the hair stretched the body of a young man, long-limbed and wide in the shoulder, and altogether very large and well-made, and altogether naked. At least, it would seem to be a body, but suddenly you noticed some two or three shallow cuts of a knife, and then you would see the body had no meat to it and no muscle and no bone—it was an empty skin.

There came some colour in the sky within the grey, and the woman, with a strange awkward turn, slipped over into the water and dragged the human skin with her, and both were gone.

And then again, as the sun came up over the hill of Dula, and Huss Hullas was still standing there, he saw the round head of a seal a half mile out on the water, with an odd wide wake behind it as if it bore something alongside itself. He did not go to fetch his gun. He never shot a seal from that day to this. Nor did he go drinking or to find women in the town. Indeed, he went inland, over the hill, to live where he might not heed the noise of the sea. He kept away from his own kind; that did not change.

Do you think it was guilt then that turned him from his outward ways, deeper into those inner ways of his? Perhaps only he saw the seal tracks on the rock and sand, or found a strip of seawrack in between the covers of the bed, and knew what he had lain with, even if it had passed for rosy Morna. The Shealcé are an elder people. It is said in the stories they can take each form as they will, the seal or the human, as it suits them, or some older form that maybe they have, which no one knows anymore who has not entered the heart of their city of coral and pearl, and remembered it.

But it is true they were in the islands long before men came there. And who knows but they will be there long after we are gone.

LEVIATHAN

The seven islands lay at various distances from the mainland, four in a sort circle, like a frozen dance, three completely isolate. The general impression, if seen from the air—birds, the occasional plane—was that they belonged to another landmass, once partnered to the original, now snapped off, carried away—then carelessly dropped, and broken on the sea.

Perhaps something had *taken* this chunk of the continent, to feed itself and its offspring? If so, it and its descendents had not finished their meal.

The Leviathan stirred slowly. It raised its head and looked about. It had no memory of anywhere. It had no memory of itself, only a sort of familiar driving force, which was its own forward motion, probably physical.

Once the Leviathan had been a monster beast of legend and myth, a symbol of vast Empires of the East. Also, a cipher for an ultimate Wickedness and Power.

Now, like a discarded, grey-silver crystal case, it lay at the shore-line.

The ground showed through its glassy body. In its eyes only the night showed, where the sweep of dawn had cast it aside.

Some time passed. A handful of fishermen landed on the beach, quietly assessed their catch, and went away, unnoticing.

A storm flew up the pebbles, and rushed shrieking into a cave, coughing with urgency.

In the end, the Leviathan rose. It looked about in all directions, at the night, the stars, the smoothing of the ocean. Into the past.

Once, the other beast had preyed here, vast, shapeless, nameless and indecipherable, battering on these isles. It had literally *fed* on them, and left them in tatters.

Then came the *other* creature. At that time, the Leviathan was deep and heavy as new gold. It sprang into the air, and grasped the predator in its jaws. The creatures perished, yowling, in seconds.

Later, the Leviathan swam away. At that hour, the world was its open country. Now and then, it would come back—but from preference, not need. Yet years and centuries go by. It is their unbreakable habit.

It was like withered crystal now, the Leviathan, colossus of gold. It needed rest and sanctuary. Spells of soft nullity, unstinting, recalling the gallant rescue of the past. The land gave it these gladly, and more.

Safe on the shore of honour, the Leviathan slept, its head between its paws, like that of a huge and savage hound, grown slow and mild with age.

But now and then, behind the sleeping eyes of it, a soft wild wonderful flash, as if new young stars ignited in its brain. Perhaps they did. For look there, the sky was full of them.

Where Does the Town
Go At Night?

"Where does the town go at night?"

"What did you say?"

Gregeris turned, but some sort of vagrant stood there, grinning at him out of a dirty, flapping overcoat. Gregeris supposed he wanted money. Otherwise the broad square was deserted in the pale grey afternoon, its clean lines undisturbed by the occasional wind-breath from the sea, which hardly even moved the clipped oleanders behind their prison-railings, or the ball-shaped evergreens on long bare stems, (like lollipops), which flanked most of the municipal buildings.

"Perhaps this will help?" Gregeris handed the man, the supposed beggar, a bank note. It was a cheerful, highly-coloured currency, and the man took it, but his smile lessened at once.

"I can't show you. You'll have to see for yourself."

"Oh, that will be all right. Don't trouble."

Gregeris turned to walk on. He had only come to the square to kill a little time, to look at the clock-tower, a sturdy thing from the seventeen hundreds. But it was smaller and much less interesting than the guide-book promised.

"Don't believe me, do you?"

Gregeris didn't answer. He walked firmly, not too briskly. His heart sank as he heard the scuffy footsteps fall in with his. He could smell the man too, that odd fried smell of ever-unwashed mortal flesh, and the musty dead-rat odour of unchangeable clothes.

"Y'see," said the beggar, in his low rough voice, "I've seen it happen. Not the only one, mind. But the only one remembers, or knows it isn't a dream. I've seen *proof*. Her, then, sitting there, right there, where the plinth is for the old statue they carted away."

There seemed nothing else for it. "The statue of King Christen, do you mean? Over there by the town hall?"

"The very one. The statue struck by lightning, and fell off."

"So I believe."

"But *she* was on the plinth. Much prettier than an old iron king."

"I'm sure she was."

The beggar laughed throatily. "Still don't believe what I'm saying, do you? Think I'm daft."

A flash of irritation, quite out of place, went through Gregeris. It was for him an irritating time, this, all of it, and being here in this provincial nowhere. "'I don't know what you *are* saying, since you haven't said." And he turned to face the beggar with what Gregeris would himself only have described as *insolence*. Because facing up to one's presumed inferiors was the most dangerous of all impertinences. Who knew what this bone-and-rag bag had once been? He might have been some great artist or actor, some aristocrat of the Creative Classes, or some purely good man, tumbled by fate to the gutter, someone worthy of respect and help, which Gregeris, his own annoying life to live, had no intention of offering.

And, "Ah," said the beggar, squaring up to him.

Gregeris saw, he thought, nothing fine or stricken in the beggar. It was a greedy, cunning face, without an actor's facial muscles. The eyes were small and sharp, the hands spatulate, lacking the noble scars of any trade, shipbuilding, writing, work of any sort.

"Well," said Gregeris.

"Yes," said the beggar. "But if you buy me a drink, I'll tell you."

"You can buy yourself a drink and a meal with the money I just gave you."

"So I can. But I'll eat and drink alone. Your loss."

"Why do you want my company?" demanded Gregeris, half angrily.

"Don't want it. Want to tell someone. You'll do. Bit of a look about you. Educated man. You'll be more flexible to it, I expect."

"Gullible, do you mean?" Gregeris saw the man had also been assessing him, and finding not much, apparently. Less than flattery, education, he sensed, in this case represented a silly adherence to books— clerkishness. Well, Gregeris had been a clerk, once. He had been many things. He felt himself glaring, but the beggar only grinned again. How to be rid of him?

Up in the sky, the fussy clock-tower sounded its clock. It was five, time to take an absinthe or cognac, or a cocktail even, if the town knew they had been invented. Why hadn't the ridiculous tower been struck by lightning instead of a statue under a third its height?

"Where do you go to drink?"

Some abysmal lair, no doubt.

But the beggar straightened and looked along the square, out to where there was a glimpse of the sky-grey rimmed, sulk-blue sea. Then he pivoted and nodded at a side street of shops, where an awning protected a little cafe from the hiding sun.

"*Cocho's*."

"Then take a drink with me at *Cocho's*."

"That's very sportive of you," said the beggar. Abruptly he thrust out his filthy, scarless and ignoble hand. Gregeris would have to shake it, or there would, probably, be no further doings. Ignore the ignoble hand then, and escape.

Compelled by common politeness, the curse of the bourgeoisie, Gregeris gripped the hand. And when he did so, he changed his mind. The hand felt fat and strong and it was electric. Gregeris let go suddenly. His fingers tingled.

"Feel it, do you?"

"Static," said Gregeris calmly. "It's a stormy afternoon. I may have given you a bit of a shock. I do that some-times, in this sort of weather."

The beggar cackled, wide-mouthed. His teeth, even the back ones, were still good. *Better*, Gregeris resentfully thought, *than my own*. "Name's Ercole," said the beggar. (*Hercules*, wouldn't you know it.) And then, surprisingly, or challengingly "You don't have to give me yours."

"You can have my name. Anton Gregeris."

"Well, Anton," (of course, the bloody man would use the Christian name at once) "we'll go along to *Cocho's*. We'll drink, and I'll tell you. Then I've done my part. Everything it can expect of me."

This was all Marthe's fault, Gregeris reflected, as he sipped the spiced brandy. Ercole had ordered a beer, which could be made to last, Gregeris ominously thought, until—more ominous still—he watched Ercole gulp half the contents of the glass at once.

It was because of Marthe that Gregeris had been

obliged to come here, to the dull little town by the sea. His first impression, other than the dullness, had been how clean and tidy the town was. The streets swept, the buildings so bleached and scrubbed, all the brass-plates polished. Just what Marthe would like, she admired order and cleanliness so much, although she had never been much good at maintaining them herself. Her poky flat in the city, crammed with useless and ugly 'objects d'art', had stayed always undusted. Balls of fluff patrolled the carpets, the ashtrays spilled and the fireplace was normally full of the cold debris of some previous fire. He suspected she washed infrequently, too, when not expecting a visitor. The bathroom had that desolate air, the lavatory unwholesome, the bath green from the dripping tap. And the boy—the boy was the same, not like Marthe, but like the flat Marthe neglected .

"Thirsty," mumbled Ercole, presumably to explain his empty glass.

"Let me buy you another."

"That's nice. Not kind, of course. Not kind, are you? Just feel you have to be generous."

"That's right."

The waiter came. He didn't seem unduly upset that Ercole was sitting at the cafe table, stinking and degenerate. Of course, Gregeris had selected one of the places outside, under the awning. And there were few other patrons, two fat men eating early plates of fish, a couple flirting over their white drinks.

When the second beer arrived, Ercole sipped it and put it down. "Now I'll tell you."

"Yes, all right. I shall have to leave at six. I have an appointment."

So after all Marthe (the 'appointment') would be his

rescue. How very odd.

"You'll realise, I expect," said Ercole, "I don't have lodgings. I had a room, but then I didn't any more. Sometimes I sleep in the old stables up the hill. But there's a couple of horses there now, and they don't like me about. So I find a corner, here or there. That's how I saw it. Then again, y'see, I might have been the type to just sleep right through it, like most of them. It's what's in you, if you ask me, in yourself, that makes you wake in the night, about a quarter past midnight."

"And what have you seen?" Gregeris heard himself prompt, dutifully.

Ercole smiled. He put his hands on the table, as if he wanted to keep them in sight, keep an eye on them, as if they might get up to something otherwise, while he revealed his secret.

"The town goes away."

"You mean it disappears?"

"Nothing so simple, Anton. No, it goes off. I mean, it *travels*."

Generally, I wake at dawn, first light, *said Ercole*. Like a damned squirrel, or a bird. Been like that for years. Sleeping rough's part of it, but I grew up on a farm. It's partly that, too. Well, when I woke the first time, which was about two months ago, I think it's dawn. But no, it's one of those glass-clear, ink black summer nights. The moon wasn't up yet, but the stars were bright, and along the esplanade the street lamps were burning cold greeny-white from the funny electricity they get here. Nothing to wake me, either, that I can hear or see.

The moment I'm awake, I'm *wide* awake, the sort of awake when you know you won't sleep again, at least not for two or three hours, and it's better to get up and do something or you get to thinking. So presently I stand up. And then, well, I staggered. Which scared me. I hadn't had anything in the way of alcohol for about five days, so it wasn't drinking bad wine. And you can't afford to get sick, in my situation. But then my head cleared, and I just thought, maybe I got up too quick. Not so young as I was.

And then I go and take a stroll along the esplanade, like the leisured people do by day, which is when a policeman will generally come to move me elsewhere, if *I* try it. But no one's about now.

The sea is kicking away at the land, blue-black. It looks rough and choppy, which strikes me as strange really, because the night is dead calm, not a cloud. A sort of steady soft *thin* breeze is blowing full in my face from the mouth of sea and sky. It has a different smell, fresher, more starry *bright*.

When I looked over, down to the beach, the sea was slopping in right across it. It wasn't the tide coming in, I've seen plenty of those. No, the sea wasn't coming in, falling back—but constant, gushing in up the beach, hitting the lower terrace of the esplanade, and spraying to both sides. Drops hit my face. It reminded me of something, couldn't think what. It looked peculiar, too, but I thought, after all tonight was a full moon and this moon would rise soon, maybe it was that making the sea act crazy.

Just then, the clock strikes on the tower in the square. It's one in the morning, and I can tell I've been up and about for around three quarters of an hour. That means I woke at a quarter past midnight. I mention this, because another time I was in the square and when I woke, I noted the clock. It's always been that time, I reckon, that I wake, and the other ones who wake, they wake up then too.

That minute, the first night on the esplanade, I see one, of my fellow awakers—only I didn't know it then, that we were a sort of select club. No, I thought there was going to be trouble.

It's a girl, you see, young, about sixteen, a slip of a thing, all flowing pale hair, and she's in her nightwear— barefoot—walking slowly along the esplanade towards me. Her eyes look like veiled mirrors, and I think she's sleep-walking or gone mad, and going to throw herself into the sea, and I'm asking myself if I should save her or let her do what she wants—have you got any more right to force someone to live that doesn't want to than to kill someone?—or if I'd better just hide, because trouble isn't what it's best for me to seek out, I'm sure you'll understand. Anyway, then she blinks, and she walks up to me and she says, "Where am I? What am I doing here?" And then I'm really scared, because she'll start screaming and God knows what'll happen then. But next she says, "Oh, but of course, that doesn't matter." And she leans on the railing and looks out at the sea, calm as you please.

The moon starts to rise then. First a line like spilt milk on the horizon's edge. Then the sky turns light navy blue and the disc comes up so fast it almost seems to leap out of the water.

"I was in bed, wasn't I?" says the girl.

"Don't ask me. You just came along."

"They call me Jitka," she says. And then she says, "I think I looked out of the window at home. I think I remember doing that. And the hill wasn't there. You know, the hill with the old palace on it."

I know the hill, because that's where the stables are, my bedchamber of old. That big hill, about half a mile inland. Where all the historic splendour of the town is, the mansions and great houses and overgrown gardens of cobwebby, bat-hung cedars. And then the slums start all round it, either side.

Gregeris mutters that he knows the area, he has his appointment near there.

Well, I say to this girl called Jitka, "You've been sleep-walking, haven't you. Best get back indoors."

"No, I don't think so," says Jitka. Not haughtily as you might expect, but kind of wistful. As if she's saying, Just let me stay up half an hour longer, Dadda. But I'm not her father, so I turn away prudently, before I start trying to see through her flimsy nightie, past the ribbons to the other pretty things inside.

Perhaps not very gallant to leave her there, but I didn't go so far, only about fifty yards, before I find another one. Another Awaker. This was a gentleman sitting on a bench. He's in his nightclothes too, but with a silk dressing-gown fastened over. "Good evening," he says, and I can tell you, by day he'd have crossed the street not to see me, let alone exchange a politeness. But I nod graciously, and when he doesn't say anything else, I walk on.

The esplanade runs for a mile, no doubt you know that from that guide-book in your pocket. I amble along it, and after another few minutes, I see these two old ducks tottering towards me, hand in hand. He's about ninety if he's a day, and she's not much less. He's got on a flannel nightshirt, the sort Grandfather would've had, and she's in an ancient thing, all yellow lace. And they're happy as two kids out of school. We pass within a foot of each other, and she calls out to me, "Oh isn't it a lovely fine night? What a lovely trip. Do you think we'll reach China?"

So I generously say, "I should think so, lady."

And they're gone, and I go on, and then I stop dead. I stare out to sea, and then down below the terrace again at the water rushing constant up the beach. What I'm thinking is this: But that's just what it's like, the way the waves are and the whole ocean parting in front of us—it's like a *bow-wave* cutting up before a ship. A moving ship, sailing quite fast. But then I think, Ercole, you've got no business thinking that. And suddenly I feel dog tired. So I turn and go back to my place under the columns of the library building, where I'd been sleeping. I lie straight down and curl up and pull my coat over my head. At first I'm stiff as a plank. Then I fall asleep. And asleep I can feel it, what I'd felt standing up when I thought I'd gone dizzy. It's the motion of a ship, you see. Not enough to make you queasy, just enough you need to get your sea-legs. Then I'm really asleep. I didn't wake again until dawn. Nothing up then, not at all. A street-sweeper, and a pony-cart with kindling, and then a girl with milk for the houses by the park. A couple of cats coming back from their prowl. Moon down, sun up, rose-pink and blushing after its bath in the sea. That's all.

Gregeris says, "A memorable dream."

S'what I thought. Course I did. You don't want to go nuts in my situation, either. They cart you off to the asylum first chance they can get.

No, I went and scrounged some breakfast at a place I know, well, to be truthful, a garbage-bin I know. Then I went for my usual constitutional round the town. It was by the church I found them.

"Found what?"

Ah, what indeed. Sea shells. Beautiful ones, a big white whorled horn that might have come from some fabled beast, and a green one, half transparent, and all these little striped red and coral ones. They were caught in a trail of seaweed up in the ivy on this wall. People passed, and if they looked, they thought they were flowers, I suppose, or a kid's expensive toy, maybe, thrown up there and lost.

"Perhaps they were."

It didn't happen again for seven days. I'd forgotten, or pretended I'd forgotten. And once when I went back to that church, the shells were gone. Someone braver or cleverer or more stupid and cowardly than me, had taken them down.

Anyway, this particular evening, I *knew*. Knew it was going to be another Night. Another *Awake Night*. I'll tell you how I knew. I was at the *Café Isabeau*, to be honest round the back door, where the big woman sometimes leaves me something, only she hadn't, but I heard this conversation in the alley over the wall. There's a young man, and he's trying to get his girl to go with him into the closed public gardens, under the trees, for the usual reason, and she's saying maybe she will, maybe she won't, and then I keep thinking I know her little voice. And then he says to her, all angry, "Oh please yourself, Jitka."

And then *she* says to him, "No, don't be angry. You know I would, only I think I ought to be home soon. It's going to be one of those nights when I have that peculiar dream I keep on having."

"Come and dream with me," he romantically burbles and I want to thump him on the head with one of the trash pails to shut him up, but anyway she goes on anyhow, the way a woman does, half the time—if you were to ask me, because they're so used to men not listening to them.

"I keep dreaming it," she says. "Five times last month, and three the month before. I dream I'm walking in the town in my nightclothes."

"I'd like to see *that*!" exclaims big-mouth, but still she goes on.

"And seven nights ago, at full moon, I dreamed it. And I knew I would, all the evening before, and I know now I will, tonight. I feel sort of excited—here, in my heart."

"I feel excited too," oozed clunk-lips, but she says:

"You see, the town slips her moorings. She sails away. The town, that is, up as far as King Christen's Hill. I watched it, I think I did, drifting back, like the shore from a liner. And then we sail through the night and wonderful, wonderful things happen—but I can't remember what. Only, I have to go home now, you see. To get some sleep before I wake up. Or I'll be so tired in the morning after the dream."

After she stops, he gives her a speech, the predictable one about how there are plenty of more sophisticated girls only too glad to go in the park with him, lining up, they are. Then he walks off, and she sighs, but that's all.

By the time I got round into the alley, she was starting to walk away too, but hearing me, she glanced back. It was her all right, even in her smartish costume, with her hair all elaborate, I knew her like one of my own. But she looked startled—no recognition, mind. She didn't remember meeting *me*. Instead she speeds up and gets out of the alley quick as she can. I catch up to her on the pavement.

"What do you want? Go away!"

"There, there, Jitka. No offence."

"How do you know my name? You were spying on me and my young man!"

Then I realise, a bit late, what I could be letting myself in for, so I just whine has she any loose money she doesn't want—and she rummages in her purse and flings a couple of coins and gallops away.

But anyway, now I know tonight is one of those Nights.

In the end, I climbed over the municipal railings and got into the public gardens myself. There's an old shed in among the overgrown area that no one bothers with. Lovers avoid it, too; there are big spiders, and even snakes, so I'm told.

I went to sleep with no trouble. Woke and heard the clock striking in the square, and it was eleven. Then I thought I'd never get off, and if I didn't I might not Wake at the *right* time—but next thing I know I am waking up again and now there's a *silence*. By which I mean the sort of silence that has a personality of its own.

Scrambling out of the hut, I stand at the edge of the bushes, and I look straight up. The stars flash bright as the points of gramophone needles, playing the circling record of the world. And now, now I can *feel* the world *rocking*. Or, the town, rocking as it rides forward on the swell of the sea. And then I saw this thing. I just stood there and to me, Anton, it was the most beautiful thing I ever saw till then. It was like the winter festival at the farm, when I was a child, you know, Yule, when the log is brought in, and I can recall all the candles burning and little silver bells, and a girl dancing, dressed like a fairy. That was magical to me then. But this.

"What did you see?" Gregeris asked, tightly, almost painfully, coerced into grim fascination.

It was fish. Yes, fish. But they were in the *air*. Yes, Anton, I swear to you on my own life.

They were wonderful fish, too, painted in all these colours, gold and scarlet, and puce, mauve and ice blue, and some of them tiny, like bees, and some large as a cat. I swear, Anton. And they were swimming about, in the air, round the stems of the trees, and through the branches, and all across the open space of the park, about five feet up in the air, or a little lower or higher. And then two or three came up to me. They stared at me with their eyes like orange jewels or green peppermints. They swam round me, and one, one was interested in me, kept rubbing his tail over my cheek or shoulder as he passed, so I put up my hand and stroked him. And, Anton, he was *wet*, wet and smooth as silk in a bath of rain. So I knew that somehow, now, we weren't only on the sea, but *in* the sea, maybe *under* the sea. Even though I could breathe the air. And I thought, That's how those shells got stranded up on the church wall.

Well, I stayed sitting there in the park, watching the fish swimming, sometimes stroking them, all night. And once a shark came by, black as coal. But it didn't come for me, or hurt the others. Some of them even played round it for a while. No one else came. I thought, Jitka will be sorry to have missed this, and I wondered if I ought to go and find her, I knew she wouldn't be scared of me now, and find those others I'd seen, the rich man and the two old ducks, and bring them here. But they'd probably seen it before, and anyway, there were other things going on, maybe, they were looking at.

I suppose I drifted off to sleep again, sitting on the

ground. Suddenly I was blinking at a grey fish flying out of a pine tree and it was a pigeon, and the sun was up.

"What's that?" said Gregeris abruptly.

The clock in the square, striking six.

"I should leave. I have an appointment." Gregeris didn't move, except to beckon the waiter. He ordered another brandy, another beer. "Go on."

After that Night, I've had three others. I've always known, either in the afternoon or in the evening, they were coming on. Like you know if you have an illness coming, or someone can feel a storm before it starts. Only not oppressive like that. Like what the girl said, an *excitement*. Only it's a sort of cool green echo in your chest. In your guts. It's like a scent that you love because it reminds you of something almost unbearably happy, only you can't remember *what*. It's like a bitter-sweet nostalgia for a memory you never had.

Oh, I've seen things, these Nights. Can't recall them all, that's a fact. But I keep more than the others. They think they dream it, you see, and I know it isn't a dream. We're Awake, and God knows there are precious few of us who do come Awake. Most of the town sleeps on, all those houses and flats, those apartments and corners and cubby-holes, all packed and stacked with sleepers, blind and deaf to it. Those buildings become like *graves*. But not for us. I've only met ten others, there are a few more, I should think. A precious few, like I said.

Jitka and I danced under the full moon once. Nothing bad. She's like a daughter to me now. She even calls me Dadda, in her dream. That was the night I saw *her*. I do remember *her*. Never forget. Even when I die, I won't forget *her*.

"The woman who was on the plinth," said Gregeris, "where

225

the statue was taken down?"

Oh but Anton, she wasn't a woman.

"You said 'She'."

So I did. It was the last Wake Night, when I woke up in the square. Something had made me do that, like it always seems to make me choose a different place to sleep, when I sense a night is coming. Full moon, like I said, already in the sky when I bedded down, just over there, under those cut trees that look like balls on sticks.

And when I woke and stood up, I was so used to it by then, the movement of the town sailing, and the smell of the sea and the wind of our passage—but then the scent of the ocean was stronger than before, and I turned and looked, across the square, to where the plinth still is. It was draped in purple, and it was *wet* purple, it poured, and ran along the square. It ran towards the sea, but then it vanished and there was just the *idea*—only the idea, mind—that the pavement might be *damp*. You see, she'd swum up from the sea, like the fish, through the air which is water those Nights, and she'd had to swim. She couldn't have walked. She was a mermaid.

Gregeris considered his drink.

I won't even swear to you now, Anton. You won't believe me. I wouldn't expect it. It doesn't matter. Y'see, Anton, truth isn't killed if you don't believe in it—that's just a popular theory put about by the non-believers.

"A mermaid, you said."

A mermaid.

She was very absolutely white, not *dead* white, but *live* white. *Moon* white. And her body had a sort of faint pale bluish freckling, like the moon does, only she wasn't harsh, like the moon, but soft and limpid. And her skin melted into the blue-silver scales of her tail. It was a strong tail, and the fork of the fins was strong. Vigorous. Her hair was strong too, it reminded me of the brush of a fox or a weasel or ermine—but it was a pale green-blonde, and it waved and coiled, and *moved* on its own, or it was stirring in the breeze-currents of the water-air. And it was like currents and breezes itself, a silvery bristly silky fur-wind of hair. Her face though was still, as if it was carved like a beautiful mask, and her great still eyes were night black. She had a coronet. She was naked. She had a woman's breasts, the nipples water-colour rose like her mouth. But you couldn't desire her. Well, I couldn't. She was—like an angel, Anton. You can't desire an angel. I've heard, the old church fathers said the mermaid was supposed to represent lust and fornication. But she wasn't like that. She was holy.

The funniest thing is, I looked at her a while and then, as if I'd no need to linger, as if the marvellous was commonplace and easy, I just turned and went off for a stroll. And on the esplanade I met Jitka, and I said, "Did you see the mermaid?" and Jitka said, "Oh yes, I've seen her." It was like being gone to heaven and you say, Have you seen God today, and they answer, But of course, He's everywhere, here. Then we danced. I don't know a thing about Jitka, but her father's dead, I'd take a bet on that. The rich man was a soldier, did I say? The old couple are in the hospital. I don't know how they get out, but maybe everyone that doesn't wake up just *can't* wake up. And they get strong those Nights, they told me. It's the cruise, they said, this bracing cruise on this liner that's sailing to the East, India or China or somesuch. And there's a little boy I see now and then. And a woman and her sister—

I do think some of them are beginning to cotton on it's not a dream. But that doesn't matter. Nor who we are, we precious few, we're nothing, there and then. We're simply The *Awake*.

Ercole had ceased to speak. They must have sat speechless, unmoving, Gregeris thought with slight dismay, for ten minutes or more.

"So you see a mermaid?" Gregeris asked now, businesslike.

"No. That was the last Night. I saw her that once. I haven't Woken since. Which means there hasn't been a Night. I don't think there has. Because I think, once you start, you go on Waking."

"You didn't speak to the mermaid. *Stroke* her."

"Come on, Anton. I wouldn't have dared. Would you? It would have been a bloody cheek. I could have dropped dead even, if I touched her. Think of the shock it would be. Like sticking your hand on the sun."

"Take off thy shoes from thy feet, this ground is holy."

"Yes, exactly that, Anton. You have it. By the way, you know, don't you, why God says that, in the Bible? It's to *earth* you, in the presence of galvanic might. Otherwise you'd go up in smoke."

Gregeris rose. "I must get on. I'll be late for my appointment." He put another of the cheerful notes on the table. "It was an interesting story. You told it well."

The beggar grinned up at him. His face was fat now, bloated by beer and talk, by importance, power. "But where does the town go to at night?" he repeated, "more to the point, *why* does the town come *back* at dawn?"

"Yes, a puzzle. Perhaps inquire, the next time."

Gregeris reached the awning's edge. Instinctively, perhaps, he glanced across the square at the plinth of King Christen's fallen statue. In his mind's eye, transparent as a ghost, he visualised the mermaid, reclining in the opal moonlight, relaxed and thoughtful, her living hair and flexing tail.

It was only as he turned and began to walk quickly inland, that Ercole called after him. "Anton! It's tonight!"

The flat-house had been stylish in the 1700's, he thought, about the time of the heyday of the clock. Now it was grimy, the elegant cornices chipped and cracked and thick with dirt, and a smell of stale cabbage soup on the stairs.

He rang the bell of her apartment, and Marthe came at once. She confronted him, a thin woman who had been slender and young twelve years ago, her fair hair now too blonde, and mouth dabbed with a fierce red, which had got on to her front teeth.

"You're so late. Why are you so late? Was the train delayed? I was worried. I have enough to worry about. I thought you weren't coming, thought you'd decided to abandon us completely. I suppose that would be more convenient, wouldn't it? I can't think why you said you'd come. You could just send me another money order. Or not bother. Why bother? It's only me, and him. What do we matter? I've been just pacing up and down. I kept looking out of the window. I got some ice earlier for the wine but it's melted. I smoked twenty cigarettes. I can't afford to do that. You know I can't."

"Good evening, Marthe," he said, with conscious irony.

To Gregeris it sounded heavy-handed, unnecessarily arrogant and obtuse. But she crumpled at once. Her face became anxious, pitiable and disgusting. How had it been he had ever—? Even twelve years ago, when she was a girl and he a younger man and a fool.

"I'm sorry. Forgive me, Anton. It's my nerves. You know how I get. It was good of you to come."

"I'm sorry, too, to be so late. I met an old business acquaintance at the station, a coincidence, a nuisance, an old bore who insisted we have a drink. He kept me talking. And of course, I couldn't make too much of it, of being here, or anything about you."

"No, no, of course."

She led him in. The apartment wasn't so bad, better than her last—or could have been. Everywhere was mess and muddle. The fair-ground knick-knacks, some clothes pushed under a sofa cushion. Stockings hung drying on a string before the open window. The ashtrays were as always. Twenty cigarettes? Surely a hundred at least. But there was the cheap white wine in its bucket of lukewarm water. And she had made her bed. She had said, she gave the bedroom over to the boy.

"How is Kays?"

"Oh—you know. He's all right. I sent him for some cigarettes. Oh, he wanted to go out anyway. He'll be back in a minute. But—I know—you don't like him much."

"What nonsense, Marthe. Of course I like him. He's only a child."

Taking him by surprise, as she always did for some reason, when she flared up, she shrilled, "He's your *son*, Anton."

"I know it, Marthe. Why else am I here?"

And again, the shallow awful victory of her crumbling face.

Once he had sat down, on a threadbare seat, the glass of tepid vinegar in his hand, she perched on the arm of the sofa, and they made small talk.

And why had he come here? The question was perfectly valid. It would have been so much simpler to send her, as she said, a cheque. That too, of course, was draining, annoying. Keeping it quiet was sometimes quite difficult, too. He was generally amazed no one had ever found him out, or perhaps they had and didn't care. His brief liaison with this woman had lasted all of two weeks. Two months later, when she reappeared, he had known at once. It was damnable. He had taken every precaution he could, to protect both of them from such an accident. He wondered if her pregnancy owed nothing to him at all, he was only a convenient dupe. The story-telling beggar, Ercole, had had him to rights, Gregeris thought, bourgeois politeness and the fear of a sordid little scandal. It was these which had made him set Marthe up in the first flat, made him pay her food bills and her medical expenses. And, once the child was born, had caused him to try to pay her off. But however much he awarded her, in the end, she must always come creeping back to him, pleading penury. Finally he began to pay her a monthly sum. But even that hadn't been the end of it. Every so often, she would send a frantic letter or telegram—and these, if ignored, had on two occasions persuaded Marthe to appear in person, once with the child, (then a snivelling, snotty eight years old, clinging to her hand), in the doorway of Gregeris's mother's house, during her sixtieth birthday dinner.

That time Gregeris had considered having Marthe, and very likely the boy, murdered. Just as he had, for a split second, considered murdering her himself that day by the canal when she announced, "You've put me in the family way, Anton. Fixed me up, good and proper, and you're the only one can set me right. Oh, not an abortion. I won't have that. One of my friends died that way. No, I need you to look after me."

And probably, thought Gregeris now, sipping the dying (really unborn) wine, only bourgeois politeness and the fear of a scene, that which had passed Marthe off to his mother as an 'employee', had also saved her neck.

"I'm sorry about the wine," she fawned. "Of course, I could have asked you to bring some, but I didn't like to," (now fawning slipping seamlessly to accusation), "it would have been nicer than what *I* can afford, though, wouldn't it? I can see you don't like this one. It was better, cold. If you'd come sooner."

Poor bitch, he thought. Can't I even spare her a few hours, some decent food and drink? She's got nothing, no resources, she can barely even read. And I need only do this, what? Once or twice a year... once or twice in all those days and nights. He glanced at her. She had washed and was not too badly dressed, her bleached hair at least well brushed. Somehow she had even got rid of the lipstick on her teeth.

"When the boy comes back, why don't I take you to dinner, Marthe?"

Oh God. She flushed, like a schoolgirl. Poor bitch, poor little bitch.

"Oh yes, Anton, that would be such fun... But I can't leave Kays—"

"Well, bring Kays. He can eat dinner too, I suppose?"

"Oh—no, no, I don't think we should. He gets so restless. He's so—awkward. He might embarrass you—"

Gregeris raised his brows. Then he saw she wanted to be alone with him. Perhaps she had some dream of reunion, or even of love-making. She would be disappointed.

At this moment the door to the flat opened, and his son walked in.

My son. The only son, so far as he knew, that he had. Kays.

"Good evening, Kays. You seem well. How are you going on? "

"All right."

Marthe looked uncomfortable, but she didn't reprove or encourage the monosyllabic, mannerless little oaf. Come to think of it, her own social graces weren't so marvellous.

As usual at a loss with children, "How is your school?" Gregeris asked stiffly.

"Don't go."

"Don't you? You should. Learn what you can while you have the chance—" The wry platitudes stuck in Gregeris's throat. It was futile to bother. The boy looked now less sullen than—what was it? Patient. *Bored,* by God.

What was that quaint adjective Gregeris had thought of for the sea? *Sulk*-blue, that was it. The boy's eyes were *sulk*-grey. Nearly colourless. Pale uneven skin, he would get spotty later no doubt, and perhaps never lose it, greasy tangled hair and unclean clothes that probably smelled. The child would smell, that unwashed-dog odour of unbathed children, redolent of slums everywhere. Like the beggar...

Take this child to dinner? *I don't think I will.* The mother was bad enough, but in some gloomy ill-lit café it would be tolerable. But not the weedy, pasty, morose brat.

My son. Kays. *How can he be mine*? He looks nothing like me. Not even anything like Marthe.

(For a moment, Gregeris imagined the boy's life, the woman leaning on him, making him do her errands, one minute playing with his dirty hair—as now—then pushing him off—as *now*. Always surprising him by her sudden over-sentimental affections and abrupt irrational attacks—perhaps not always verbal, there was a yellowish bruise on his cheek. And the school was doubtless hopeless and the teachers stupid and perhaps also sadistic.)

This was the problem with coming to see her, them. *This*, this thinking about her, and about Kays. The town by the sea should have taken them far enough away from Gregeris. It had required three hours for him to get here.

"Well, Kays." Gregeris stood over him. The top of the child's crown reached the man's ribcage. The child's head was bowed, and raised for nothing. "Here, would you like this? Another cheerful note. Too much, far too much—someone would think the boy had stolen it. "Your mother and I are going out for some air. A glass of wine."

And she chirruped, "Yes, Kays, I'll take you over to Fat Anna's."

After all the boy's head snapped up. In his clutch the lurid money blazed, and in his eyes something else took pallid fire. "*No.*"

"Oh yes. You like Fat Anna's."

"Don't want to."

"Don't be a baby, Kays. Fat Anna will give you pancakes . "

"No, she doesn't. No, not now."

Held aside in a globe of distaste, Gregeris watched the venomous serpent rise in Marthe and glare out from her eyes. "You'll do as I say, d'you hear?" The voice lifted, thin and piercing as the doorbell. "Do as I say, or I'll—"

checking now, not to reveal herself as hard or spiteful, unfeminine, unpleasant, before the benefactor— "Be a good boy," tardy wheedling, and then her hand gripping on the thin arm, working in another dark-then-fade-yellow bruise. "I don't see your Uncle Anton, except now and then. He's too busy—"

Kays was crying. Not very much, just a defeated dew of tears on the white cheeks. But he made no further protest, well lessoned in *this* school at least.

Later, in the restaurant, among the nearly clean table-cloths, the wax stains and smell of meat sauce, Marthe confessed, "Anna locks him in the small room, she has to, he runs away. But I have to have him protected, don't I, when I'm not there—"

Gregeris, who had helped escort the prisoner to the woman's tenement cave, (in one of the nastier streets, behind King Christen's Hill), considered that perhaps Marthe was often out, often away, at night. Or, more likely, often had company in at night. (The boy shoved in the bedroom and warned not to leave it.) It had been a man's shirt pushed under the sofa cushion. What a curious article to leave behind. Had Gregeris been meant to notice it?

He had intended to return that night to the city. But when he got free of Marthe it was almost ten, and Gregeris felt he was exhausted. The dinner, naturally, had been a mistake. They had parted, she with false sobs, and acrimony, Gregeris restrained, starchy, and feeling old.

What on earth had they said to each other? (Her excuse for demanding Gregeris's presence had been some conceivably-invented concern over Kays, that he slept poorly or something like that. But presently she said that he often ran away, even at night. And then again she said that she thought Kays was insane—but this was after the second bottle was opened.)

Otherwise, the conversation had been a dreary complaining recital of her burdensome life, leaving out, as he now thought, her casual encounters with other men, her possible prostitution. When at last he had been able to pay the bill, and put her in a taxi-cab for the flat-house, her face was for an instant full of dangerous outrage. Yes, she had expected more. Was *used* to more.

After this, surely, he must keep away from her. During the meal, watching her scrawny throat swallowing, he had again wondered, with the fascination of the dreamer who could only ever fantasise, how much of a challenge it would be to his hands.

He found quite a good hotel, or his taxi found it for him, on the tree-massed upper slope of the hill. It nestled among the historic mansions, a mansion once itself, comfortable and accommodating for anyone who might afford it. Thank God for money and hypocrisy, and all those worthless things which provided the only safety in existence. He must never visit Marthe again. Or the. awful boy, who surely could now only grow up to be a thug, or the occupant of some grave.

Gregeris took a hot bath and drank the tisane the hotel's housekeeper had personally made for him. He climbed into the comfortable, creaking bed. Sleep came at once. Thank God too for such sleep, obedient as any servant.

Gregeris woke with a start. He heard a clock striking, a narrow wire of notes. Was it midnight? Why should that matter to him?

He sat up, wide awake, full of a sensation of anxiety, almost terror—and excitement. For a moment he couldn't bring himself to switch on the lamp. But when he did so, his watch on the bedside table showed only eleven. He had slept for less than a quarter of an hour, yet it had seemed an eternity. The confounded clock in the square had woken him. How had he heard it, so far up here, so far away—sound had risen, he supposed.

In any case, it was the beggar, that scavenger Ercole, with his tales of midnight and the town and the sea, who had caused Gregeris's frisson of nerves.

Gregeris drank some mineral water. Then he got up and walked over to the window, drawing back the curtains. The town lay below, there it was, stretching down away from the hill to the flat plain of the sea. There were fewer lights, all of them low and dim behind their blinds, only the street lamps burning white, greenish-white, as Ercole had said. The clock-tower, the square, were hidden behind other buildings.

When did the town, that part of the town beyond the hill, which went sailing, set off? Midnight, Gregeris deduced. That would be it. And so the motion would gradually wake those ones who did wake, by about a quarter past. After all, that hour, between midnight and one in the morning, was the rogue hour, the hour when time stopped and began again, namelessly, like a baby between its birth and its first birthday—not yet fully realised, or part of the concrete world.

It was quite plausible, the story. Yes, looking down from the hill at the town, you could credit this was the exact area which would gently unhook itself, like one piece of a jigsaw, from the rest, and slip quietly out on the tide.

Gregeris drank more water. He lit a cigarette, next arranged a chair by the window. Before he sat down, he put out his bedside lamp, so that he could see better what the town got up to.

This was, of course, preposterous, and he speculated if months in the future, he would have the spirit to tell anyone, some business crony, his elderly mother, jokingly of course, how he had sat up to watch, keep sentinel over the roving town, which sailed away on certain nights not always of the full moon, returning like a prowling cat with the dawn.

"A beggar told me. Quite a clever chap, rough, but with a vivid, arresting use of words."

But why had Ercole told him anything? Just for money? *Then I've done my part,* he had said. *Everything it can expect of me.*

It? Who? The town? Why did the town want its secret told? To boast? Perhaps to *warn*.

Gregeris gazed down. There below, hidden by the lush curve of the many-gardened hill, the slum where she lived, Marthe. And the boy. There they would be, sleeping in their fug. And the town, sailing out, would carry them sleeping with it.

Gregeris couldn't deny he liked the idea of it, the notion of this penance of his carried far out to sea.

Well. He could watch, see if it was. Half amused at himself, yet he was strangely tingling, as if he felt the electricity in the air, which had galvanized Ercole's filthy palm, and, come to think of it, the boy's, for when Gregeris had put the bank note into Kays' fingers, there had been a flicker of it, too, though none on Marthe.

Certainly I never felt more wide awake.

He would be sorry, no doubt, in the morning. Perhaps

he could doze on the train, although he disliked doing that.

It was better than lying in bed, anyway, fretting at insomnia.

Avidly Gregeris leaned forward, his chin on his hand.

The sound was terrible, how terrible it was. What in God's name was it? Some memory, caught in the dream—oh, yes, he remembered now, after that train crash in the mountains, and the street below his room full of people crying and calling and women screaming, and the rumble of the ambulances—

Horrible. He must wake up, get away.

Gregeris opened his eyes and winced at the blinding light of early day, the sun exploding full in the window over a vast sea like smashed diamonds.

But the sound—it was still there—it was all round him. There must have been some awful calamity, some disaster—Gregeris jumped to his feet, knocking over as he did so the little table, the bottle and glass, which fell with a crash. Had a war been declared? There had been no likelihood of such a thing, surely.

Under Gregeris's window, three storeys down, (as in the comfortable hotel all about), voices rose in a wash of dread, and a woman was crying hysterically, "*Jacob—Jacob—*"

Then, standing up, he saw. That was, he *no longer* saw. For the sight he would see had vanished, while he slept, he who had determined to watch all night, the sight which had been there below. The view of the town.

The town was gone. All that lay beyond the base of the hill was a great curving bay of glittering, prancing, sun-dazzled sea. The town had sailed away. The town had not returned.

Gregeris stood there with his hands up over his mouth, as if to keep in his own rash cry. *Marthe—Kays—* The town had sailed away and they had been taken with it, for their slum below the hill was the last section of the jigsaw-piece, and they were now far off, who knew how far, or where, that place where those asleep slept on in the tombs of their houses, (would they ever Wake? There was a chance of it now, one might think), and the air was sea, and fish swam through the trees and the creatures of the deeps, and the mermaid floated to the plinth, blue-white, white-blue-green, contemplative and black of eye—

Someone knocked violently on the door. Then the door burst open. No less than the manager bounded into the room, incoherent and wild eyed -

"So sorry to disturb—ah, you've seen—an earthquake they say—the police insist we must evacuate—the hill's so near the edge—perhaps not safe—hurry, if you will— No! No time to dress, throw on your coat—quickly! Oh my God, my God!"

Some big ugly building accommodated the group in which Gregeris found himself. He thought it must be a school of some sort, once a grand house. It was cluttered with hard chairs, cracked windows, and cupboards full of text books. No one was allowed yet to leave. Everyone, it seemed, must given their name and address, even visitors such as Gregeris, and then be examined by a medical practitioner. But the examination was cursory—a light shone in the eyes, the tempo of the heart checked—and although three times different persons wrote down his details, still they refused to let him go. Soon, soon, they said. You must understand, we must be sure of who has survived, and if you are all quite well.

Several were not, of course. The fusty air of the school was thick with crying. So many of the people now crowded in there had 'lost'—this being the very word they used—families, friends, lovers. Some had lost property, too. "My little shop," one man kept wailing, blundering here and there. "Five years I've had it— opened every day at eight—where is it, I ask you?"

None of them knew where any of it was. They had woken from serene sleep to find—*nothing*. An omission.

It was an earthquake. That area had fallen into the sea. An earthquake and tidal wave which had disturbed no one, not even the pigeons on the roofs.

Had any others had a 'warning', as Gregeris had? He pondered. Some of them, through their confusion and grief, looked almost shifty.

But his mind kept going away from this, the aftermath, to the beggar, Ercole. What had become of him, Awake, and sailing on and on? And those others, the girl called Jitka, the old couple from the hospital, and the rich soldier, and the ones Ercole hadn't met or hadn't recollected?

Was the town like one of those sea sprites in legend, which seduced, giving magical favours and rides to its chosen victims, playing with them in the waves, until their trust was properly won. Then riding off deep into the sea and drowning them?

The thought came clearly. *Don't mislead yourself.* It isn't that. Nothing so mundane or simple.

God knew. Gregeris never would.

It was while he was walking about among the groups and huddles of people, trying to find an official who would finally pass him through the police in the grounds outside, that Gregeris received the worst shock of his life.

Oh, decidedly the worst. Worse than that threat in his youth, or that financial fright seven years ago, worse than when Marthe had told him she was pregnant, or arrived in the birthday dinner door. Worse, much, much worse than this morning, standing up and seeing only ocean where the houses and the clock-tower and the square had been. For there, amid the clutter of mourning refugees from world's edge, stood Kays.

But was it Kays? Yes, yes. No other. A pale, fleshless, dirty little boy, his face tracked now by tears like scars, and crying on and on.

Some woman touched Gregeris's arm, making him start. "Poor mite. His mother's gone with the rest. Do you know him? Look, I think he knows *you*. Do go and speak to him. None, of us can help."

And in the numbness of his shock, Gregeris found himself pushed mildly and inexorably on. A woman did, he thought, always manage to push you where she decided you must go. And now he and the boy stood face to face, looking up or down.

"How—are you here?" Gregeris heard himself blurt. And as he said it, knew. Fat Anna's street, where the boy had been penned, was the other, the wrong side, of the hill. And Marthe, damn her, drunk and selfish to the last, hadn't thought to fetch him back. Gregeris could just picture her, her self-justifying mumbles as she slithered into her sty of bed. *He'll be all right. I'm too upset tonight. I'll go for him in the morning.*

Good God, but the boy had *known*—his panic, for panic it had been, his rage and mutiny that he was too small to perpetrate against the overbearing adults. And that fat woman locking him up so he couldn't escape, as normally he always did from Marthe—Ercole had said,

"And there's a little boy I see, now and then."

"You were Awake," Gregeris said.

They stood alone in the midst of the grey fog, the misery of strangers.

"I mean, you were Awake, those special Nights. Weren't you, Kays?"

Sullen for a moment, unwilling. Then, "Yes," he replied.

"And so you knew it was a Night, and you wanted to be able to go with the town, to see the fish and the mermaid—to get *free*."

Kays didn't say, How do you know? You, of all people, how can *you* know?

His face was so white it looked clean. It was clean, after all, clean of all the rubbish of life, through which somehow he had so courageously and savagely fought his way, and so reached the Wonder—only to lose it through the actions of a pair of selfish blind fools—

"Did you know—did you know this was the last chance, the last Night?"

The boy had stopped crying for a minute. He said, "It could have been, any Night. Any Night could have been the last chance."

Oh God, when we dead awaken—the last trump sounded and the gate of Paradise was flung wide—and we kept him from it. Just because we, she and I, and all the rest, have always missed our chance, or not seen it, or turned from it, despising. She slept like a stone, but he, my son, he Woke. And I've robbed him of it forever.

"Kays... " Gregeris faltered.

The boy began to cry again, messily, excessively, but still staring up at Gregeris, as if through heavy rain.

He wasn't crying for Marthe, how could he be? But for

Paradise, lost.

"I'm so sorry," said Gregeris. Such stupid words.

But the child, who saw Truth, his child, who was Awake, knew what Gregeris had actually said. He came to Gregeris and clung to him, ruining his coat, weeping, as if weeping for all the sleeping world, and Gregeris held him tight.

XOANON

It is a bleak village for sure, held there in that arm of the land, against the acres of the cold, grey sea. Stones on that beach as great as the pale seals that swim by in summer. Hills behind, worn bare through their grass that has no colour. Not a tree to be seen, for they cannot withstand the winter gales. And the little houses, brown and white, with their little narrow windows, and the winding street where now and then some cart goes up and down, pulled by a dark and steadfast horse. And, on the slope, the white church, with its pointed roof and thick wooden door. No stained glass in its walls, but that is not what the stranger comes seeking. It is the carvings you visit.

The village lives by the fish, and has done so for three or four hundred years, and maybe longer. Along the shore, the boats are drawn up, painted with their names that cannot be read, unless you speak the language of this place. But some of the boats are painted not with words but pictures. They do not all read and write here. They do not find much use for it, even now when there are books and newspapers to be had on the mainland. Nor do you find a television anywhere, and only two or three radios that give a poor reception—the sea and the sky are between them and all things, and the weather. But in the pub there is a gramophone with a horn, and three hundred records.

Crossing over is best done in the summer, or on a calm day of late spring. You arrive in a black boat painted with a girl in a long blue dress, with a wreath of shells on her yellow hair. The boat is called *The Girl in the Blue Dress*.

Old Aelin hands you out, courteous and unspeaking. His face is like hard driftwood, brown and grey and torn in wrinkles, and his teeth are black. But he smells cleanly of the sea, and his eyes, where the driftwood has been opened to reveal them, are the blue of the girl's dress, clear and sane and strange and old. The eyes of a good man, or perhaps a woman, for they have here no manner of the coarse old men you will meet elsewhere, the men who think women are betrayers and fools, useful only by a crib or stove. And indeed, the women of the village are not of that sort, and the men are none of them of the coarser sort. They sing and tell stories, and in these fluid tales you will hear of the pitiful sweet mermaids who have gifted human lovers of both genders with immortal life beneath the water, of men who have died for their women, and women who have died for their men, of the true love of man for man and woman for woman, of the value of daughters, and the virtues of gentleness, and how the seals have their own tongue, which may be learned, and that in the world beyond death, all are equal forever, and sometimes they call God She, and sometimes He, and sometimes They, or It. But they speak of God, as of all things, with respect, and interest. You learn, before you come, of Japanese visitors and black students, who have been unnerved that no one noticed, in the village, or so it seemed, their physical differences, in which they rightly took pride.

There was also a woman, once, who pointed out that the value the village set on animals was flawed, for they live by fishing the seas and eating the fish. But the villagers nodded politely to this woman, and since she could not speak their language, and they only a little of hers, she did not hear of their service, which is held twice a year, in which they bless the fish and ask pardon of them, as too they do when they catch them. In the service, the priest explains that the world is, in some ways, not well made, which is not the fault of God, since She, He, They and It did not construct all the world's laws, in fact only those laws which are benign, tidy and pleasing to everyone. Through their own fault, or error, man and beast must sustain themselves, and cannot always do so without meat in some form. Until a new world is made, this cannot be put right. In truth, most of what the village catches is taken to the mainland, and before the winter closes the sea, the seals are fed a catch to assist them on their journey.

Most visitors leave *The Girl in the Blue Dress* tired from the hour's crossing, which can be a discomfort even in summer, and go up the street to the public house, which has a painted sign of a strong, handsome man with the tail of a shark. This pub is called *The Guest*.

Here they serve you local drink, white whisky with the scent of turf, a thimbleful powered like any triple measure elsewhere, and a milder pale yellow ale. Or there is tea to be had. On broad plates they will bring you golden loaves whose dark inner flesh tastes of nuts, pickled apples from the village orchard tucked behind the houses, trees crooked and little, that produce a sharp red fruit, cheeses like the best of Northern France, and, if asked, flakes of smoked fish with whipped fried eggs.

In winter, the fire burns in the huge fireplace of the pub, but in summer the dense stone walls keep out a blistering heat. The rafters are low enough to stun you, if you should be more than short, and they have hung about them long ribbons that check you, should you forget, and so save you a headache. Almost no one in the

247

village is more than five and a half feet tall, it is true. But they are formed all in proportion, on a smaller scale. Aelin is probably the tallest of them, for he is five feet ten inches, and in the pub he walks bent over.

When you have dined and rested, you can go through the village, and up the slope of the first hill, towards the church. On this slope, it seems you must look back, and down below, the village is, and the huge sea beyond. There comes the sense of immensity, as when you gaze up into the sky, perhaps the sky of night with all its million, billion stars. How small is the village, the land itself, and from that vast firmament of silver water, what may not come?

When you resume your climb, you may think how bare the church is, so stark and white, and inside you anticipate few ornaments, and you are correct to do this, for there is almost nothing at all. The windows are narrow and plain, and have shutters against the storms. Though there is an altar it has on it only ever a bare white cloth. There is no crucifix, though—once you have grasped their language—you will hear them speak of Jesus Christ, and as if He were well known among them, the son perhaps of some grandmother a couple of generations gone. But they speak too of others, and it may occur to you to wonder how they have heard here, cut off as they are, uninvolved as they are in television and telephone, of Mohammed and Buddha. And then again there are names they will speak you will not recognise, probably. And besides you may mistake these names for those of their forefathers, these sons of grandmothers, until maybe there is mention of what might be termed a miracle—conception without intercourse, ascents to heaven, transformations and healings, resurrection and rebirth. All these matters are apparently as normal to the villagers as the boiling of a kettle or the turning tides of the sea. The only way indeed you may be sure that they are speaking of some great one, some One who has come from God, is by the tone of pride in their voices. For they are *proud* of Mohammed and Jesus and Buddha, and all the others. They smile as they speak, as if they told you instead how rich and powerful and beautiful their ancestors have been.

On the altar, however, there is a cup made of iron, and from this they drink water during the services, a sort of communion, perhaps. The stranger too, if he or she is present and so wishes, may join in the ritual. But the services are held irregularly, you cannot be sure you will arrive at the right time.

Usually the church stands empty and unlocked, full of light, cool in summer, frozen cold in spring. You look about, and so regard the nine long pews, which are all that are ever needed here, though once, there were more. The wooden carvings are placed one at the left or south end of each pew. Finding them, it may be you are surprised that they are so small. You may need to bend close, to put on spectacles, or produce a magnifying glass.

Then you will see that the carvings are, in their own manner, very simple, although perhaps attractive to the eye. Perhaps they will seem at once mystical, imbued with all that is provoking and inexplicable. Or sinister; they might seem to be that. Or, you may be disappointed. Having come so far and so uncomfortably to this pared spot, despite the good food and drink you may have taken, and the looks of the villagers, their kindness, their glowing stained glass eyes.

Yes, you may think. Well, and is this all? This little

curved fish creature that has something about it of the whale, and which symbolizes the sea, for on its back it carries a tiny carven boat. And, moving forward up the aisle, to the west, there is the carving of a goblet, not unlike that which stands on the altar, but upturned, so some visitors have asked if it was not wrongly attached. Beyond the upturned cup is a carved sun, emblematic, an image seen very often and in many areas, even on the wrapping paper sold for birthdays. At the end of the fourth pew a tiny man and woman stand embracing, and a tinier child clings to the woman's long skirt. From their costume, these three, the carvings can be dated, to some mid-point of the 1700's, as the villagers do date them. At the end of the fifth pew is a skull, Spare and universal as the previous sun. And at the end of the sixth, something more complex, an angel, apparently, a winged being. Its face is so small it has no features but a suggestion of eyes, although minutely the feathers are scored into the wings. On the seventh pew is another fish, this one roaring like a lion. On the eighth pew a presentation that may defeat even the youngest eye, the strongest spectacles, and the magnifying glass. After much study, if you have the patience, you may behold an amalgam of things, cows and sheep, fish and cats, snakes, dogs, men and women, and countless other icons, most not decipherable. In the scramble of shapes it will eventually come to be seen that everything here is winged. On the ninth pew however, there is no use in study. This carving, it seems, is an abstract pattern, something not often demonstrated at that era, conceivably the invention of a broken mind. This final woodwork is disturbing, insulting to some, like a cheat. To come so far and find only these little things, and this last thing, so meaningless, therefore unimportant.

Besides, have you not seen all this already in the pamphlet on the mainland, or reproduced in some glossy book that deals with the carvings of churches? Why then did you come? But, yes, there is still the ultimate bizarre object.

Out from the church then you go, an hour or five minutes after you entered it, and walking on the path that they have shown you from the village pub, you ascend the rest of the barren hill, and the white church falls behind.

In summer there will be sheep out on the hills, and three or four cows, brown cows with heavy heads bearing each the white crescent of the moon. The sheep are shaggy, and they have been described as pink. Their colour is old and washed by rain, but their faces, like those of the cows, are profound. They graze placidly, and let you by without fear or sullenness. If you should like animals and wish to touch them, they will come up to you at a call. Sometimes the horses from the carts are there also, and they gallop, but again they are careful not to alarm, or so you may think, and let you caress their rough electric manes. Under or upon the stones on the hills you might see a spotted snake, harmless. You may stroke these as easily as the cats in the village street, if you care for snakes or cats. You may have heard that the seals too will let you approach them, though only the villagers feed them by hand. It is the same with the birds, and with everything wild that lives thereabouts. Do not be amazed that a fox trots to you out of the bushes, sniffs at your foot or knee. The rabbits that feed in the low fields between the hills never run away, unless by accident you almost tread on one.

Over the third hill, and you will be glad of your

walking shoes, you find the last curiosity of your trip. To some this has more value, to others less, than the carvings attached to the pews in the church.

Much has been said of it, the ruin of the boat. Firstly, that it is a ship and not a boat at all, with the bone of her strong mast still sticking up, formed of the wood that must come from far away, where the gales do not reach, formed of that wood which made the carvings. Her shell is intact, though the weather has leached it all to a grey that is almost white. But there are holes in the flanks of her and in the deck, and the cabin amidships has mostly fallen down. The metal on the wheel is red with rust bright as flowers.

Of course, reason tells you, that they brought her here, the villagers, though for what purpose? Perhaps straightforwardly to abet their peculiar story. In the story, the ship or boat fell down from the sky, fell slowly enough that many saw her, and, when she met the earth, slowly enough she did not entirely shatter to bits.

On the side no mark remains, but you will know that, like the boat of Aelin, this one was also called *The Girl in the Blue Dress*, and so painted. In those days of the eighteenth century, not one man or woman in the village could read or write.

The spar, or part of the spar, remains, and perhaps a gull or greenfinch will perch there. It will watch you as you circle round the boat, look at the places where they hauled in their nets heavy with fish, at the wreck of the planking. Before the bird flies off, probably you will be weary of the ship that is a boat, but you will sit on the warm hillside if it is summer, to rest before returning to the village. In spring even you may rest. It is a hard walk, going and coming down.

No one in the village will tell you the story of the carvings and the boat, unless you ask, and then Aelin will return and tell you. You will discover then that Aelin has a blind dog that can nevertheless somehow see, or seem to, for it knows everywhere so well. It will sit by his side, but if you wish it, it will sit by you, and you will comb its coarse silk with your fingers, should you want to, and maybe buy it a dish of the yellow ale, as you will doubtless want to buy some drink for Aelin. The prices in the pub called *The Guest* are absurdly cheap, and they employ the currency of the mainland. You may notice that the locals do not seem to pay, but maybe an account is kept. If it happened, as once it did, that you had lost your wallet or your purse, neither would you pay anything, and some money would be found in your pocket or under your glass, when you came back from the clean little pub latrine, with its cracked white enamel wash-basin, and the large cake of amber soap. Even if you had lied, they would do this. They would not care that you had lied.

Aelin will tell you, quietly and mildly, in your own language, whatever that is, the tale of the boat and the carvings, which is in the books, but there is no reason you should not hear it twice, and he will tell it the best.

Two hundred years and more ago, the boats went out each day, the five or six or seven of them, out to reap the fishes from the sea. And sometimes it would be that a boat would not come back. The women would wait upon the shore, wrapped in their shawls, cold even in summer, looking to see if the boat their man was in would reappear at last. There were some five men to each boat, and so the lost boat meant five lost men, and five families of women, and too their children often enough, standing there at the edge of the water. They would weep, or not, but the salt sea is made of tears.

One summer the water was calm as blue silk, and the boats went out at dawn, and all came back at sunfall but one, that boat called *The Girl in the Blue Dress*.

It had been a long day, for the days are long here in the summer, but down to the beach the five women came, and with them four children, two with one woman, and one each with two of the other women, while two women walked alone. They stopped at the fringes of the sea that now was half red, as the sun burned out inland, and half the dark blue the eastern sky was going.

Who has seen beyond the shore at night, where no lamp or light can reach it, however bright, knows that it becomes finally one with the sky, and then it cannot be found, the end of one, the commencement of the other. Only the land is different from them both. But then the moon rose, and made a silver road upon the sea, yet nothing moved on that road. And when the moon had gone over, it left again the darkness, which was void. Later came the sun, like a golden beast rising out of the water. But the sun brought nothing either, though its passing was longer.

Some days and nights the five women waited on the shore. Now and then other women brought them a little food, or took the children away to sleep. At the entering and retreat of the tides, the women moved back or forward like figures on a clock. One or two might lie to sleep an hour on the stones, while the others watched. After about seven days, the men came, and the priest, and took them softly back into the village. There they cried and railed their anger and bitterness and pain. Others comforted them who had themselves lamented in the same way, and others who understood that they too might one day so lament. Presently they got up, the five widows, from the rock of their grief, and took on their empty lives, where every moment is like every other and, as before the passage of God, there is no sundering of day from night.

A month or two passed, and it was harvest time in the few fields between the hills. As the men and women worked, they heard a strange note sounding in the sky, and in the village they heard it too, and the women that were there came out of their doors.

The sky was clear as the blue eye of a child. Nothing was in it, not a cloud, not a bird. And then there appeared a tiny dot, which began to grow bigger, and soon those that looked saw how it grew bigger since it fell towards the earth.

Slowly it fell, as if it had no weight, or very little, yet directly down. And before it reached the earth, the watchers saw plainly that it was a boat, a boat having one sail, and from her sides floated out the rent nets like a web. And those that were close enough saw too how on the curve of her side there was the painting of her name, a girl with a blue gown and shells in her yellow hair.

She settled light as a leaf over the third hill, and they went running to see, leaving their scythes in the fields, and in the village the pots to burn.

When they reached her, they knew her for sure. They were afraid, how not? But going near, they started to call out the names of her crew. None answered. None were there. The boat was empty of everything, all vanished but the spoiled nets, not a bucket, not a rope, and nothing of the men, even when the villagers got up their courage and mounted the deck, and stepped into the little cabin. All was gone, even the compass, even the lamp. And of the crew not a trace.

The five widows had come up by then, and the four children. It was one of these children that remarked on the odour of the boat. It had naturally smelled of tar and of fish, and now it did not. Now they did not know what it smelled of, although the child had said that it was flowers.

The fifth widow, one of the two who had no children, saw the small wooden things that lay under the wheel. They had mostly gone back from the boat by then, but one of the men got over into her again, and took the things up and brought them out.

Sometimes the fishers would carve in wood, to pass time as they waited on a still sea, or by night at home before the fire. They recognised the carvings as their own, that is, the carving of the men who had been lost, who had disappeared. They did not know what the carvings meant, except, four of them. That is, the fish bearing the boat, which was the sea, the roaring fish, which meant a storm, the upturned cup which was the symbol of want, hunger and thirst, and the skull, which, to most of the world, has always signified death.

The other carvings, the amalgam of flying creatures, the sun, the man and woman who embraced, even the angel, these perplexed them, while the abstract pattern made them uneasy. They carried the enigmas to the village, and put them in the church, where the priest bent over them and asked God for help.

At this point in the story, Aelin will tell you that, when at last the carvings were set on the ends of the nine pews, they were placed deliberately out of order. This is because their force is so enormous, even in mere simulation, that it is considered best that it does not run in the correct sequence. So it comes about you can never properly deduce the tale merely by examining the carvings. You can only ever be told.

That night, the village slept restlessly, yet sleep it did, for the sea's sound induces sleep for those who have always lived within hearing of it, the lullaby that is heard perhaps in the womb. And the five widows and the four children slept, and they dreamed, each of them, the same dream, and waking up in the darkest hours of morning, they ran out into the street and stood there, those nine humans, as they had stood before at the edge of the sea, looking for the boat that instead dropped down from heaven.

They did not know which of their men had carved the wood, or if all of them had done it, as maybe all of them had. But, without the skill of writing, it had been their only method to reveal what had gone on. And in their dreams the women and the children had seen these men, each one her husband, or the child its father, and showing the carvings, they had explained with care the nature of events.

They had sailed, the fishermen, on a calm sea, which was the fish with the vessel on its back. But soon, they had lost sight of the other boats, as might happen. Then without warning the sky turned black, and a storm blew up—the roaring fish—worse than they had known on such a morning. They rode it out as best they could, and eventually, the wind sank, and the clouds melted, and the day was as before, blue and calm, and still now as a thing deeply asleep.

They sensed that they were far from land, and worse,

most strangely, as if they had gone somewhere far from everything that they had known. The boat could not sail, there was no wind. They waited for the going of the sun at last, and for the sunset wind that almost always rises. But the day did not alter, the sea did not, nor the sky, and at length they must admit the sun itself did not move from the centre of heaven.

One man had a pocket watch, and by this thereafter they timed the days and nights. They drank the ale they had brought, only a jug of it, and they had some bread to eat, but it was quickly consumed, though they tried to make it persist. Nor did any fish approach the nets. The sea was bottomless and lucid, and nothing was in it, and no bird crossed the sky. Thus then, what they foresaw, the upturned cup, and so the ultimate parting from their wives and children—that last embrace—and at the end the skull of death.

They were not afraid, more dreary, resentful, for they were all young men. They raged, they prayed, and some wept. But then they were too weak for anything, and sat on the deck, their spines against the sides of the boat, under the lovely, perfect sky. After this they forgot to measure the passage of time.

Maybe they sank into a sort of trance or faint. They woke as one, and everything was changed. Their weakness had left them, each man felt refreshed as if from a fine meal, and a sweet slumber. They stood up, and as they did so, an enormous light enveloped them, a light whiter than snow, more brilliant than the heart of the sun, a light which should have blinded and slain them, but it did not, no, it was like a balm, and they laughed aloud. In the middle of the light they presently saw a creature that they took for an angel, for it was very beautiful and had wings, yet there were no features to its face, only two most wonderful shining eyes, and even this, the form of it, its eyes and wings, they knew in those moments were more the manner of their seeing, than the reality. Nevertheless, it touched them gently with its hand, and all at once, the boat was lifted up into the sky, up with the glory of the light, up and up and so to the place that now, speaking to their wives and children in the dream, they were powerless to describe, and shook their heads, smiling, and indicating the carving which had no form, was only a pattern, and that not regular, or similar to anything. An inexplicable place—but a place that was, to the world. Heaven.

In the dream then, the women had asked, and the children had asked, would they not return, these men, since they still lived? The men replied that this was not possible, now, but they had sent a sign at least, and the sign should be heeded. Not as a promise or reward, but as a certainty. Look at the final carving, which had attempted to show how everything in the world grew wings and flew upward—save that these were not wings, nor was it upward, though it might seem to be—all was not as it appeared, yet better, much, much better, as a blind man who had imagined sight, should he be able suddenly to see, or as true love is better than loneliness, or children grow up into men and women, or summer comes after winter, and there has always been a morning after night.

The village, Aelin will then say, stands where it has always stood, and the boat lies between the hills, but the carvings were attached to nine of the pews in the church, the nine pews that remain.

He will not then argue or, shamed and smirking,

apologise for any foolishness, or what you might desire to call whimsy. He will not try to answer any questions to do with religion or faith, although he will be silent only in the most courteous way. If you ask him what became of the five widows, he will say that he believes, in time, they remarried. If you ask if he credits the story of the carvings and the boat, he will nod.

Then you may stay drinking, and he will stay with you if you request it, but no longer allow you to pay for his drinks, but this is done so simply and in so friendly a fashion, it will not be a rebuff, and is not a rebuff, not even if you have sneered and cackled, and said he was an imbecile. He does not mind. Why should he mind? There is nothing to mind about. Words are not always facts.

If you wish, you may sleep that night in one of the three large herbal-scented beds at *The Guest*, and tomorrow he will take you back across the sea. Or he will do so by night even, if you crave for it.

Even he will go walking with you, back to the church, and stand by as again you observe the carvings, or he will go up the hills with you, and proceed with you about the boat. He will reply to such questions as are pertinent—the vanished painting on the side, the type of birds that fly over in the dark, singing, what he supposes might have been the thoughts of those villagers two centuries off, after the dream was revealed, how the carvings were fixed to the pews—with great ease, apparently—his age, which is almost ninety, the names of the stars above.

If you are angry he will speak softly of little things. If you are sad he will murmur that all will be well. But he has already told you that. Perhaps this is his only concession.

When, that evening or night, or that next day, he has

taken you back over the water, and you get out on the mainland, hard as concrete, built high and blown loud with life, then you will be in a position of examining properly, if you mean to, what you have seen and heard. You will decide then, and possibly in a different form from your decision in the village. You may find you believe it all, or some of it, or none of it. Or next year you may. One dusk, or dawn. Or never. You may never ever believe a word.

I do.

Xoanon: Primitive, usually wooden image of deity supposed to have fallen from heaven.

Concise Oxford Dictionary (1987)

LAND'S END,
THE EDGE OF THE SEA

Have you ever seen them? Many have. *I* have. Once I saw two very young children. Her hair was the colour of honey, his like molasses. The morning sky was blue and the sun shone with summer. They were playing, running to and fro, throwing little sticks, each for the other to catch, laughing and careless as the young, if possible, should always be.

Intuitively, having watched them a moment, smiling, pleased with their pleasure, I glanced beyond them to see if some nearby cottage, their home, stood there, just above the line of the water and the sand.

No house was to be seen. It must be farther off, then, or a little further inland. No matter. They were in the prime of health and high spirits, obviously cared for.

Presently, together, they ran away along the surf-line fizzing on the beach, sprinting towards the early west.

The second time, about three months later, I saw a young couple, he perhaps twenty or so, and she a little less. There they were, strolling there, at the brink of the land, the water, alternately leaving their elegant footprints in the sand, or splashing through the foam.

Her hair was black as a crow's wing, and his was pale as barley. They laughed gently and talked intently, the way, still, lovers may.

The next couple I beheld, it was quite a few years later. I had been elsewhere. They too held hands, like lovers, and both their sets of hair were iron grey. They were some eighty or ninety years in age, I thought. They did not chatter or murmur, but in a while he picked up a cream-white shell, and they passed this delicately and respectfully between them, as if it were some great treasure.

He walked then on the inside of the way, tending left and nearest to the land. But the fourth time I saw them, I was in company with two or three friends. We had come from a village feast a little farther up the coast. It was almost midnight and we bore a single flaming torch. She, now was on the inside of the way. Her dress had spangles on it and none that saw them could doubt it was a wedding dress, and that they had been joined together that very day. They were in age about thirty.

One of the strangest times, perhaps, was when she was far older, and he a little boy, running up to her, smiling. Their skins then were smoky dark but their eyes a pale blue. Sister and brother? Mother and child?

How delighted they were in each other's company, but nothing smug or excluding about this—if they caught your eye, they would willingly exchange talk with you. There was one time, an old fellow from my own birthplace had stumbled and hurt his ankle, and carefully and good-humouredly, the man and woman, then about twenty years old perhaps, helped him to the nearest house. He said later, he felt he knew them, was even related to them, but did not know how, or from where.

Another acquaintance of mine, a young fisher-woman, glimpsed the couple at midday, out in the full bright sun, and on this occasion, they were two babies, rolling and chortling, as ever at the border between land and water. My friend was concerned for they were so *very* young and no one with them... but they seemed, she said, to dissolve into the midday glow.

No one I know has seen them either swimming or walking inland. They paddle through the surf, or walk the land side about four feet in.

It is the border, the literal seam that connects land and ocean. Where the glittering and restless join of white stitchwork is, of surf and sand. The sea never fully empties there. The land never encroaches.

Water and earth have married. They became each other, and new things, and human things, and doubtless too others, marine and harder to perceive—fish and sea-crabs, limpets and beings of the rock-pools, blue serpents like ropes.

The very last time I beheld them was a year back. Her skin was black as iron, her hair like golden thread. His skin was tanned to copper and his hair like silver silk. She was about eighteen years young, and fresh as the spray and the first spring flowers. And he, despite his colouring, plainly was as old as the hills inland, and old as the tides beyond the surf.

None of us really know their purpose, if even they have one.

It is enough they are there. As it is enough the fluid sea is there, and the water's edge, and the solid land, the sky, night and day and time. And the air and the void of space. Every one with its join, its border, its compact, its marriage.

All things are separate. And all things: One.

Publishing History of the Stories

Girls in Green Dresses
Weird Tales. No 321 (Vol 57, No 1), Fall 2000.
Octocon Souvenir Programme. The National Irish Science Fiction Convention 2004, Dublin.

Magritte's Secret Agent – *Rod Serling's The Twilight Zone Magazine*. Vol 1 No 2, May 1981.
Dreams Of Dark And Light: The Great Short Fiction of Tanith Lee, Arkham House, USA, 1986.
The Gorgon And Other Beastly Tales, DAW Books, New York, 1985. New edition Fantastic Books, USA, 2013.
Mermaids And Other Mysteries Of the Deep. San Francisco: Prime Books, 2015. Edited by Paula Guran.

Paper Boat – Arts Council Anthology – New Stories, 1978
Realms Of Fantasy. Vol 3 No 3, February 1997.

Lace-Maker, Blade-Taker, Grave-Breaker, Priest – *Lace and Blade*, Leda, an imprint of Norilana Books, 2008, edited by Deborah J Ross.

Under Fog (The Wreckers) – *Subterfuge*. NewCon Press, England 2008.
The Mammoth Book Of Best New Horror 20. New York: Running Press, 2009. Edited by Stephen Jones.

The Sea Was In Her Eyes – *Octocon Souvenir Programme*. The National Irish Science Fiction Convention 2004, Dublin.

Because Our Skins Are Finer
Rod Serling's The Twilight Zone Magazine. Vol 1 No 8, November 1981.

The Gorgon And Other Beastly Tales, DAW Books, New York, 1985. New edition Fantastic Books, USA, 2013.
Dreams Of Dark And Light: The Great Short Fiction of Tanith Lee, Arkham House, USA, 1986.

Leviathan – original to this collection

Where Does The Town Go At Night
Interzone. No 147, September 1999.
H.P. Lovecraft's Magazine Of Horror. Vol 1 No 2. (Spring 2005). Pages 62-74.
Tempting The Gods: The Selected Stories Of Tanith Lee Volume One, Wildside Press, USA, 2009.

Xoanon
H.P. Lovecraft's Magazine of Horror. Vol. 1, No. 1 Spring 2004.

Land's End, The Edge Of The Sea – original to this collection

About the Author

As written by her

Tanith Lee was born in North London (UK) in 1947. Because her parents were professional dancers (ballroom, Latin American) and had to live where the work was, she attended a number of truly terrible schools, and didn't learn to read – she is also dyslectic – until almost age 8. And then only because her father taught her. This opened the world of books to Lee, and by 9 she was writing. After much better education at a grammar school, Lee went on to work in a library. This was followed by various other jobs – shop assistant, waitress, clerk – plus a year at art college when she was 25-26. In 1974 this mosaic ended when DAW Books of America, under the leadership of Donald A Wollheim, bought and published Lee's *The Birthgrave*, and thereafter 26 of her novels and collections.

Since then Lee has written around 95 books, and over 300 short stories. 4 of her radio plays have been broadcast by the BBC; she also wrote 2 episodes (*Sarcophagus* and *Sand*) for the TV series *Blake's 7*. Some of her stories regularly get read on Radio 4 Extra.

Lee writes in many styles in and across many genres, including Horror, SF and Fantasy, Historical, Detective, Contemporary-Psychological, Children and Young Adult. Her preoccupation, though, is always people.

In 1992 she married the writer-artist-photographer John Kaiine, her companion since 1987. They live on the Sussex Weald, near the sea, in a house full of books and plants, with two black and white overlords called cats.

CPSIA information can be obtained
at www.ICGtesting.com
Printed in the USA
BVOW09s1610290717
490579BV00002B/132/P